A

REASONABLE

DOUBT

ALSO BY PHILLIP MARGOLIN

A
REASONABLE
DOUBT

Phillip Margolin

Minotaur Books
New York

First published in the United States by Minotaur Books, an imprint of St. Martin's Publishing Group

A REASONABLE DOUBT. Copyright © 2020 by Phillip Margolin. All rights reserved. Printed in the United States of America. For information, address St. Martin's Publishing Group, 120 Broadway, New York, NY 10271.

www.minotaurbooks.com

Designed by Omar Chapa

The Library of Congress Cataloging-in-Publication Data is available upon request.

ISBN 978-1-250-11754-0 (hardcover)
ISBN 978-1-250-11755-7 (ebook)

Our books may be purchased in bulk for promotional, educational, or business use. Please contact your local bookseller or the Macmillan Corporate and Premium Sales Department at 1-800-221-7945, extension 5442, or by email at MacmillanSpecialMarkets@macmillan.com.

First Edition: March 2020

10 9 8 7 6 5 4 3 2 1

For Julie Young, the recently retired Executive Director of Chess for Success. Thank you for your extraordinary service to an extraordinary nonprofit program that has been serving Oregon and Washington's children for a quarter of a century. Your brilliant leadership made the program what it is today.

A
REASONABLE
DOUBT

PROLOGUE

2020

For her fifth birthday, Robin Lockwood received a magic kit with one hundred easy-to-learn tricks and proceeded to "astonish" her parents and brothers whenever she could trap them. After that, she was hooked, and she begged to see celebrated magicians whenever they appeared on television. Tonight, one of her clients was going to debut the Chamber of Death, his greatest illusion, in front of a packed house in the Imperial Theater.

Robin had a personal interest in seeing Robert Chesterfield perform this illusion. Several years ago, she had been present at Lord Chesterfield's seaside mansion when the dress rehearsal of the trick had ended in a truly bizarre manner. She hoped that she would see the finished product tonight.

The lights dimmed and Robin focused on the stage, determined to figure out how the seemingly impossible trick was done. Three women in hooded robes pushed a sarcophagus down the aisle and onto the stage, and Lord Chesterfield, dressed like an Egyptian high priest, was locked inside. Two of the magician's assistants lifted handfuls of poisonous snakes and scorpions out of glass cages and fed them into the coffin. Robin knew what was going to happen next, but she still tensed when hideous screams issued from the coffin and Chesterfield begged to be released from his prison. Then the screams stopped and eerie music floated through the theater. One of Chesterfield's assistants unlocked the padlocks that secured the lid of the sarcophagus and raised it.

Robin expected Chesterfield to have vanished from the coffin, only to miraculously appear in the back of the theater, but that didn't happen. One of the magician's assistants looked in the coffin. Then she screamed. Moments later, everyone in the theater knew that there was a dead man in the sarcophagus.

What Robin couldn't figure out was how the man had been murdered in front of three thousand people without anyone knowing who had killed him.

PART ONE

THE CHAMBER OF DEATH

2017

CHAPTER ONE

On a Monday morning in March of 2017, Robin Lockwood rose before the sun and ran the five miles from her apartment to McGill's gym.

For years, the Pearl had been a decaying warehouse district. Then the developers invaded and expensive condos, boutiques, art galleries, and trendy restaurants sprang up like mushrooms after a heavy rain. The old brick building in which McGill's gym was housed was one of the few places that had evaded the agents of gentrification.

Barry McGill, the gym's owner, had been a top ten middleweight many moons and pounds ago, and his idea of what a gym was supposed to be had gone out of fashion about the same time he started ballooning up to heavyweight. McGill's wasn't air-conditioned, it stank from sweat, and it didn't have a pool or spa. That turned off the millennials and young professionals who worked out so they would look good in the Pearl's singles bars, but it did attract professional boxers and mixed martial arts combatants, masochistic weight lifters, and serious bodybuilders. Anyone wearing spandex need not apply. Robin fit right in.

Robin had been the first girl in her state to place in a boys' high school wrestling championship. She didn't try out for the wrestling team in college, because her university fielded a top NCAA Division I squad, but there was a gym near the school that taught mixed martial arts. By Robin's first semester at Yale Law School, she was ranked ninth in the UFC in her weight class and her fans sang the old rock and roll song "Rockin' Robin" when she walked into the octagon.

Robin's UFC career ended shortly after law school started. Mandy Kerrigan, a top contender, had a fight scheduled on a pay-per-view card in Las Vegas. When her opponent was injured a week before the fight, Robin was asked to fill in. Robin saw the fight as a chance for fame and glory. Her manager told her it was a huge mistake. Robin admitted he had been right, as soon as she regained consciousness. Short-term memory loss convinced her that it was time to stop fighting, but she still loved to work out.

Barry McGill was a crusty old bastard, but he had a soft spot for Robin. "Your gal pal, Martinez, is over by the weights," he called out when he spotted her heading for the locker room. "Think you two girls can stop gabbing long enough to work up a sweat?"

"Let us *girls* know when you're ready to go a few rounds, Barry, and I'll put the EMTs on notice," Robin shot back. "They have a special rate for AARP members."

McGill chuckled and Robin gave him the finger.

After she changed into her workout gear, Robin joined Sally Martinez, who was doing curls in front of a floor-to-ceiling mirror. Martinez was a CPA who had won all-American honors wrestling for Pacific University and had trained in mixed martial arts. Sally and Robin sparred together occasionally, but Sally usually worked out in the evening.

"What are you doing here so early?"

"Tax season. I've got to get my workouts in while I can."

Robin and Sally were a study in contrasts. Robin was five eight with a wiry build; a midwesterner with blond hair and blue eyes that proclaimed her Nordic ancestry. Sally's brown skin and straight black hair were clues that her parents had emigrated from Mexico. She was shorter than Robin but more muscular.

After Robin warmed up, they walked over to the mats and began circling each other. Robin saw an opening and snapped a front kick. Sally slipped past it, grabbed Robin's ankle, kicked her other leg out from under her, and put Robin in a submission hold.

Robin tapped out and they got to their feet. Sally shot a double leg tackle and threw Robin to the mat. They scrambled for a few seconds before Sally wrapped her legs around Robin's waist in a figure four and put her in a choke hold.

"You're slow as molasses this morning," Sally said when they were standing again.

"A case kept me tossing and turning all night," Robin answered.

"You sure it wasn't Jeff?"

Robin blushed. When Sally laughed, Robin took her down with a single leg tackle.

"Hey, that's cheating," Sally complained.

After her workout, Robin showered and changed into the clothes she kept in her locker before walking across town to the law offices of Barrister, Berman & Lockwood.

The walls of the firm's reception area were decorated with photographs of Haystack Rock, Multnomah Falls, Mount Hood, and other Oregon landmarks, and it was furnished with several chairs, a sofa, and end tables covered by magazines. When Robin entered the waiting area, Linda Garrett, the receptionist, motioned her over.

"What's up?" Robin asked.

Garrett nodded toward an elegantly dressed gentleman who was thumbing through a magazine.

"He wanted to see Miss Barrister. I told him that she'd retired, so he asked if he could see one of the other attorneys. Mark is out of town taking depositions, and I wasn't sure you could fit him in."

When Robin walked over to him, the man put down the magazine and stood up.

"I'm Robin Lockwood, one of the partners."

"Pleased to meet you," the man said in a charming British accent. "I'm Robert Chesterfield, and I was hoping to discuss a legal matter with Regina Barrister."

"Miss Barrister has retired."

"So I was told. I must say that I was surprised to hear that. She was in her late thirties when she represented me, which means she would only be sixty-something now. I assumed she'd still be practicing."

"She was able to take early retirement," Robin said, not wanting to reveal the real reason Regina had been forced to leave the practice of law. "Is there something I can help you with?"

"Perhaps."

"Why don't we go back to my office?"

When Regina left to travel the world, Mark had graciously given Robin Regina's corner office. The floor on which the firm did business was high enough above the lobby of a glass-and-steel high-rise in downtown Portland to give Robin a spectacular view of the Willamette River, the foothills of the Cascade Range, and the snowcaps that crowned Mount Hood and Mount St. Helens.

"Why did you want to see Regina?" Robin asked when Chesterfield was seated across the desk from her.

"I'm a professional magician, and I want to get a patent for the Chamber of Death, a new illusion I'm developing for a show I'm going to perform in Las Vegas."

Robin smiled. "That sounds terrifying."

Chesterfield returned the smile. "My hope is that it will also be mystifying."

Robin laughed. Then she grew serious. "Unfortunately, even if Regina were still practicing, she wouldn't have been able to help you. She specialized in criminal defense. I don't think she ever handled an intellectual property case."

"What about you? Can you help me?"

"I'm afraid not. Criminal law is also my specialty. I wouldn't know the first thing about patenting a magic trick. I don't even know if you can get a patent for a magic illusion."

"What about Mr. Berman? Could he secure my patent?"

"Mark specializes in civil litigation. I doubt that he's ever handled a case involving a patent."

"Miss Lockwood, if I retained your firm to represent me in a patent case, would you be my attorneys if I became embroiled in a matter in a completely different field of law?"

"What area are you talking about? It would have to be something our firm is competent to handle."

"Are you a good criminal defense attorney?"

"I do okay."

Chesterfield gestured toward the wall where Robin's diplomas were displayed. "I see you're an Eli. I've heard that it is incredibly difficult to gain admission to Yale's law school, so you are both brilliant and modest, a charming combination for someone in your profession."

"I love flattery, Mr. Chesterfield, but, unfortunately, we won't be able to take on your case. I can give you the names of some excellent intellectual property attorneys."

"I've decided that I want your firm to represent me."

"That doesn't make any sense."

Chesterfield held up his right hand and pulled his sleeve up to his elbow. He turned the hand so she could see the palm and the back. Then he said, "Abracadabra."

When he rotated his hand again, a check appeared.

Chesterfield laid it on Robin's desk. "If Regina thought enough of you to make you a partner, I know I can trust you to handle my affairs. All I'm asking is that you keep an open mind. Research the patent question for me, then decide what you want to do. This check is for five thousand dollars made out to your firm. Put it in your trust account. If you decide you can't represent me, return the balance after deducting your fee for this meeting and for any research you might do on my behalf."

Five thousand dollars was a decent retainer, but Robin had doubts about whether it was ethical to take the magician's money.

Chesterfield seemed to read Robin's mind. "I can see you have concerns, so I'm willing to sign a document in which I state that you have fully informed me about your lack of experience in the field of patent law and that I am retaining you despite this fact." Chesterfield made a business card appear out of thin air and handed it to Robin. "I'm staying in town for a few days. Give me a call when you've reached a decision."

As Chesterfield stood up to leave, Robin thought of something. "You said Miss Barrister represented you many years ago. What type of case was it?"

"One she was definitely competent to handle," Chesterfield said. Then he walked out of Robin's office.

As soon as Chesterfield left, Robin walked to Mary Stendahl's office. Mary had been Regina's secretary and was the only person in the office who had been with Regina from the time she started her practice until she retired.

Stendahl was one of those women who look great with gray hair. Though she was in her late sixties, she looked ten years younger, and she kept in the tip-top shape she had to be in to keep up with six grandchildren by hiking and mountain climbing.

"Did you see the man who just left?" Robin asked.

"No."

"He said that Regina represented him when she was in her late thirties. You were with her then, weren't you?"

"Yes."

"I'm curious about the old case."

"What's the man's name?" Stendahl asked.

"Robert Chesterfield. He's a magician."

Stendahl's hand flew to her mouth. "Oh my goodness! Robert Chesterfield. I definitely remember that case. He was charged with murder. Actually, it might have been more than one."

"What can you tell me about the case?"

"Not much. I started as a receptionist, so I didn't know the details. I do remember that it got a lot of publicity, but if you want the inside scoop, you'd better talk to Regina."

"Would we still have the case files?"

Mary thought for a moment. "We might. If we did, they'd be in the basement in storage."

"Can you check to see if they're there?"

"Do you want them now?"

"There's no rush. We're probably not going to represent him. I'm just curious."

Robin left Mary's office and headed for the coffee room, preoccupied with thoughts of Robert Chesterfield. She loved magic, and the idea of representing a professional magician excited her. But she was also aware of the rules of ethics that governed her profession. It was a no-no to take on a client when you weren't competent in the area of law in which they needed help, and Robin didn't know a damn thing about patent law.

Robin was so preoccupied by thoughts of Robert Chesterfield that she started to pass Jeff Hodges's office without looking in. The firm's in-house investigator was six two with long, shaggy reddish blond hair, green eyes, pale freckled skin, and a face covered with telltale scars that were reminders of the injuries he'd suffered in an explosion in a meth lab when he was a police officer.

When Robin joined the firm, she had wondered about the origin of the scars and Jeff's limp. The more she got to know Jeff, the more she found herself attracted to him. Then someone tried to kill her. In the aftermath, she asked Jeff to make love to her. Jeff had turned her down gently. He told her that it was her adrenaline talking, and reminded her that office romances were a very bad idea. Robin appreciated Jeff's gallantry, but there was a mutual attraction they couldn't ignore. After another life-and-death situation, they had made love. Jeff had moved in with her a few months ago.

"You were up and out early," Hodges called to her.

Robin stopped. "I went to the gym. I needed to cleanse my system after last night's drunken orgy."

"You call a few beers and a roll in the hay an orgy? You're betraying your small-town origins."

"Hey, we had tons of orgies where I grew up."

Jeff laughed and Robin remembered Chesterfield.

"You have a second?"

"For you, always."

Robin walked into Jeff's office and plopped down on one of Jeff's client chairs. "I just had a really weird experience," she said. Then she told Jeff about the magician's visit.

"Do you know anything about the Chesterfield case?" she asked when she was through.

"That was way before I joined the firm. Are you going to try and get him his patent?"

"I don't think I should. I feel like I'd be asking for a malpractice suit. Although, I must admit I'm tempted. I love magic, and it would be really cool to know the secret behind one of these amazing illusions."

"You should watch that television show. You know, the one where Mysterioso, the magician in the mask, reveals how famous magic tricks are done."

Robin flushed with anger. "I hate that show and I think Mysterioso is disgusting. He's ruining the fun of millions of people by destroying the wonder other magicians create."

"Whoa. Why don't you tell me what you really think?"

"Giving away the secret behind a magician's tricks should be a criminal offense."

"Sorry I brought it up."

Now Robin blushed. "No, I'm sorry I went off. I shouldn't have gotten so worked up, but that guy really pisses me off. Anyway, I'm going to wait to talk to Mark before I decide if we should turn down Chesterfield."

"Are you going to ask Regina about the case she handled for him?"

"I was planning on visiting her today. I can ask her this afternoon."

CHAPTER TWO

Robert Chesterfield was disappointed that Regina Barrister was no longer practicing law because he knew that he might need a top-flight criminal attorney very soon. He'd also looked forward to seeing Regina again because she was one of the most beautiful and intriguing women he'd ever met. The combination of brains and looks had been very exciting. Over the years, he'd fantasized about what she might have been like in bed.

Chesterfield sighed. She'd have to be better in the sack than Claire. God, what a mistake he'd made marrying her. She was attractive and rich, but she was a controlling bitch who used her pocketbook as a whip. Unfortunately, he had not discovered this until after they tied the knot. The one lucky break he'd gotten was not having a prenup. When they wed, Claire thought he had more money than she did because he was a headliner at a major casino on the Las Vegas Strip. That was all over now, and the only way he could solve his financial problems was by getting his wife to loosen the purse strings. Unfortunately, once Claire discovered his real net worth, she had secured an unbreakable lock on her cashbox.

To make matters worse, there were rumors that she was in a hot and heavy relationship with David Turner, a rival magician, whom he loathed. Chesterfield wouldn't mind getting rid of Claire if he could find another woman with a lot of money who would help him out of his current predicament, but he had no idea who that might be.

Chesterfield was so distracted by thoughts of doom and gloom that he didn't notice the two men until they were next to him. He didn't recognize the muscle-bound ape with the shaved skull and shoulders so wide that they threatened to rip out the seams of his black leather jacket. But the second man was no stranger.

Rafael Otero was slender, clean shaven, and dressed in a suit. His sunken cheeks and narrow jaw gave him a slight resemblance to a wolf. Chesterfield knew that Otero was the more dangerous of the duo.

Augustine Montenegro had sent the men to intimidate Chesterfield, but the magician had dealt with bullies since he was a mere lad in Manchester. If push came to shove, Chesterfield could make a very sharp knife materialize. He'd started carrying it when Roger Bergson tried bullying him in primary school, and it had been a successful solution to the occasional difficulty over the years. Unfortunately, Auggie had many more enforcers in his stable. If these two disappeared, two more would take their place.

"Hello, Rafael. To what do I owe the pleasure of your company?" Chesterfield asked.

"Cut the shit, Bobby. You know damn well why I'm here. You owe Auggie a lot of money and he's getting antsy waiting for it."

"He shouldn't be worried, old chap. Didn't I send him some of what I owe quite recently?"

"What you sent barely covered the interest. Auggie doesn't want drips, Bobby. He wants you to fill his tank."

Chesterfield smiled. "You are very adept at turning a phrase, Rafael."

"I'm also immune to bullshit."

"You can tell Augustine that he has nothing to worry about. You know I've got a show that's going to open at the Babylon Casino in a few months. I'll soon have more than enough money to pay my debt."

"Yeah, about that. We went to the Babylon and talked to Lou Holt. He says the gig is dependent on you coming through with a new illusion, which he hasn't seen yet."

"That is not a problem. The Chamber of Death is ready for a test run. Augustine will receive an invitation to a private showing quite soon."

"Auggie's not interested in magic, Bobby. He's interested in cold, hard cash, which you'd better make appear very soon or we'll be unveiling our own magic trick, the Vanishing Magician."

Chesterfield laughed. "That was another excellent bon mot. Did you think that up on the spur of the moment? Perhaps you should leave the leg-breaking trade and become a poet."

"Don't be cute. Be responsible. If Auggie doesn't have the money soon, you'll be in no condition to perform magic or do anything else."

With that remark, the two enforcers walked away.

Chesterfield hadn't shown fear, because you could never do that with predators, but he was afraid. And Montenegro wasn't the only cause of his unease, merely the most dangerous one. What Chesterfield hadn't told Rafael was that the salary the casino was offering wouldn't come close to covering his gambling debt. His one hope was his backers. The money he'd sent to Montenegro had been skimmed from their account. If they didn't catch on to what he'd been doing with their investments, he might come out okay in the end. But that was a big *if*.

Chesterfield knew he was being backed into a corner, but he'd always been good at extricating himself from dangerous situations. He was worried, but there was always plan B.

CHAPTER THREE

Regina Barrister lived in a Tudor house on an acre of land in Dunthorpe, Portland's most exclusive neighborhood. Regina had left the practice of law after being diagnosed with dementia. Although she was taking medication that temporarily held the disease in check, it wasn't a cure, and the once brilliant attorney was often lethargic or depressed. Robin didn't know what to expect when she rang the doorbell.

Stanley Cloud smiled when he saw who was at the door. Robin smiled back, but she couldn't help noticing the toll caring for Regina had taken on her former boss, the retired chief justice of the Oregon Supreme Court.

Stanley and Regina had been lovers for years. When Regina faced the fact that she was losing her mind, Stanley had resigned from the court and taken Regina on a yearlong trip around the world while Regina could still appreciate the experience. They had returned to Portland a few months ago and Stanley had moved in to take care of her.

When he was chief justice, Stanley Cloud had been filled with energy, a handsome man who was often mistaken for being much younger than his chronological age. The Stanley Cloud who greeted Robin looked old. His once chiseled features had rounded, he had put on weight, and he looked worn out. Robin could not imagine what it would be like to watch the love of your life slowly lose her mind and fade away.

"How's my senior partner doing?" Robin asked.

"She's having a good day."

"Terrific. I had a meeting with a potential client this morning. Regina represented him over twenty years ago, and I wanted to ask her about the case."

"Long-term memory lasts a lot longer than short-term, so she might be able to help you. She's in the backyard. Go on out. I'll leave you two alone."

Robin walked across the living room and through French doors onto a wide flagstone patio. Regina was lying on a lounge chair staring across her lawn at a sailboat that was drifting along the river. Regina looked so peaceful that Robin waited for a while before disturbing her.

"Hi, boss," Robin said.

Regina turned her head when she saw that she had a visitor. This house used to be filled with people invited to parties and intimate dinners, but Regina didn't get many visitors these days. Robin hoped that Regina's memory loss made her forget how completely she had been abandoned.

"Mind if I join you?" Robin asked.

"Please," Regina answered with a smile.

Robin dragged a lawn chair to a spot next to Regina and they sat in silence for a while. Watching the river was restful and a good break from the hectic pace of Robin's practice.

"I had an interesting visitor today," Robin said after a while. "An old client of yours."

Regina didn't say anything. Robin had gotten used to that. She suspected that Regina was afraid to engage in a conversation because she was terrified that she wouldn't be able to remember something that she should know.

"His name is Robert Chesterfield. He's British and he's a magician. He wanted me to secure a patent for a magic illusion he's going to perform in Las Vegas. When he came to the office, he asked for you. He told me that you represented him in a case more than twenty years ago."

When Regina didn't respond, Robin forged on.

"I asked Mary Stendahl, your secretary, about him."

Robin told Regina Mary's position with the firm and her relationship to Regina so Regina wouldn't worry if she had no idea whom Robin was talking about.

"Mary said it was a murder case, maybe two murders, but she doesn't remember a lot about it. I was hoping you could fill me in."

Regina stared at the river for so long that Robin wasn't certain she was going to answer. Then she said, "I remember the case."

PART TWO

EVIDENCE OF OTHER CRIMES

1997–1998

CHAPTER FOUR

If you were casting a movie and needed someone to play a British lord, you would give Robert Chesterfield the part before he'd read a line. Chesterfield stood ramrod-straight like a graduate of the Royal Military Academy at Sandhurst, which he sometimes claimed he had attended. He had curly blond hair that always looked windblown, teeth so white they belonged in a toothpaste commercial, and the ruddy complexion of a man who rowed on the Thames and hunted quail. Then there was his Oxbridge accent, which made him sound like an upper-class Brit.

Chesterfield was always cheery. And why wouldn't he be? After moving from London to Portland, he had wooed and wed Lily Dowd, who was plain, plump, a tad slow, twelve years his senior, and the heir to a grocery chain fortune. Chesterfield thought of his wife as Dowdy Dowd, though he never called her that to her face. A master of sexual techniques, Chesterfield knew that frequent orgasms and praise for his spouse's beauty—no matter how unbelievable—translated into XK-Es, country club memberships, a seaside mansion with servants, and entrée into Oregon society.

While Chesterfield cut an imposing figure, Samuel Moser, the manager of the Westmont Country Club, did not. Sam was of medium height, balding, and overweight. Unlike Chesterfield, who always looked like he was modeling for a men's fashion magazine, Moser dressed in the dull gray suits, plain white shirts, and drab ties that made him look like the accountant he'd been before securing his position at Oregon's most prestigious country club.

As soon as Moser left the meeting with the club's board of directors, he told the valets to notify him when Chesterfield arrived. Four minutes after Chesterfield brought his classic Jaguar XK-E to a halt at the club's porticoed entrance, Moser waylaid him beneath the crystal chandelier that illuminated the lobby.

"Mr. Chesterfield, may I have a moment of your time?"

"Of course, Sam."

"Why don't we step into my office," Moser said.

"My, this sounds ominous," Chesterfield answered with a smile.

Moser led Chesterfield down a carpeted, wood-paneled hall without saying another word. When they entered the anteroom of his office, Moser saw Chesterfield cast a quick glance at his secretary's desk. Sophie Randall was not seated at it. Moser had told her what he planned to do, and he knew that she would not want to be anywhere near Chesterfield when he did it.

When they were seated with the door closed, Moser folded his hands on his desk and stared at Chesterfield. "I noticed that you looked at Mrs. Randall's desk when you walked by it."

Chesterfield smiled again. "I did. She's an attractive woman, and the sight of a pretty woman always brightens my day."

"You do know that she's married?"

"Yes."

"Then why did you make a pass at her?"

"Me? I never did."

"That's not what she says. She said your request was quite graphic. She was very upset."

Chesterfield flashed a self-satisfied smile. "I think Mrs. Randall has been engaging in wishful thinking."

"I've had similar complaints about lewd language and unwanted sexual advances from the female staff and the wives of club members."

Chesterfield looked offended. "You're kidding!"

"Unfortunately, I am not. I've also had complaints about cheating at cards. We do not tolerate any of that at the Westmont."

"Where is this going, Moser?"

"Nowhere, if you cease your behavior."

Chesterfield leaned back and folded his arms across his chest. "And if I don't cease this *alleged* behavior?"

"Then I shall bring the complaints to the attention of the membership committee."

Chesterfield studied Moser for a moment. Then he laughed. "Really, Sam, old boy?" He laughed again. "Do you think the committee is going to expel the husband of the wealthiest member of the Westmont because of the complaints of a secretary?"

"I believe that they will take her complaints and the other complaints quite seriously considering their source, the sheer number, and your reputation."

Chesterfield leaned forward and jettisoned all pretense of civility. "Listen to me, you little shit. Fuck with me and you'll be the one who's out on his ass."

Moser stared back, unfazed. "This is exactly the type of behavior that we do not tolerate at the Westmont, sir. Continue along this path, and you will no longer be welcome here."

Chesterfield stood up so quickly that his chair almost toppled over. "We'll see who's not here, Sammy boy," he shot back before stomping out of the office.

Moser closed his eyes and took a deep breath to calm himself. Then he picked up his phone and dialed Landon Crawford.

Retired Federal Judge Landon Crawford was still an imposing figure at seventy-three. He had been six two when he played linebacker for Harvard. Age had taken away several inches and he'd lost a little muscle mass, but his chest and shoulders were still thick, and his hair, though gray, was mostly there. More important, he continued to project the force of personality that had cowed opposing linemen and recalcitrant attorneys.

The judge sat in his favorite spot at a corner of the terrace that overlooked the eighteenth hole. In the distance, maple trees, birches, and evergreens shaded the lush green fairways. It was an idyllic setting, but Crawford was certain that his peace would soon be disrupted. Everyone knew where he held court, and ten minutes after Crawford ended the call with Sam Moser, Robert Chesterfield walked onto the terrace, looked around, and spotted the board chair.

"Landon, we have to talk," Chesterfield said as he sat opposite Crawford.

"Should I signal the waiter? Do you want something to eat or drink?" Crawford asked.

"I do not, old chap. I am too upset to eat or drink."

"What's the problem?"

"Samuel Moser. The little cretin just accused me of engaging in disreputable conduct and threatened to toss me out of the club."

"Sam can't toss you out of the club. He's an employee."

"Exactly, and I will not tolerate an employee speaking to me the way he did."

"It would take a recommendation of the membership committee and the vote of the board to discontinue your membership."

"Right."

"What is it you want me to do, Robert?"

"I want you to fire that impudent little toad."

Crawford frowned. "Because he brought complaints by club members and employees to your attention?"

"The accusations are completely unfounded."

"Robert, I have to tell you that you have been the subject of much discussion since Lily asked us to grant you a club membership. Maybe you've noticed that several members have excluded you from their bridge and poker games. That's because they suspect you cheat."

"Who says I'm cheating? Tell me who said that."

"I'm afraid that the complaints were told to me in confidence, but there have been several, and the people making them have sterling reputations."

"And I don't."

"Look, Robert, I'm going to be frank. There were a number of board members who were not pleased to have you join our club, but Lily is a dear woman and everyone was deeply saddened when Frank passed away. So we let you in because it made Lily happy. Your conduct has made many people regret their decision.

"You are Lily's husband and your behavior is not the sort of behavior in which a married man should be engaged. The Westmont Club is not a pickup bar in a seedy section of Portland. Our members are the cream of Portland society and we value our employees. I've had several members of the female staff complain that you've made lewd suggestions and groped them. I've had similar complaints from some of the wives. And this was before Sam came to me with Sophie Randall's complaint."

"So you're siding with that obese bookkeeper?"

"I'm not taking sides, Robert. I am telling you that several members of the club and staff are not enamored of your conduct. I am also telling you that steps will be taken if this conduct does not cease immediately."

"Then let me tell you that I'm going to resign my membership unless Moser is fired. Think of what that will do to Lily. She'll be disgraced. Think of how much you'll be hurting her if she has to leave the Westmont, because that's what she'll do if I tell her how I'm being treated."

"Listen to me, Robert. You're going about this the wrong way. There's no need for confrontation. Change your behavior and this will all be forgotten."

"By you maybe, but not by me."

Chesterfield stood up.

"You people think you're so high-and-mighty. Well, we'll see who comes out on top," Chesterfield said before he made a military about-face and left the terrace.

The judge sighed. Everyone knew that Lily's marriage to Robert Chesterfield had been a terrible mistake. Lily's children, Crawford's wife, and several other women in the club had tried to make her see how big a mistake it would be, but Lily was not that bright and she could be incredibly stubborn. The word was that Lily had been drinking and taking antidepressants since her husband's heart gave out unexpectedly. Crawford believed that Lily had fallen for the debonair and exciting Robert Chesterfield to escape the extreme depression that was crushing her. The judge didn't want to hurt Lily, but Chesterfield was an intolerable blot on the club's reputation. Everyone wanted him gone and he hoped that goal could be accomplished without subjecting Lily Dowd to more grief.

In addition to her mansion on the coast and homes in Aspen, London, and the Caribbean, Lily Dowd owned a five-thousand-square-foot penthouse in Portland. Chesterfield drove to the condo in a rage, barely avoiding two accidents. All his life, people like Crawford and Moser had treated him like something you find on the bottom of your shoe. He had not put up with it before and he didn't intend to start now.

"What's wrong?" Lily asked when her husband stormed in.

"We're resigning from the Westmont," Chesterfield said, his face flushed with anger.

"I . . . I can't leave the Westmont. All my friends are there."

"It's those prissy bastards who pretend to be your friends who've defamed me." Chesterfield gripped Lily's shoulders. "They don't care for you, Lily. They only care about the prestige you bring to the club, and your fortune."

"What happened, Bobby?"

"I've been accused of cheating at cards, of making sexual advances to secretaries. It's disgusting and it's a lie, and I won't stand for it."

"They said you made sexual advances?"

Chesterfield looked into Lily's eyes for a moment, then pulled her into his embrace. "There's only one woman in my life and that woman is you."

"But the Westmont . . . I can't, Bobby. Please don't ask me."

Chesterfield pushed Lily to arm's length. "I will never ask you to do something that you do not want to do. But I will not set foot in that den of liars again."

"Oh no. Please don't resign."

"They've made it impossible for me to stay. How can I show my face at the club, knowing that everyone will be whispering falsehoods behind my back?"

"But, Bobby, it has to be a mistake. I'm sure if we talk to Landon—"

"I talked to him after Samuel Moser insulted me. He backed that offensive toad."

Lily looked lost. "The Westmont. Frank and I were married there. I just can't quit."

"You must do what you think is best, Lily. I would never force you to leave a place that means so much to you. But I can't stay a member and maintain my dignity."

CHAPTER FIVE

Beauty can be a curse. When Regina Barrister was in her twenties, she was tall and slim with ivory skin, sparkling blue eyes, golden hair, and a dazzling smile. She also had an IQ that put her in the top one percent of the top one percent, but men could not see an IQ. Even though she had finished first in her high school and college classes, her nickname had been "The Cheerleader" when she arrived at Harvard Law in the mid-eighties. She hadn't been taken seriously until she finished—once again—at the top of her class at the end of her first year.

Regina had encountered some of the same problems when she returned to Oregon to practice law. Male judges and attorneys made passes and treated her with disdain until she started winning case after case. Within a few years of opening her practice she had a new nickname, "The Sorceress," because of her uncanny ability to win unwinnable cases. At thirty-seven, Regina's looks still made men pause in midsentence and women commit the sin of envy, but now that Regina was one of the best criminal defense lawyers in the state the sexist attitudes that had dogged her early years were a thing of the past, unless she was trying a case against an insecure, narcistic chauvinist like Peter Ragland.

Peter Ragland was the son of Jasper Ragland, the legendary United States Attorney for Oregon. No detective who had worked on a case with Peter had anything nice to say about him. He was a mental midget who thought he knew everything and would not listen to advice. The general consensus was that Ragland was trying to prove that he was just as good as his brilliant father. If that was his goal, he was failing miserably. Ragland lost cases he should have won and had victories reversed on appeal by committing stupid errors of law.

Regina loved going up against Ragland. He was obnoxious, but he was also incompetent and so ego centered that he made terrible errors of judgment, like the one he had made when he had treated Regina with disdain a month earlier when she had come to his office in an attempt to get him to drop a DUI case against the majority leader in the state senate.

"What can I do for you, Regina?" asked Peter, who had begged for the case because of the publicity it was going to get.

"I'm representing Bridget O'Leary."

"She must really be desperate if she's willing to pay your fees."

"She's also innocent."

Ragland had laughed. "Everybody I charge is innocent. Unfortunately for Senator O'Leary, my case is open and shut. Good stop, alcohol on the senator's breath, a point-eight breathalyzer, and a cop who is a great witness."

Regina had placed a sealed manila envelope on Ragland's desk. "You might want to read my expert's report before you make a firm decision."

Ragland had made no move toward the envelope.

"You can't win this case, Peter, and I want to save you the embarrassment you will experience if Bridget is acquitted."

"Which she won't be." Peter smirked. "I know all about your

nickname. You may be a Sorceress, but even your magic wand won't make the evidence go away."

"Aren't you even going to look at the report?"

"Maybe later. Thanks for dropping by."

For a moment, Regina had thought about trying to reason with Ragland, but she knew her efforts would be wasted. Regina had hoped to save her client the stress and expense of a trial, but, barring a miracle, they were headed to court, where she looked forward to humiliating Peter Ragland.

Judge Richard Ogilvie's courtroom was packed because of the news coverage it had received. As soon as the case was called, Regina waived a jury and elected to try it to the judge. Ragland didn't expect this and he protested, but a defendant could waive his constitutional right to a jury trial and there was nothing Ragland could do about that, except wonder what Regina was up to.

Ragland's only witness was Harriet Moreland, the arresting officer, who testified that she had stopped Senator O'Leary because one of her taillights was broken. When the senator lowered her window, the officer smelled alcohol on her breath. Moreland had asked the senator if she had been drinking. O'Leary said that she'd had one beer at a dinner meeting that had finished shortly before the stop.

"Did you have the defendant take a breathalyzer test?" Ragland asked.

"I did."

"What was the result?"

"Mrs. O'Leary blew a point-eight."

"Was that significant?"

"According to our statutes. A person with point-eight blood alcohol is under the influence."

"When you got that reading, what did you do?"

"I arrested the defendant for Driving Under the Influence."

"No further questions."

"Miss Barrister?" Judge Ogilvie asked.

"Thank you, Your Honor."

Regina's investigator had interviewed Officer Moreland, so Regina knew that Ragland had left some important pieces out of her narrative.

"Officer Moreland, you didn't stop Mrs. O'Leary because she was driving erratically, did you?"

"No."

"In fact, you noticed nothing improper with the way she drove."

"I did not."

"Isn't it true that the odor of alcohol alone is not proof that a driver is under the influence?"

"Yes."

"Did you ask Mrs. O'Leary to perform a series of field sobriety tests in order to see if she was affected by alcohol?"

"Yes."

"Did she agree to take the tests?"

"Yes."

"Did these tests include walking a straight line, repeating the words Methodist and Episcopal, and touching her nose with her head back and her eyes closed."

"Yes."

"Did Mrs. O'Leary pass the field sobriety tests?"

"Yes."

"Am I correct in saying that Mrs. O'Leary was not driving erratically, she performed the field sobriety tests perfectly, and the point-eight breathalyzer reading was the sole basis for the arrest?"

"Yes."

Regina was certain that Ragland was oblivious to the way the case was going and her suspicions were confirmed by the smug look on the prosecutor's face when he rested.

"Do you have any witnesses, Miss Barrister?"

"Just one, Your Honor. Mrs. O'Leary calls Oscar Benitez."

A slender man with a coffee-colored complexion and a leading man's good looks walked to the stand, dressed impeccably in a dark suit, a yellow and navy-blue striped tie, and a white silk shirt.

"How are you employed, Mr. Benitez?"

"I am the owner of Pacific Northwest Forensic Services."

"What does your company do?"

"We provide help to attorneys and others who have questions about forensic evidence."

"Before opening your own business, where were you employed?"

"I worked at the Oregon State Crime Lab for fifteen years."

"Do you have any experience with the breathalyzer machines that are used to determine the amount of alcohol in a person's blood?"

"My experience with breathalyzers is extensive. I've used breathalyzers hundreds of times; I've tested them to make sure they are accurate, and I've read countless pieces of literature that discusses them."

"Mr. Benitez," Regina asked, "Is there an error factor in these machines?"

"Yes."

"My client took a breath test and the result was a reading of point-eight. Can you please tell Judge Ogilvie what that means?"

Benitez turned to the judge. "The reading the machine prints out is never exact and a point-eight, maybe a point-nine, and a one."

"Those would both be proof that a person is driving under the influence, wouldn't it?" Regina asked.

"Yes."

"Is there another percentage that a point-eight could be?"

"Yes. A point-eight reading could be a point-seven."

"And that would mean a person was not breaking the law, wouldn't it?"

"Yes."

"The State has to convince Judge Ogilvie beyond a reasonable doubt that Mrs. O'Leary was driving under the influence. If the only evidence against her was the point-eight reading on the breathalyzer, would the reading constitute proof beyond a reasonable doubt of intoxication?"

"No, because of the error factor."

"No further questions."

Peter Ragland flailed around during his cross-examination and accomplished nothing. While he gave his closing argument, Regina glanced at his table. Among the papers spread across the prosecutor's table was the unopened manila envelope Regina had given him with Oscar Benitez's report. When Ragland's witness list did not contain the name of an expert witness, Regina guessed that Ragland had not bothered to read it or couldn't find an expert to refute it.

Regina stood to argue for acquittal, but Judge Ogilvie waved her down.

"I don't have to hear any argument from the defense, Miss Barrister. Mrs. O'Leary was not driving erratically; she passed the field sobriety tests and the odor of alcohol alone is not proof of intoxication. The only evidence that the State produced that would tend to prove that Mrs. O'Leary was driving while intoxicated is the breath test and your expert's uncontested testimony is that we can't say beyond a reasonable doubt that the real percentage wasn't point-seven, which is below the blood level you have to prove to convict. So, I have to find Mrs. O'Leary 'Not Guilty.'"

Regina hoped that Peter Ragland would leave the courtroom so she wouldn't have to talk to him, but he came up to her on his way out.

"You got lucky you had Ogilvie for your judge. No one else would have bought your argument."

Regina was mad at Ragland for wasting everyone's time, but she reined in her anger.

"I tried to tell you that you had no case. You should have listened to me. It would have saved us both a lot of time."

Ragland turned red with anger. "We both know the senator is a drunk. She may have beat the rap this time, but the voters will remember that the senator was charged with drunk driving, and a lot of them won't remember the verdict when it comes time to vote."

Ragland stomped off and Regina stared after him. He was a vindictive prick, and she hoped she wouldn't have to deal with him again.

CHAPTER SIX

The parties and special dinners at the Westmont always made the holiday season hectic, but Sam Moser's obsessive preparation helped him get through the days between Thanksgiving and New Year's Eve. Moser envisioned the holiday season as a battle between chaos and order. There would always be screwups, but you could deal with them if you worked out all possible scenarios in advance.

With Thanksgiving and Christmas in the rearview mirror, only the New Year's Eve festivities remained, and Moser believed that he had all things New Year well in hand. That enabled him to take a deep breath and relax even though it was two days before the last major party of 1997.

Moser was in a particularly jolly mood when his secretary brought him his mail, which included a package gift-wrapped with paper displaying Santa and his reindeer and bound by a bright red bow. Moser looked for the name of the person who had sent the gift, but there was none. He tore off the wrapping paper and smiled when he saw that his gift was a box of chocolates. He opened the box and saw a dozen delicious-looking pieces. A legend on the inside of the lid described the treats. One was filled with caramel, and Moser's fingers were halfway to the tempting square when he remembered that he was supposed to be on a diet in which cakes, candies, and all things fattening were strictly forbidden. The diet had been imposed by his doctor after his last physical. He had promised to keep to it, but he had failed in his resolve. Soon after, there had been a minor cardiac incident that scared the hell out of Sam, his wife, and their children. As soon as he left the hospital, Moser vowed to stay on the straight and narrow path to health and a long life.

Moser closed the box with great reluctance and retied the bow. Then he carried the box to the anteroom. Unlike her boss, Sophie Randall did not have to watch her weight. Even though she was married with a three-year-old daughter, the attractive redhead had a teenager's figure.

"A gift?" Sophie asked with a smile of delight when Moser set the box down on the edge of her desk.

"You, my dear, are the beneficiary of my horrible but mandatory diet. Enjoy."

Sophie grinned. "Thanks, boss."

Moser returned the smile and went back into his office.

Ten minutes later, his door opened and Sophie staggered in. She was starting to say something when she grasped her stomach with both hands and vomited on Moser's rug. Moser leaped to his feet, but Sophie went into convulsions before he could reach her and was dead within minutes.

The Westmont Country Club was walled off from the hoi polloi by a ten-foot-high, ivy-covered wall. While the guard at the front gate examined Morris Quinlan's shield, Roger Dillon looked through the car window at the beautifully manicured grounds.

Homicide Detectives Dillon and Quinlan were separated by

almost twenty years of age, oceans of experience, and appeared to have nothing in common. Quinlan's clothes were mismatched and off-the-rack, and there was a faint coffee stain over the left breast of his wrinkled white shirt. The detective's gut flopped over his belt; his jowls, which were covered by a gray-black stubble, were fleshy; his salt-and-pepper hair was cut close to his scalp; and a badly reset broken nose decorated a face with the reddish hue of the recovering alcoholic.

Where Quinlan was overweight, sloppy, and self-indulgent, Roger Dillon, who ran distances and pumped iron, was trim, self-disciplined, and dressed to look like a businessman or an attorney.

Where Dillon and Quinlan were similar was in their IQ scores. Dillon's high school grades and SATs were good enough to get him into a top college, but he was the sole support of his disabled single mother and three siblings, so he'd ended up working a full-time job and going to night school. In later years, Dillon would get the nickname OED because his breadth of knowledge reminded people of the *Oxford English Dictionary*.

People usually assumed Quinlan was a Neanderthal, but the older man was an excellent detective with a gift for logical thinking, who was capable of making brilliant intuitive leaps.

"Have you ever been in a place like this?" Roger asked as they drove down the winding, tree-lined lane to the clubhouse.

"Do I look like I hang out at country clubs?"

When his partner didn't answer, Quinlan glanced at him and saw that he was nervous. Places like the Westmont were as alien to Dillon as a raja's palace or the wilds of Borneo. He had grown up in Portland's poorest neighborhood and graduated from its worst high school. Portland State, where he went to night school before the police academy, was not known as a destination for the rich and famous.

"Look, Roger, I've dealt with these country-club types before. They may dress better than we do and drive fancy cars, but they take a shit just like you and me. So anytime they start talking down to you, imagine them sitting on the crapper."

Dillon smiled, but he wasn't entirely convinced that people who belonged to places like the Westmont didn't have their servants go to the bathroom for them.

And it wasn't just the setting that was making Roger nervous. He had made detective a year ago and had just been promoted to Homicide, a rapid rise from newbie to the most sought-after assignment in the Portland Police Bureau. There were whispers that the promotion had been made so that Homicide could have a token African American, but no one who wasn't jealous would seriously assume that was the reason for Dillon's promotion.

Roger's arrest record as a police officer had been among the best and his solve rate as a detective had been exceptional, but those successes didn't stop the butterflies from flapping in Roger's stomach as he approached the scene of his first murder case.

A section of the parking lot had been cordoned off for official vehicles, and a uniformed officer showed Quinlan where to park. As Roger followed his partner up the steps and through the front door of the club, he nervously adjusted his tie and pulled down on his jacket.

"Hey, Garrity," Quinlan said to a young officer who was stationed in the club lobby. "Where's the scene of the crime?"

Garrity threw a thumb over his shoulder. Quinlan and Dillon walked by a policewoman who was taking down a statement from a distraught middle-aged man and down an oak-paneled hallway crowded with forensic experts. A door was open at the end of the hall. An officer handed the detectives Tyvek suits, booties, and surgical masks. Dillon put on all three, but Quinlan carried his mask in his hand. When the detectives walked through the anteroom, they saw Dr. Max Rothstein, the state medical examiner, bent over the body of a young woman. His face was partially concealed by a surgical mask.

"What have you got for us, Doc?" Quinlan asked.

"Put on your mask, Morris. I won't know for certain until I get the toxicology report, but I smelled a bitter almond odor when I got close to the victim, so I'm putting my money on cyanide poisoning. You can develop clinically significant cyanide concentrations by inhaling cyanide gas from the body of a victim."

"Got it," Quinlan said as he slipped on his mask.

"Who's the victim?" Dillon asked.

"Sophie Randall."

"Is this her office?"

"Her boss's. She's his secretary."

"How was she poisoned?" Quinlan asked.

"See that box of candy on her desk?" Dr. Rothstein answered.

The men looked. A lab tech was taking photographs of the box.

"Two pieces are missing. Samuel Moser, Randall's boss, received the candy as a gift from an unknown person. He's on a diet so he gave the candy to Mrs. Randall. Moments after she ate the candy, she came into this office, went into convulsions, and died. I'm betting we'll find cyanide in the candy."

"We passed a heavyset guy in a suit at the end of the hall. Is that Moser?"

Rothstein nodded. "He saw Mrs. Randall die and he's really upset, so go easy on him."

"Got it. We'll get out of your hair. Let me know as soon as you have more on the cause of death."

The detectives discarded their Tyvek suits and walked back toward the lobby.

"Hi, Gloria," Quinlan said to the policewoman who was taking Moser's statement. "We'd like to talk to Mr. Moser. Are you about done?"

"I am."

"Mr. Moser, I'm Morris Quinlan and this is Roger Dillon. We're with Homicide. Is there someplace quiet where we can talk, an office or conference room?"

"There's a conference room on the second floor."

"Okay. Lead the way."

Moser walked toward the stairs with Quinlan following and Dillon bringing up the rear. Dillon was about to climb the stairs when Quinlan swore so quietly that only Dillon heard him.

A deputy district attorney was always assigned to a homicide as soon as possible to observe the crime scene. Dillon turned and saw a short man with styled blond hair, wire-rimmed glasses, and a thin mustache walking toward them. As soon as Dillon recognized Peter Ragland, he knew why his partner was upset.

Ragland spotted Quinlan and waved.

"What are you doing here, Pete?" Quinlan asked.

"I'm a member of the Westmont, Morris. When the boss heard there was a homicide at the club, I was the natural pick to handle the case."

Moser turned when he heard Quinlan speak to Ragland.

"Mr. Moser," Quinlan said, "this is Deputy District Attorney Peter Ragland."

"No need for an introduction, is there, Sam?" Ragland said. "Fill me in. What have we got here?"

"Mr. Moser's secretary, Sophie Randall, was poisoned and we're going upstairs to get some background."

"It looks like I got here just in time."

Ragland followed the trio, and a few minutes later, the four men were seated at one end of a long oak table.

"How are you doing?" Quinlan asked Moser.

"Not great."

"I noticed what looks like a liquor cabinet when we walked in. Any chance there's a bottle of Scotch in there?"

Moser flashed a sad smile. "Yes, but that's not necessary. Ask your questions."

"Okay. So, what's your position at the Westmont Country Club?"

"I manage the Westmont."

"What's that entail?"

Quinlan didn't care about Moser's duties, but he hoped that leading him away from memories of the murder and into familiar territory would help Moser relax.

"How long has Mrs. Randall been your secretary?" Quinlan asked when Moser had explained the duties of a club manager and the detective thought he was ready to answer relevant questions.

"Seven years."

"What can you tell me about her?"

Moser started to talk, but he choked up. Quinlan didn't push. After a few moments, Moser took a deep breath and answered the question.

"Sophie was a lovely person. She was smart, efficient, everyone liked her."

"Did she have any enemies?"

"God, no. I've never heard anyone say a bad word about her."

"Do you feel up to telling me what happened?"

Moser nodded. "Someone sent me a box of chocolates in the mail."

"Do you know who sent it?"

"No. There was no return address and no card. I assumed it was a member of the club."

"Any wrapping?"

"Yes. I gave it to an officer."

"Did you eat any of the candy?" the detective asked.

"No. I'm on a strict diet, so I gave them to Sophie."

Moser choked up again and Quinlan waited for him to regain his composure.

"I'm sorry," Moser apologized.

"Don't be," Quinlan said. "I take it that you cared for Mrs. Randall."

"She was so nice, happily married, they have a five-year-old girl." He shook his head. "If I hadn't given the candy to her—"

"You'd have given it to someone else and they would be dead. This is not your fault. Get that straight. It's the fault of the bastard who murdered Mrs. Randall. Now, can you think of who that might be?"

Moser shook his head. "Everyone liked Sophie."

"What about you, Mr. Moser? The candy was sent to you, so I have to believe you were the intended victim. Did everyone like you? As the manager of a large establishment, you must have had run-ins with employees, club members—"

Moser started to say something. Then he hesitated.

"Have you thought of someone, Sam?" Ragland asked.

"I'm very reluctant to accuse anyone, especially in a situation as serious as this."

"You're not accusing anyone," the deputy DA said. "You're helping us gather information."

"There is someone who comes to mind, but . . ."

"We're not going to rush out and arrest someone without evidence," Quinlan assured Moser. "The last thing we want to do is charge an innocent person with committing a serious crime. Now, who were you thinking about?"

"Robert Chesterfield."

"Who is that?" Quinlan asked.

"Robert Chesterfield is a thoroughly detestable individual who resigned from the club several months ago after a series of accusations of sexual harassment from female members and female employees. There were also suggestions that he cheated at cards.

When I brought these complaints to his attention, he grew out-raged and threatened me. One of the complainants was Mrs. Randall.

"What really concerns me is something that happened roughly two years ago. Lily Dowd is a very wealthy widow. She may have been the wealthiest member of the Westmont, and that is saying a lot."

"'May have been'?" Quinlan asked.

"Mrs. Dowd resigned when Mr. Chesterfield did."

"Go on."

"Mr. Chesterfield claims to be British. He's also hinted that he has some sort of connection to the royal family, that he's a lord or something."

"You don't believe him?"

"I would take anything Robert Chesterfield said with an entire sack of salt."

"Okay. Go ahead. What happened two years ago, and what does it have to do with what happened today?"

"I've been told that Mrs. Dowd met Chesterfield in London about a year after her husband, Frank Dowd, passed. Chesterfield moved to Oregon a few years ago. He's very smooth and he talked his way into the club one evening. Mrs. Dowd was at the club that night. I have no proof, but I am willing to bet that the meeting at the Westmont was no coincidence.

"In any event, Mrs. Dowd and Mr. Chesterfield began seeing each other, but Mrs. Dowd was also being courted by Arthur Gentry, another club member. Then Arthur died unexpectedly."

"Why was his death a surprise?" Quinlan asked.

"Mr. Gentry was in his sixties but he always appeared to be in excellent health. Mrs. Dowd was very distraught at the news of Mr. Gentry's passing, and Mr. Chesterfield was always there to comfort her. Within months of Mr. Gentry's death, Mrs. Dowd married Chesterfield."

"So, Gentry dying opened the door for Chesterfield?" Quinlan said.

"Yes."

"Do you know what caused Arthur's death?" Quinlan asked.

"No. I just heard that he passed suddenly."

"Who can we talk to about Mr. Chesterfield?"

"Mrs. Dowd has two adult children, Iris and Andrew. Iris is a doctor at Saint Francis Medical Center and Andrew is an attorney with the Reed, Briggs firm. They're both members of the Westmont. From what I've been told, they were horrified when Mrs. Dowd married Chesterfield. Chesterfield has caused a rift between Mrs. Dowd and her children, and her resignation from the Westmont has isolated her from many of her friends."

"Can you get us a list of people who might help us in our investigation?" Quinlan asked.

"I'll have it to you by tomorrow."

"Thank you. Can you think of anyone else who might have a grudge against you or Mrs. Randall?"

Before he could answer, the door opened and Landon Crawford walked in.

"My God, Sam, I just heard."

"Who are you, sir?" Dillon asked.

"It's okay, Roger. I know the judge," Quinlan said.

Before his appointment to the federal bench, Crawford had been a trial judge on the Multnomah County Circuit Court. Crawford took a hard look at Quinlan. "You're a detective, Quinlan, right? You testified in a few of my cases."

"That's right, Judge. What are you doing here?"

"He's the chair of the Westmont board," Ragland said.

"I just learned that Sophie Randall is dead," Crawford said. "What happened?"

"She was poisoned, Landon," Moser answered.

"Poisoned? How could that happen?"

"We just started our investigation," Quinlan said. "We have an idea about what happened, but I don't like speculating."

"Quite right," Crawford agreed. Then he looked at Moser. "Are you okay?"

"Not really," Moser answered as a tear welled up.

"I can see how upsetting this has been for you," Quinlan said. "Do you have any more questions, Pete, Roger?"

"Not right now," the deputy DA said. Roger shook his head.

Quinlan handed Moser his card. "Why don't you go home. If you think of anything that might help us, please call."

Moser nodded and stood up to go. Crawford started to follow him

"Can you wait a moment?" Quinlan said. "I have a few questions for you."

"Certainly. Do you want me to drive you home?" the judge asked Moser.

"Thanks, but I'm okay."

"How can I help?" Crawford asked as soon as the door closed behind Moser.

"From what we know, someone sent a box of poisoned chocolates to Mr. Moser. He's on a diet so he gave the candy to Mrs. Randall, who ate some and died."

"My God. Do you have any idea who sent them?"

"No. Do you? Can you think of someone with a grudge against Mr. Moser or Mrs. Randall?"

The judge went quiet and the detectives let him think. After a few minutes, Crawford's brow furrowed and they could tell he'd thought of something.

"One person does come to mind."

"Who's that?" Quinlan asked.

"There's a man named Robert Chesterfield, an ex-member

who resigned under pressure. He'd been cheating at cards, accosting the female staff. It was pretty sordid. Sam and I confronted him and he threatened Sam."

"That's the only name Mr. Moser could come up with. He told us that Mr. Chesterfield and a Mr. Gentry were courting a Lily Dowd and mentioned that Mr. Gentry died shortly before Chesterfield and Dowd married. Do you know anything about that?"

"My wife is a friend of Lily's and she might know something of use."

"I'd like to talk to her."

"I'll set up a meeting."

"I have a question," Peter Ragland interjected. "Were there ever any rumors about Sam and Sophie?"

"What type of rumors?" the judge asked, although it was obvious from his facial expression that he knew exactly what the deputy district attorney was getting at.

"Were they having an affair?"

"You're way off track with that."

Ragland shrugged. "I've got to ask. If something was going on and she was calling it off or threatening to tell Sam's wife, there's a scenario where Moser sends the candy to himself, then gives the box to Sophie under the pretext of being on a diet."

"No, no, Pete. I've been to Sam's house and seen him at social occasions. He's been married for twenty-plus years. He talks glowingly about his wife all the time. And Sophie has . . . had an equally happy marriage. She doted on her husband and their daughter."

"Okay. Good to know."

"Can I ask you a question, Judge Crawford?" Roger interjected.

"This is Roger Dillon, my new partner. This is his first homicide case."

"Pleased to meet you," Crawford said. "Listen to Detective

Quinlan. He's one of the bright spots in the bureau. Now, what did you want to know?"

"Is Mr. Chesterfield really British and from London?"

"That's what he claims. Why?"

"Just an idea. Can you tell me anything more about his background?"

"Sorry, but I don't know him well. For that matter, I don't think any of the members did."

Crawford left and Quinlan turned to his partner. "What's your idea?"

"I met a Scotland Yard inspector at a conference a year ago. I thought I'd give him a ring to see if he knows anything about Chesterfield. He seems to be our only lead."

"I'm not so sure about Moser," Ragland said. "He seemed a little melodramatic. It could be he was putting on an act."

"I didn't get that impression, Pete. His grief seems genuine," Quinlan said. Dillon could tell that his partner was restraining himself.

"Yeah, well, he could be a good actor. Let's not cross him off our list yet."

"Sure thing," Quinlan said. "Say, Pete, do you know Chesterfield?"

"I know who he is. I have a bridge group I play with every Wednesday night when I can. We were short a man one evening and he sat in. That's about it."

"What are your impressions?" Quinlan asked.

"I don't really have any. He seemed to know his bidding, if I remember correctly, but I can't recall anything he said. I don't know if I spoke to him after that."

"Did you witness any of the behavior that led to Chesterfield leaving?"

"No. This job keeps me pretty busy, so I don't get to the club as much as I'd like to."

"Okay. The lab techs should be done with the crime scene by now, so Roger and I are going to take a look."

As soon as Ragland and the detectives left the conference room, they heard someone yelling on the floor below. When they got to the bottom of the stairs, they saw two police officers blocking a muscular young man in a garage mechanic's uniform, who was trying to get around them.

Samuel Moser put a restraining hand on the distraught man's arm. "Please, Gary," he pleaded.

The man shook off Moser's hand. "Let go of me."

Ragland and the detectives joined the group.

"What's going on?" the deputy DA asked.

"This is Gary Randall, Sophie's husband," Moser explained.

"Is she . . . When Margie called, she said she was . . ."

"She didn't suffer," Moser lied. "It was very fast."

"Please, I have to see her," Gary pleaded. "I won't cause any trouble."

Quinlan stepped between the officers and Randall. "I know you want to see your wife, but she's passed and she's at peace. You don't want to see her now. You should remember her the way she was the last time you saw her, when she was happy. That's the memory you want."

Randall's shoulders sagged and he started to sob. Quinlan escorted Randall into a room off the lobby and sat him on a sofa. Moser sat beside him.

Randall looked up, his eyes filled with tears. "Who would want to do this?"

"That's what we're going to find out," Quinlan assured him. "We have our best people looking for evidence that will lead us to the person who hurt your wife."

"Where's Jane?" Moser asked.

Randall looked as though he'd been punched in the gut. "Oh

God. How can I tell her that Sophie is—?" He broke down again, unable to say the word.

"Jane?" Quinlan asked.

"Their daughter," Moser explained.

"Is someone with her?" Moser asked Randall.

"She's in school."

"You should go to her," Quinlan said. "Your daughter needs you now. Do you feel up to driving?"

Randall wiped his eyes and took some deep breaths. "I'll be okay. When can I see Sophie to say goodbye?"

"Give these officers your contact information and I'll make sure it's soon," Quinlan said.

"Thank you."

Quinlan squeezed Randall's shoulder. Then he led Dillon and Ragland out of the room.

"Poor bastard," Dillon said.

"This is the part of this job I hate," Quinlan told him. "And it never gets easier."

CHAPTER SEVEN

Morris Quinlan had been sitting in the reception area of the accounting firm of Fisk & Combe for fifteen minutes when a severe-looking woman in a gray business suit walked out of a long hall and stopped in front of him.

"Mr. Quinlan?" the woman asked.

"Actually, it's Detective Quinlan." He stood up. "And you're Eileen Paulson?"

"Yes." Paulson frowned. "Is this about a client?"

"No. I'm with Homicide, and it concerns your father, Arthur Gentry."

Paulson's features hardened. "It's about time. Come back to my office."

Paulson's office was halfway down the hall. She had a window with a view of the Willamette River and enough space to let you know that she was a partner in the firm. The decorations were austere, mostly college degrees and professional certificates. The few personal items were a picture of Mrs. Paulson, her husband, and their child, and a framed crayon drawing of a stick figure father, mother, and child standing in front of a house that Quinlan assumed was a tribute to the daughter's artistic talent.

"Why did you say that it was about time when I said I was from Homicide?" Quinlan asked when they were seated.

"Two years ago, when it happened, I told the investigating officers that there was something suspicious about my father's death, but they brushed me off."

"What made you think something was wrong?"

"My mother passed away several years ago and my father was horribly depressed. We had a wonderful relationship and he moved in for a while. Being around Jill, his granddaughter, was a tonic. After a while, he moved back to his house, but we spoke or visited all the time. But what really pulled him out of his depression was his relationship with Lily Dowd.

"Dad and Mom were longtime members of the Westmont Country Club, and they were very good friends with Lily and her husband, Frank. Frank passed away a year after my mother, and Lily and my father grew close. They started showing up at club events together and I thought they might get married. Then Robert Chesterfield showed up.

"Lily met him in London. She had a place there and she moved to London to get away from Oregon for a while because of the bad memories of her husband's death. I don't know what happened in London, but Chesterfield showed up in Portland shortly after Lily returned and started going after her. Lily is very wealthy and Chesterfield is a predator. That was obvious from the get-go, only Lily couldn't see that.

"My father tried to warn her about him, but Lily was infatuated. Chesterfield was much younger than Lily. He was dashing and sophisticated and he swept her off her feet. She wouldn't hear anything against him. When my father tried to wake her up, it soured their relationship.

"My father was very concerned about Lily's welfare and he started looking into Chesterfield's background. I don't know what he found, but he told me that he was going to talk to Chesterfield and get him to back off. The next thing I knew, my father was dead."

"I read the police report," Quinlan said. "The investigators concluded that your father died from natural causes."

Paulson's posture became rigid. She folded her hands on her desk and stared into Quinlan's eyes. "My father was sixty-two but he had the physique of a man in his early fifties. When he was in college, he swam so well that he almost made the Olympic team, and he never stopped working out. Those workouts were strenuous. His physicals never showed any danger signs. He didn't smoke, he was a social drinker and rarely had more than a glass of wine. There is no way he would have just keeled over."

"The police report said that you found your dad."

Paulson nodded and briefly lost her composure.

"Tell me how that happened and what you saw."

"Jill is ten and she's on a swim team. My husband works at Intel and my job keeps me pretty busy, so we often asked Dad to pick up Jill from school and take her to swim practice." Paulson smiled. "He loved Jill and he loved doing it. On a Monday, the day before I found him, I called to ask if he could take Jill, and the call went to his answering machine. I tried later, but I never got through, so I had to take her. My husband and I both had meetings the next afternoon, so I called again and the calls went straight to voice mail. That's when I got nervous and drove to his house. I have a key. When I went in, he was lying in the living room."

"Was there any indication of how he died?"

"There was a pool of vomit. It had dried. It looked old."

"Was there any food nearby or in the kitchen? Something he might have eaten?"

"Why do you ask?"

"I'd rather not say."

"Does this have anything to do with Sophie Randall's death? I heard that someone gave her poisoned chocolates."

"Who told you that?"

"It's all they're talking about at the Westmont."

Quinlan wondered if Peter Ragland had been opening his big mouth.

"Is it true?" Paulson asked.

"I'm afraid I can't discuss Mrs. Randall's case, except to tell you that she was poisoned."

"And you think the same person poisoned my father? Is it Robert Chesterfield? Do you think he killed Sophie Randall? Everyone knows about the run-in he had with Sam Moser."

"I really can't discuss the Randall case."

"Oh my God, I just remembered something. My father called me two days before I found his body. This would have been in the afternoon. He said he'd just gotten a box of chocolates in the mail and he wanted to know if I'd sent it. I said I hadn't. When I found my father, there was a pile of mail on a table in the entryway next to the mail slot, but I never saw the box of chocolates."

"I didn't see any mention of a box of chocolates in the police reports."

Paulson stared into space for a moment. Then her features hardened. "The back door was open," she said.

"What?"

"Father always locked all the doors. But the back door was open. If there was poison in those chocolates, the person who sent them could have taken the box away after he died."

"There was no mention of the back door being open in the police report."

"I didn't discover it until I came back to the house to get some clothes for the funeral, a few days after the police had left. It didn't occur to me that it might be important until now. I don't even know that Father wasn't responsible. It's also possible that one of the investigators forgot to lock the door when he left."

"That's a possibility. But the info about the door is helpful. Thank you." Quinlan handed Paulson his card. "If you think of anything else, please call me."

"Thank you for caring," Paulson said.

CHAPTER EIGHT

The office of the state medical examiner was in a tree-shaded, two-story, redbrick building that had once been a Scandinavian funeral home. The roof over the front porch was supported by white pillars, and the porch was partially hidden from view by arborvitae, split-leaf maples, and other shrubs.

Max Rothstein came out to greet Morris Quinlan as soon as the receptionist announced him. The state medical examiner was a Santa Claus look-alike with a beer belly and full white beard. His deep voice, sense of humor, and ability to make the most obscure medical facts understandable made him an excellent witness.

"What can you tell me about the cause of death in Sophie Randall's case?" Quinlan asked when they were seated in Rothstein's office.

"It was definitely cyanide poisoning. I found traces during the autopsy, and the chocolates were all doctored."

"Was there anything special about the chocolates?"

"I had the lab look at them. It's a national brand. The killer could have bought them in any state in the union. And there's nothing distinctive about the box or the wrapping paper that would let us narrow down where it was purchased. The chocolates were mailed a day before Christmas so the odds on anyone re-membering who mailed them is next to zero. There were no prints on the wrapping paper, the box, or anything else."

"Did you get a chance to look at the autopsy report in Arthur Gentry's case?"

"I did."

"And?"

"Arthur Gentry had been dead for several days before Eileen Paulson discovered his body, which makes a conclusive diagnosis of cyanide poisoning difficult. Cyanide has a relatively short half-life, anywhere from minutes to hours. That means toxicological detection of cyanide to conclusively confirm cyanide poisoning is feasible only within the first few hours following exposure.

"However, there were some findings consistent with cyanide poisoning. Gentry vomited, and the vomit around his lips was black. The tissue of the liver, lungs, spleen, and heart was bright pink, and the stomach lining was badly damaged and blackened. This is consistent with cyanide poisoning. And there's one other finding that may help you. Gentry ate chocolate before he died."

"The same type that killed Randall?"

"No. I asked the lab to look into that, and they concluded that the chocolate that Gentry and Randall ate were different brands."

The Justice Center was a sixteen-story building in downtown Port-land that housed the Multnomah County jail, some circuit and dis-trict courts, state parole and probation, the state crime lab, and the central precinct of the Portland Police Bureau. The Detective Divi-sion was a wide-open space that stretched along one side of the thirteenth floor. Each detective had their own cubicle separated from the other cubicles by a chest-high divider. Morris Quinlan had just returned from talking to Dr. Rothstein when Roger Dillon walked into his cubicle.

Quinlan swiveled his chair and looked up at his partner's smiling face. "What's got you all excited?" Quinlan asked.

"I just got off the phone with Scott Bentley, my contact at Scotland Yard, and he had some interesting things to tell me."

"Don't keep me in suspense."

"Robert Chesterfield is British. He called himself Lord Chesterfield when he performed in London as a stage magician, but he's no lord. He was born in a slum in Manchester to abusive, alcoholic parents and was in trouble from an early age. Chesterfield ran away from home on several occasions and earned money by gambling in high-stakes, back-alley poker games. Scott says that Chesterfield is a whiz at card manipulation. He was arrested for assault when he stabbed a man who accused him of cheating, but witnesses said that the other player attacked Chesterfield. No charges were brought, because the police concluded that Chesterfield acted in self-defense.

"Chesterfield developed his persona as an English gentleman when he began performing. Scott told me that Lord Robert is quite the ladies' man and his favorite prey is wealthy older women like Lily Dowd. He used these women to get him into several private clubs, where he made a living at cards. Scott tells me that he stayed under the radar by winning but not winning so much that he called attention to himself."

A magician might be able to pick the lock on Arthur Gentry's back door, Quinlan thought. Out loud, he asked Dillon if he knew why Chesterfield had left London and come to Oregon.

"Scott wasn't certain. There were rumors of a scandal but he didn't have time to follow up. We know he met Lily Dowd in London, so he may have moved to Oregon with the idea of marrying her."

"Nice work."

"Thanks."

"I did a little detecting myself," Quinlan said, and he proceeded to tell Dillon what he'd found out at the medical examiner's office and during his meeting with Eileen Paulson.

"Before I visited Max, I spoke to Jan Crawford, the judge's wife," Quinlan continued. "She had some interesting things to tell me."

"Such as?"

"When her husband told her that Chesterfield was going to resign from the Westmont and take Lily with him, she tried to talk Lily out of it, but Dowd wouldn't listen. A few weeks after she resigned, Lily called Mrs. Crawford. Mrs. Crawford said that Dowd sounded drunk or drugged. She told Mrs. Crawford that she regretted resigning and had found out that many of the accusations about cheating at cards and with women were true. She said that she was at their home on the coast, which is isolated, and that Robert watched her all the time.

"Mrs. Crawford asked if she was afraid and if she needed help, but Mrs. Dowd suddenly said that she didn't mean what she'd said, and she hung up. Mrs. Crawford called back but her calls went to voice mail. Then Dowd called again and asked Mrs. Crawford not to call anymore."

"Should we go out there?" Dillon asked. "This sounds serious."

"Dowd's home is out of our jurisdiction. Even if she lived in Portland, we wouldn't have any grounds to believe that a crime is being committed."

Dillon sighed. "You're right. But what about the murders? Do you think we have enough evidence to show that Chesterfield murdered Randall or Gentry?"

"No. He's our chief suspect but I don't see enough here to go for an indictment."

Dillon started to say something, when Quinlan's phone rang. Quinlan answered it, and Dillon could tell that he wasn't pleased.

"Grab your coat," Morris Quinlan said when he hung up.

"Where are we going?"

"Ragland wants to brainstorm the Randall case."

CHAPTER NINE

An icy wind raced inland from the river, and threatening black clouds hovered over the detectives, who hunched their shoulders as they walked to the Multnomah County Courthouse. The district attorney's office was on the sixth floor. Peter Ragland had one of the exterior offices with a view of downtown Portland and the West Hills that were assigned to higher-ranking deputies.

Photographs of Ragland with politicians and celebrities took up part of one wall, giving visitors the impression that Peter hobnobbed with the rich and famous. Ragland's father appeared in most of the photographs, and Quinlan thought that Peter was probably just along for the ride.

Next to the photographs was a diploma from Georgetown, an elite law school. Rumor had it that Peter had been admitted as a legacy because Jasper Ragland was one of the school's famous alumni. Another rumor held that he had barely scraped through.

"Sit, sit," Ragland said, pointing at the two client chairs on the other side of his desk. "What have you got for me?"

Quinlan laid out what they had discovered.

"Good job," Ragland said when Quinlan finished his briefing. "I think it's time we confronted Mr. Chesterfield, don't you?"

"I don't know, Pete," Quinlan said. "There are still big holes in our case."

"Such as?"

"We don't have any evidence connecting Chesterfield to the poisoned candy in the Randall murder, and the evidence is even weaker in Gentry's case."

Ragland leaned back in his chair and grinned. "That's the beauty of having two murders with the same MO and a defendant with a motive to kill both victims. I'll introduce evidence of the Gentry murder at Chesterfield's trial for the murder of Sophie Randall and vice versa. That will give the jurors in both trials strong circumstantial evidence that Chesterfield killed Randall and Gentry."

"I still don't see proof beyond a reasonable doubt," Quinlan said. "We don't even have conclusive evidence that Gentry died from cyanide poisoning."

Ragland flashed Quinlan a patronizing smile. "Leave proving the case to me, Morris. I've got the law degree."

"Yes, you do."

"What do you think, Roger?" Ragland asked.

"You make some good points," Dillon said in an attempt to be diplomatic, "but I don't think we have enough to go for an indictment."

"Maybe we can get that extra something when we talk to Chesterfield."

"Aren't you worried that you'll tip him off?" Dillon asked.

"It's too late to worry about that. I called him and he's expecting us to visit this afternoon." Ragland stood up. "Gentlemen, let's take a trip to the coast. Oh, and when we arrive, let me handle the questions. I'm used to dealing with the class of people who gain admission to the Westmont."

Most of Oregon's four million citizens live close to I-5, the highway that runs north to south from Canada to Mexico, so Oregon is sparsely populated east or west of the interstate. The road from Portland to the Pacific passed through small towns, farmland, forests, and mountains. Morris Quinlan drove along it in a driving rain.

When they crossed the Coast Range, Roger Dillon saw patches of snow in the forest. Once they turned south onto the highway that ran along the coast, he distracted himself by watching violent waves crash into the massive rock formations that jutted out of the churning Pacific.

Several miles south of Lincoln City, Quinlan turned seaward onto a narrow, unmarked, gravel driveway bounded by evergreens and shrubbery. The unpaved driveway stopped at a high stone wall divided by a gate. Quinlan lowered his window and pressed a button embedded in an intercom. Ragland was expected, and the gate swung open as soon as the detective identified their party. As they continued along a paved driveway, gaps in the foliage gave Dillon fleeting views of an unruly ocean. A final turn revealed a modern glass, steel, and weathered wood house that sprawled along a cliff. Below the cliff was a sandy windswept beach.

Quinlan parked and the three men rushed under an overhang that shielded the front door from the fury of the storm. Moments later, the door opened into a flagstone entryway where they were greeted by Robert Chesterfield, who was dressed in neatly pressed slacks, a tan sweater, and a sky blue shirt. Chesterfield asked the deputy DA and the detectives to come in. Their host had a charming British accent, and Dillon imagined him standing in the vaulted hall of an English castle, welcoming members of a fox hunt before the chase.

"How are you, Peter? I don't think I've seen you since we battled over bridge. Sorry you had to drive out in this ghastly weather."

"The drive wasn't so bad. Thanks for seeing me on such short notice."

"It's no trouble. We're quite isolated out here, and I welcome the company."

"This is Morris Quinlan and Roger Dillon. They're the detectives who are investigating Sophie Randall's murder."

"Pleased to meet you. Can I get you anything to drink, coffee, tea? In the movies policemen always reject spirits when they're working, but we're out of the public eye. Can you imbibe when you're on duty? I've got some exceptional, fifteen-year-old, single malt Scotch."

"Coffee would be great," Peter said.

"I'm good," Quinlan said.

"Coffee for me, if it's not too much trouble," Dillon told Chesterfield.

"The houseman and maid are off today, so I'll have to do the honors. Why don't you get comfortable while I get the coffee?"

The detectives and the prosecutor walked down three steps into a spacious sunken living room where floor-to-ceiling windows gave a panoramic view of the ocean. The burning logs in a stone fireplace radiated heat into the cavernous space. Ragland chose an armchair near the fire, and the detectives sat on a couch.

"Is Mrs. Dowd going to join us?" Quinlan asked when Chesterfield returned carrying a silver tray with coffee, sugar, and cream.

"Unfortunately, Lily is indisposed. A vicious bug has attacked her. Not unexpected in this inclement weather."

"Give her my regards," Peter said.

"I will. She'll be sorry she missed you."

Chesterfield sat in a comfortable armchair across from the deputy DA and the detectives. "How can I be of assistance, Peter?"

"We're trying to get background information about anyone who might have had a reason to poison Sophie Randall or Samuel Moser. You knew Sophie Randall, didn't you?"

"I saw her around the club."

"And you know Sam Moser?"

"I do."

"I understand that you and Sam had a row."

"We did."

"It concerned Mrs. Randall, didn't it?"

"In part."

"Didn't she accuse you of making a pass at her?"

"That's what Moser said. It wasn't true."

"Then why did she accuse you?"

"We only have Moser's word that she did accuse me, and the poor girl is deceased. I assure you that contrary to the vicious rumors Moser's been spreading, I never said or did anything inappropriate where Mrs. Randall was concerned."

"Mr. Moser was the recipient of the chocolates that poisoned Mrs. Randall. Obviously, he was the intended victim. You don't deny that you threatened him, do you?"

Chesterfield looked amused. "Really, Peter, you're playing this hand as badly as you play bridge. There's no need to beat around the bush. If you think I tried to kill Moser, why not come out and say so."

"Well?"

"No, Peter, I did not send poisoned chocolates to Samuel Moser."

"What about Arthur Gentry?"

"What about him?"

"Did you cause his death?"

"Why would I poison Arthur Gentry? I barely knew the man."

"Arthur Gentry was an old friend of your wife's. He wanted to marry her. Gentry stood between you and Mrs. Dowd's fortune."

Chesterfield shook his head. "Really, Peter, I don't know where you get your information. Lily and Gentry were friends, but she had no romantic feelings toward him. Believe me, I didn't have to poison Arthur Gentry to get him out of the picture when I was courting Lily."

Chesterfield looked sad. "I'm sorry you have such a poor opinion of me, Peter. You could have saved yourself the trouble of a drive in this awful weather if you'd told me why you wanted to talk to me when you called."

Chesterfield cast a condescending look in Ragland's direction. "And, if I did kill someone, do you think I would confess to you and these nice gentlemen?"

Quinlan couldn't believe how badly Ragland was botching the interview. Chesterfield was making a fool of him. Even worse, he now knew that they suspected that Arthur Gentry had been murdered and he was a suspect.

"You've got me all wrong," Ragland stammered as he scrambled to save the situation. "We're not accusing you of anything. We just want to know if you have any information that will help us solve these murders."

"How could I? I resigned several months before Mrs. Randall was poisoned, and I had no contact with the Westmont after I resigned. I'm not surprised that someone tried to murder Moser. He is thoroughly unlikable and he treated me with a total lack of respect. I'm sure I'm not the only person who was upset by his superior attitude—an attitude that I don't appreciate in an employee. Do you have any more questions for me?"

Quinlan was fed up. "Yeah," he said, "I got a few. How did you know Arthur Gentry was poisoned?"

For the first time since they'd entered his house, Chesterfield looked flustered. "I . . . I didn't. We've been talking about poisoning and it just came out. If Sophie Randall had been stabbed, I would probably have denied stabbing Arthur. Was he poisoned?"

"Nice catch," Quinlan said. "By the way, that accent, it's phony, right?"

Chesterfield's jaw tightened. "Pardon me?"

"This whole business about being an English lord, that's a load of shit, isn't it? Aren't you really little Bobby Chesterfield from the Manchester slums who cheats at cards and fucks women old enough to be his mother?"

Chesterfield's hands curled into fists, and Dillon could tell that it was taking him every ounce of energy to keep from exploding.

"I've had enough of this interrogation. It's time for you gentlemen to leave. If you wish to speak to me again, you can contact me through my solicitor."

Quinlan smiled as he stood. "We don't have solicitors in the US of A. We got attorneys, and you should look into hiring a good one who's up on his criminal law."

"That went well," Quinlan said sarcastically when they were back on the highway.

"That son of a bitch," Ragland fumed. "We'll see how smug he is when he's rotting on death row."

"Look, Peter, you've got to start being objective," Quinlan said. "Chesterfield is a horse's ass, but he's a very intelligent horse's ass. He was baiting you because he knows you don't have a prosecutable case."

"That's where you and I disagree. I think I can get an indictment with what I have. Once Chesterfield is in custody, dressed in an orange jumpsuit instead of an Armani, we'll see how fast he changes his tune."

Quinlan was smart enough to know that he wasn't going to change Ragland's mind, so he stopped trying. Getting an indictment would not be a problem. Any prosecutor worth his salt could convince a grand jury to indict the pope for John Kennedy's assassination. Winning this case when it went to trial was something else.

CHAPTER TEN

Morris Quinlan was sound asleep when his phone rang.

"My hunch paid off," Peter Ragland bragged as soon as Quinlan answered.

"What hunch?" Quinlan asked, groggy and annoyed at being jarred out of a deep sleep.

"You know I got the murder indictments for Chesterfield last week?"

"I testified at the grand jury, Peter."

"Well, I don't just want to arrest His Lordship, I want to shake him up. I knew a guy like Chesterfield wouldn't be able to keep it in his pants, so I called in a favor from an undercover at Vice and had a tail put on him. Guess what?" Ragland asked gleefully.

"You woke me from a deep sleep, Peter. I'm too tired for games. Please cut to the chase."

"Lily Dowd is at her house on the coast. About an hour ago, Chesterfield escorted an attractive young woman up to Dowd's Portland condo. They're probably in the sack, doing the dirty right now, so I thought that this would be a perfect time to come calling.

I'm in the lobby of the condo with two uniforms. Hustle on down, and you'll be just in time to get in on the bust."

Robert Chesterfield had just finished giving a young woman whose name he couldn't remember her second orgasm when loud banging on the front door interrupted a most enjoyable evening.

"Stay here, my dear," Chesterfield said as he got out of bed and slipped on a robe.

"Open up, police!" a familiar voice shouted.

Motherfucker, thought Chesterfield, who remained outwardly composed. "Is that you, Peter?" he asked through the door.

"Open up, Robert."

"Why should I do that? It's the middle of the night and I have a guest."

"Tell your guest to get dressed. Playtime is over. I have a warrant for your arrest."

"Put on some clothes, dear. The police are calling!" Chesterfield shouted. Then he sighed and opened the door. "Did you plan this bit of theater in the hopes of embarrassing me?" Chesterfield asked wearily. "Because you haven't succeeded."

Ragland walked into the penthouse and handed Chesterfield the arrest warrant. "Robert Chesterfield, I am arresting you for the murders of Arthur Gentry and Sophie Randall and the attempted murder of Samuel Moser," the deputy DA said.

While Chesterfield was reading the warrant, Ragland told him his Miranda rights. He was just finishing when a frightened young woman walked out of Chesterfield's bedroom.

Chesterfield turned toward her and flashed a reassuring smile. "Megan—" he began.

"It's Mary," the woman corrected.

"I apologize. This dapper young man is Peter Ragland, and he's arresting me for several murders."

Mary's eyes grew wide.

"Don't worry. I didn't murder anyone, so you were never in any danger. Peter just loves to grab headlines." Chesterfield turned to Ragland. "May Mary leave? I only met her a few hours ago."

Ragland hesitated and Quinlan stepped in. "Let the young woman go, Peter, so we can get on with this."

Ragland gestured toward the door. "Give these officers your name, address, and phone number. Then you can take off."

Mary gripped her purse tightly to her chest and scurried out of the condo. One of the uniforms followed her.

"What shall we do now?" Chesterfield asked. "Would you and your companions like some tea?"

Ragland reddened. "Don't you ever get tired of this phony Brit act? Put your hands behind your back so we can cuff them. You'll have your tea and crumpets in the jail."

"May I dress first?"

Quinlan was afraid Ragland would try to take Chesterfield to jail in his birthday suit, so he stepped in. "Go with him while he dresses," the detective told the other uniform.

Ragland frowned, but he didn't countermand the order.

"This has been a productive evening, if I do say so myself," Ragland gloated when Chesterfield was out of sight.

"I hope you're right," Quinlan said. Ragland had acted rashly, and Quinlan was very worried that the case was going to blow up in Peter's face.

CHAPTER ELEVEN

For the past four days, Regina Barrister had been in court in a county located in the desert, a five-hour drive from Portland. Her client was charged with murder, and the case was anything but easy. When the jury brought in the not guilty verdict, Regina had been relieved and subdued. That had not been the case when she was alone in her car. As soon as the engine started, Regina broke into a massive grin, put on *Jump Back: The Best of The Rolling Stones*, and sang along at the top of her lungs all the way back to Portland.

Regina arrived home a little before midnight and crawled into bed. She had just fallen asleep when the ringing of her phone jerked her awake again.

"I have a Mr. Chesterfield on the line, Miss Barrister," said the operator at the answering service that put through urgent calls after hours. "He's an inmate at the jail."

"Have I the pleasure of talking to Regina Barrister?" a man asked when the call was put through.

"I'm Regina."

"My name is Robert Chesterfield and I've just been arrested for two murders."

Regina walked out of the jail elevator. Moments later, a guard opened a thick steel door and led her into a narrow corridor that ran in front of three contact visiting rooms. When she stopped in front of the middle room, Regina looked through a large window of shatterproof glass into a narrow concrete room where Robert Chesterfield was sitting at a table that was bolted to the floor. He was dressed in an orange jumpsuit that should have made him look common. Instead, he brought to mind the handsome British prisoners of war in World War II movies who faced captivity with a stiff upper lip while they plotted their escape.

"What an appropriate name for a successful trial attorney," Chesterfield said when Regina was seated across from him.

"When my parents emigrated from Russia to the US, my family name was Batiashvili. My father learned English by reading British mystery novels. When he realized that Americans had a hard time with his last name, he changed it to Barrister."

"Ah yes, Dorothy Sayers's Lord Peter Wimsey and Agatha Christie's Hercule Poirot, not to mention the immortal Sherlock, the heroes of my youth. I believe that your father and I would have gotten along."

Regina flashed an indulgent smile. "That's enough about me, Mr. Chesterfield. You said you've been charged with two murders. Tell me what the police think you did."

"Are you by any chance a member of the Westmont Country Club?"

"No."

"Did you read about the secretary at the club who was poisoned?"

"I did, but I don't usually pay much attention to a murder case when I'm not involved."

"Busman's holiday, eh?" Chesterfield said with a smile. Then he stopped smiling. "I moved to Oregon from London several years ago and began seeing Lily Dowd, who was a widow and a member of the Westmont. A gentleman named Arthur Gentry was also courting Lily. Mr. Gentry passed away quite suddenly. I married Lily soon after and became a member of the Westmont.

"Several months ago, Samuel Moser, the manager of the club, accused me of sexually harassing female members and staff, including his secretary, Sophie Randall. He also accused me of cheating at cards. There was no truth to these accusations, and I told him so. Mr. Moser continued to insult me, and I demanded that he be fired. When the board refused, my wife and I resigned.

"In December, someone sent Mr. Moser a box of chocolates. He gave the box to Mrs. Randall. She ate a few pieces and died. The papers reported that the chocolates contained cyanide. Now I've learned that the police believe that Mr. Gentry may have been poisoned."

"Are you being accused of murdering both victims?" Regina asked.

Chesterfield nodded. "Do you know a prosecutor named Peter Ragland?"

"I do."

"Have you had any cases against him?"

"I have."

"How did you do?"

"Of the four cases I tried against Peter, three ended in not guilty verdicts. I lost one case, but I appealed, and the Oregon Court of Appeals reversed because Peter failed to tell me that his key witness had not identified my client at a lineup and a photo throwdown. When the case was sent back for a new trial, Peter's boss told him to dismiss it. Is Peter the DA on your case?"

"Yes. He's also a member of the Westmont and he seems to be having the time of his life harassing me with these ridiculous charges. Recently, Mr. Ragland drove to my house on the coast with Detectives Quinlan and Dillon and tried to interrogate me. When I realized what he was up to, I sent them packing. Then he showed up at my condominium tonight while I was entertaining a young woman and dragged me downtown. If it hadn't been for Detective Quinlan, I'm sure he would have perp-walked me out of my building in the nude."

"Did they tell you why you're a suspect?"

"It has to be because of the argument I had with Moser. Ragland asked me about it. And, of course, if Arthur Gentry and I were both courting Lily and he was also poisoned . . ." Chesterfield shrugged.

"If you decide to retain me, I'll contact Peter and get discovery. Then we'll know the state's evidence."

"I understand that there's no bail in a murder case."

"There's no automatic bail, but I can get bail for you by asking for a bail hearing and convincing the judge that the DA doesn't have a strong case. That doesn't always work. Judges are reluctant to release defendants charged with murder."

"How much will you want as a retainer if I hire you today?"

"We're talking six figures if you're charged with murder and high six figures if you're facing the death penalty. There could be further expenses for expert witnesses and investigators."

"That shouldn't be a problem. My wife is quite wealthy."

"Didn't you just tell me that you were in bed with a young woman when Ragland arrested you? Won't your wife be angry?"

Chesterfield smiled. "Lily is very understanding. Give her a call and tell her I'm in jail, and I'm sure she'll come to the rescue. But I trust you'll treat the circumstances of my arrest as an attorney-client confidence."

After Regina left the jail, she caught a few hours of sleep before going to her office. When she got there, Regina called the number Chesterfield had given her for his wife.

"Am I speaking to Lily Dowd?" Regina asked when a woman answered the phone.

"Yes?"

"My name is Regina Barrister. I'm a criminal defense attorney in Portland, and I have some disturbing news for you. Your husband has been arrested. I talked to him at the jail last night."

"Bobby is in jail?" Dowd asked as if she had not heard Regina correctly.

"I'm afraid so."

"What are the charges?"

"They're very serious. I think it would be better if we discussed them in person."

"I'm not a child, Miss Barrister. Tell what's going on."

"The district attorney is accusing him of poisoning a woman named Sophie Randall, attempting to poison Samuel Moser, and poisoning another man named Arthur Gentry."

"Arthur!" Dowd gasped. Then there was silence on Dowd's end of the phone.

"Mrs. Dowd, are you all right?"

"Yes. This is just a shock. And it can't be true. Bobby would never do anything like that."

"He's told me that he's innocent."

"Of course, he is."

"I'm sure you understand that it is very expensive to defend a murder case. One of the reasons I'm calling is because your husband wants to retain me. He told me to call you to make the financial arrangements so I can represent him."

"What amount are we talking about?"

Regina quoted a figure and explained why it was high. Dowd was silent again for a moment.

"That's a lot of money. I'd like to talk to you in person before I write a check."

"Of course. Can you come to Portland, or would you rather I go to you?"

"Will they let me see Bobby?"

"Yes. There are visiting hours."

"Very well. I'll come to Portland. Can I see Bobby this afternoon?"

"I'll try to set up a visit. We can talk after you see your husband."

CHAPTER TWELVE

Regina was standing at the front door of the Justice Center when a black Mercedes limousine stopped at the base of the steps. A light rain was falling. A chauffeur opened the rear door and held an umbrella over Lily Dowd, who was wearing a dull gray overcoat and sensible shoes. If it weren't for the limo and the chauffeur, Regina would not have known that Dowd was one of the wealthiest women in Oregon.

"Mrs. Dowd," Regina said as she walked down the steps.

Dowd and the chauffeur met Regina halfway.

"Let's get inside," Regina said.

"I'll be all right now, Greg," Dowd said. "I'll call you when I'm ready to go."

The chauffeur shielded Dowd until she was out of the rain. Then he walked back to the car and drove off. Dowd opened her coat when she was inside. Her dress was as drab as her coat.

"How is Bobby doing?" Dowd asked.

"Remarkably well for someone facing the most serious charges the State can bring."

Dowd smiled. "That's Bobby. He's always so cheerful. When can I see him?"

"Right away. You won't be able to be in the same room with him. They have noncontact rooms where you can talk on a phone through shatterproof glass."

"But I'm his wife."

"It's the best I could do. Very few people other than a defendant's lawyer can have a contact visit."

"I shall talk to John about this. It's ridiculous."

"John?"

"The governor. I'll call him later today and straighten this out."

Regina didn't know what to say to that, so she changed the subject. "I'll take you to Reception and set up the meeting. Then I'll wait for you so you can have privacy when you visit. We can go back to my office when you're finished."

"That's very nice of you," Dowd said.

Regina smiled and walked Lily Dowd into the jail reception area.

"How are you holding up?" Robert Chesterfield asked his wife.

"Oh, Bobby, look at you."

"Now, don't you worry. I'm just fine. I can't say much for the cuisine, and the accommodations don't match up to the Ritz, but I'm being treated quite well."

"I met Miss Barrister. Do you think she can help you?"

"She has an excellent reputation. I have confidence in her. I think it would be in our best interest to hire her."

"Then I'll do that, right away."

"Thank you, dear."

"Can she get you out of here quickly?"

"Probably not. She was very clear that it's difficult to get bail in a murder case."

"But you're innocent."

"I am, so everything will come out well in the end. Meanwhile, you must be patient and let my attorney do her job."

Lily dabbed tears from her cheeks. "I can't bear to see you like this."

"I'm fine. Just know that I love you and that there is no truth to these charges. We'll be together soon."

Regina walked Lily Dowd to her law office. Lily gave Regina a check for the retainer and Regina explained what would happen in her husband's case.

As soon as Lily Dowd left, Regina dialed Peter Ragland.

"Hi, Regina. What's up?"

"Robert Chesterfield just retained me."

Ragland chuckled. "I think I can have that fact introduced in evidence as an admission of guilt."

"Cute, Peter."

"Is he calling himself Mr. Chesterfield or Lord Chesterfield?"

"Plain old *mister*. Is your comedy monologue over? Can we discuss the case?"

"What happened to your sense of humor?"

"It deserted me when I was awakened from a sound sleep and had to go to the jail at one in the morning because you decided to arrest my client in the middle of the night."

Ragland chuckled again. Regina took a deep breath and counted to ten.

"When can I get discovery?" she asked.

"Anytime you want it."

"Care to tell me why you think you have a case?"

"It's all laid out in the police reports."

"What about bail?"

"Not happening. Chesterfield isn't an American citizen. If he gets out of custody, he'll flee. Of course, I'd make all sorts of concessions, like taking the death penalty off the table, if Mr. Chesterfield admits he killed Mrs. Randall and Mr. Gentry and pleads guilty in both cases."

"My client is adamant that he's not involved with either case."

"I'd expect nothing less. Isn't it amazing how many innocent victims of our justice system are serving time at the penitentiary?"

CHAPTER THIRTEEN

The Multnomah County Courthouse is an ominous, eight-story, gray concrete building that takes up an entire block in downtown Portland. The courtroom of the Honorable Henry Beathard was on the fifth floor. Regina led Lily Dowd past the reporters who crowded the corridor and into a room with high windows and marble columns. The grim faces of judges past stared down at them from the walls.

Regina guessed that the courtroom would be packed, so she'd asked the bailiff to reserve a seat for Lily behind the defense table. As she led Lily down the aisle, Regina noticed Morris Quinlan sitting on the back bench. Regina respected Quinlan, so she smiled at him as she passed by.

"Chesterfield's called in the A team," Roger Dillon said.

"Yeah," Quinlan answered. "This could get embarrassing. Regina is the last person you want on the other side of a case if you have the IQ of a gnat."

When they were almost to Lily's seat, Regina saw Gary Randall, Sophie Randall's husband. He glared at Regina, but Regina was not offended. She felt very sorry for him and understood why he would hate her for helping the man accused of murdering his wife.

The guards had brought Robert Chesterfield over from the jail after letting him change into a hand-tailored suit that Lily had provided. He was waiting at one of the two counsel tables that stood within the bar of the court.

"It's so good to see you," Chesterfield said as he reached out to take Lily's hand.

"No touching," one of the guards said, and Chesterfield pulled his hand back.

"Sorry," he apologized.

"Why can't I touch my husband?" Lily demanded.

"It's a rule, dearest," Chesterfield said. "These gentlemen are just performing their sworn duty."

Peter Ragland sat at the other counsel table. Regina nodded at the deputy district attorney as she passed through the gate that separated the spectators from the attorneys and the judge. After setting out her notes, law books, and statutes, she took a seat next to her client.

"How does it look?" Chesterfield asked.

"We lucked out. Henry Beathard is going to hear our bail motion and motion in limine."

"Why is that lucky?"

"Beathard taught Evidence before being appointed to the bench, and our motion in limine is based on an interpretation of a rule of evidence. If we win the motion in limine, the judge will probably grant our motion for bail."

Before Chesterfield could ask another question, a door opened behind the bench, and a barrel-chested man with thinning black hair, old-fashioned horn-rimmed glasses, and a goatee stepped out.

Regina had loved law school. She had been fanatic about preparing for class, and she relished the battle of wits with her professors when they called on her. Henry Beathard conducted motion hearings the way he had conducted his law school classes, and Regina had prepped extra hard for this one.

"Good morning, Mr. Ragland and Miss Barrister," the judge said. "Miss Barrister, you want me to decide your motion for bail and your motion in limine at this hearing. That's a bit unusual."

Regina stood. "It is, Your Honor, but the State can't hold Mr. Chesterfield without bail under ORS 135.240 unless it convinces you that the proof is evident or the presumption is strong that Mr. Chesterfield is guilty of the crimes charged in the indictment. If we prevail on our motion to exclude evidence of the Gentry case from Mr. Chesterfield's trial for the murder of Sophie Randall, it will have a major impact on the State's ability to convince you that Mr. Chesterfield should be denied bail."

"Very well," Judge Beathard said. "I'll hear the motion in limine first. Mr. Ragland, let me see if I understand the facts you hope to establish in our trial, and please correct me if I don't get this right.

"As I understand it, you intend to present witnesses who will testify that a few months before the new year, Samuel Moser accused the defendant of misconduct at the Westmont Country Club. Mr. Chesterfield was very angry and resigned from the club. Then, two days before the new year, someone sent a box of poisoned chocolates to Mr. Moser. He was on a diet and gave the candy to Sophie Randall, his secretary. Mrs. Randall ate some of the candy and died of cyanide poisoning. You think you can prove that Robert Chesterfield put cyanide in the candy and sent it to Mr. Moser because he was angry at Mr. Moser, and this is the basis for the murder charge involving Mrs. Randall and the attempted murder charge involving Mr. Moser. How am I doing?"

"Just fine, Your Honor," Ragland said.

"Okay. Now, there is another indictment containing charges our jury will not be asked to decide. In that case, you're alleging that Mr. Chesterfield and Arthur Gentry were courting a woman named Lily Dowd and that Mr. Chesterfield poisoned his rival for Mrs. Dowd's affections so he could get rid of him and marry Mrs. Dowd. Am I good so far, Mr. Ragland?"

"Yes."

"Mr. Ragland, is it your contention that you should be able to tell the jurors about Mr. Gentry's death when it's deciding whether Mr. Chesterfield is guilty of killing Mrs. Randall and attempting to kill Mr. Moser?"

"Yes, Your Honor."

Beathard turned to Regina. "You don't think Mr. Ragland should be allowed to tell the jury about the evidence in the Gentry case, do you, Miss Barrister?"

"No, I don't."

"And you want me to rule that the Gentry evidence is inadmissible in this trial?"

"Yes."

"Since this is your motion, Miss Barrister, you have the burden of convincing me that the State is wrong when Mr. Ragland argues that the Gentry evidence should be heard by our jury. Proceed."

Regina stood and addressed the court. "Your Honor, it's a well-established rule that the State can't introduce evidence of crimes not charged in an indictment to prove that the defendant is guilty of the crimes charged. The reason for this rule is obvious. If a person is charged with murder and the State introduces evidence that he committed other unrelated crimes, the jurors might conclude that he must be guilty because he has criminal tendencies.

"If the crimes are similar, though unrelated to the crime alleged in the indictment, it would be a natural human tendency to conclude that the defendant must be guilty of the crime charged because he has committed the same type of crime in the past."

"Aren't there exceptions to this rule, Counselor?" Judge Beathard asked.

"Yes, five, but none apply in the case at bar."

"What are the exceptions, and why don't they apply to the Gentry evidence?"

"You can get evidence of other crimes before a jury if the evidence tends to establish the following: motive; intent; the absence of mistake or accident; a common scheme or plan embracing the commission of two or more crimes so related to each other that proof of one tends to establish the others; or the identity of the person charged with committing the crime on trial. It is Mr. Chesterfield's contention that none of these exceptions apply in this case."

"I think we can all agree that no one sends candy laced with cyanide to someone by mistake or accident," the judge said. "Would you need to introduce evidence from the Gentry case in our case to prove that Mr. Chesterfield didn't send the candy by mistake or accident, Mr. Ragland?"

"I might, Your Honor, if the defendant admitted sending the poisoned candy to Mr. Moser but claimed he didn't know there was poison in the candy."

"Is that what your client will say, Miss Barrister?" the judge asked.

"Mr. Chesterfield adamantly denies sending the candy to Mr. Moser."

"Very well, Miss Barrister," Judge Beathard said. "Let's move to intent. Mr. Ragland, if you had solid proof that Mr. Chesterfield knowingly sent poison candy to Mr. Moser, it would be crystal clear, wouldn't it, that he intended to kill Mr. Moser?"

"Yes."

"So why would you need to introduce evidence from another poisoning case to make your point with the jury?"

Ragland fidgeted for a moment before conceding that he wouldn't need to introduce evidence from Gentry to show intent under those circumstances.

"Tell me why the motive exception doesn't apply, Miss Barrister."

"Mr. Ragland is going to argue that Mr. Moser accused my client of cheating at cards and making unwanted advances to female members and employees of the Westmont Country Club, among other things, and that made Mr. Chesterfield so angry that he gave up his membership in the club. Then Mr. Ragland will argue that Mr. Chesterfield sent the poisoned candy to Mr. Moser because he hated Mr. Moser and wanted revenge.

"In the Gentry case, the State will try to prove that my client and Mr. Gentry were courting Lily Dowd, and Mr. Chesterfield killed Mr. Gentry to get rid of a rival for Mrs. Dowd's hand.

"These motives are very different and have no relation to each other. Evidence from the Gentry case will not throw any light on the motive that prompted the attempt on Samuel Moser's life."

"What do you have to say about motive, Mr. Ragland?" Judge Beathard asked the prosecutor.

"I contend that Mr. Chesterfield hated both men, so hate was the motive for both murders."

"Can't you be a rival in love without hating the other suitor?" the judge asked.

"I . . . It's possible, I guess," Ragland conceded grudgingly.

"Even if you established that Mr. Chesterfield did hate his romantic rival, is mere hatred sufficient to get other crimes' evidence before a jury? Wouldn't that open the door to admitting any crime in a defendant's life where he hated the victim?"

"Well, that's too broad," Ragland answered.

"Do you have any evidence that Mr. Chesterfield hated Mr. Gentry? Are there phone calls, threatening letters?" the judge asked.

Ragland looked flustered. "Not that we have discovered so far."

"Why can't Mr. Ragland introduce the Gentry evidence to prove a common scheme or plan?" the judge asked Regina.

"To bring a case within this exception to the general rule, the two crimes must be connected as parts of a plan or so related as to show a common motive or intent running through both," Regina said. "The case before the court provides an excellent example of a situation where the exception applies. Evidence of the attempted murder of Mr. Moser would be admissible to prove how Mrs. Randall got the poisoned candy. The murder weapon was sent to Mr. Moser and he gave it to Mrs. Randall because he was on a diet, so the two crimes are connected. But the State will try to prove that Mr. Gentry was murdered two years before Mrs. Randall for completely different reasons that are not connected to this case. The two murders are not part of a common scheme or plan."

"Mr. Ragland?"

"It's the same MO. He has a grudge against someone, and he sends them poisoned candy."

"We're talking about whether the two crimes are part of a common scheme or plan, and I don't see that they are.

"But what about using the Gentry evidence to prove the identity of the person who murdered Mrs. Randall?" Judge Beathard asked Regina.

"The cases I've cited in my memo hold that the mere fact that the two crimes are parallel as to the methods and means employed in their execution doesn't serve to identify the defendant as the poisoner of Mrs. Randall unless his guilt may be inferred from its similarity to the Gentry poisoning.

"Mr. Ragland has no evidence that proves that Mr. Chesterfield sent the candy to Mr. Moser. In the Gentry case, there is only circumstantial evidence that the cause of death is cyanide, and the only evidence that the poison, if it existed, was in candy is also circumstantial and derives from an inadmissible hearsay statement made by Mr. Gentry. No box of chocolates was found in Gentry's house.

"Furthermore, this is not a case where a killer leaves a distinctive mark on each victim, like a Z cut in the victim's cheek or a rose left at each murder scene. Using poison to kill someone is not so unique that Your Honor could conclude that the use of poison in Gentry proves the identity of the poisoner in this case.

"I'd like to make one other point, Your Honor. As soon as I understood how little evidence Mr. Ragland can present to implicate my client in this case, it became obvious to me that Mr. Ragland can't prove his case without evidence from the Gentry case, because there isn't enough evidence in either case to convince a jury beyond a reasonable doubt that Mr. Chesterfield committed any of the crimes charged.

"Mr. Ragland is hoping to bootstrap a conviction in the case that is before you by presenting the unrelated evidence in Gentry, precisely the type of behavior the rule of evidence prohibiting the use of unconnected evidence of other crimes was written to forbid."

Ragland responded to Regina's arguments, but it was clear that the judge was only listening to be courteous. When Ragland sat down, the judge made his ruling.

"I spent quite a bit of time researching the issues raised by your motion, Miss Barrister. The cases and law review articles cited in your excellent memorandum of law in support of the motion were very helpful. After giving the issue a lot of thought, I find that I agree with Miss Barrister. Her motion to prohibit the introduction in our case of evidence about Arthur Gentry's case is granted.

"I'm also going to grant Mr. Chesterfield bail."

Lily Dowd leaned forward and laid a hand on Regina's shoulder. "Thank you."

"You were fantastic," Chesterfield said. "Worth every penny."

"I'd like to see Counsel in chambers so we can work out the

conditions of release," the judge said before standing up and heading to his chambers.

As soon as Judge Beathard left the courtroom, the spectators and reporters started talking. Because of the noise and commotion, no one noticed that Gary Randall had walked into the bar of the court until he smashed his fist into Robert Chesterfield's face.

"I'll kill you!" he screamed as he pulled his fist back again. Before he could land another blow, the jail guards grabbed him and wrestled him to the ground.

"Let me go!" Randall screamed as he thrashed about on the floor.

"You've got the wrong man, Mr. Randall," Chesterfield said. "I didn't try to poison anyone."

Morris Quinlan watched the chaos caused by Gary Randall's attack. Then he shook his head in disgust and left the courtroom. "I knew Peter would fuck up this case," he told his partner.

"What can we do now?"

"We can try to find evidence that proves Chesterfield sent the candy to Moser. If we don't, he's going to walk."

"There's something I don't understand," Dillon said.

"What's that?"

"Ragland is obviously incompetent, so why is he handling major cases?"

"Politics, my boy. You saw the pictures on Ragland's wall. Daddy was one of the most respected prosecutors this state ever produced and one of its most influential politicians. He's retired now, but he still pulls a lot of strings, and people, like the district attorney, owe him big-time. As long as Jasper Ragland wants Peter in the DA's office, he'll remain in the DA's office."

Lily Dowd waited in the courtroom with one of Regina's associates until Regina came out of the judge's chambers and told her what she would have to do to obtain her husband's release. As soon as

Lily left with the associate, Regina spoke with the reporters. Then she crossed the street to the Justice Center, where Robert Chesterfield had been taken while the lawyers and the judge decided on his release conditions.

"Your wife is posting bail, so you should be out by this afternoon," Regina said as soon as she and Chesterfield were alone in the contact visiting room.

"That's great. I can't thank you enough. Can you make a guess on how the judge's ruling will impact my case?"

"It might kill it. If Ragland were smart, he would have held off on the indictments. After I read the discovery, it was obvious that he didn't have enough evidence to prove your guilt beyond a reasonable doubt. I'm guessing that he'll dismiss both cases and hold off on new indictments until he has stronger evidence implicating you."

"Which he will never have, since I am completely innocent."

"I'm thinking of making a motion for a speedy trial to force Ragland's hand. Of course, he can stall by appealing Judge Beathard's ruling to the Court of Appeals. That could keep the case on hold for a year or more."

"The law is not something I'm schooled in, so I'll leave the legal decisions in your capable hands. You've been spot-on so far. But I would like to discuss the case with you when I'm back in civilization." Chesterfield looked into Regina's eyes and smiled. "Perhaps we could have dinner together sometime next week."

"I'd love to have dinner with you and Lily," Regina answered.

"I don't want to trouble Lily. My arrest and incarceration have been a big strain for her. She should rest in our house at the coast."

Regina was certain she knew what her client was up to. "If you really want to discuss legal matters, it would be better if we met at my office, Mr. Chesterfield."

"Robert, please. I feel we've gotten to the point in our relationship where we can be on a first-name basis."

Regina looked directly at her client. "If you're talking about

the attorney-client relationship, I'd be glad to call you Robert. If you're thinking of any other type of relationship, you should stop."

Again, Chesterfield smiled. "I think you might enjoy an extra-legal relationship with me, Regina. You're a beautiful woman, and I'm guessing that you have . . . appetites."

Regina stared at Chesterfield for a few seconds more. Then she burst out laughing.

"Knock it off, will you. I'll make this as plain as I can: There is no chance whatsoever that I'm going to jump in the sack with you. Is that clear?"

Chesterfield smiled once more. "You can't blame a chap for trying."

"Fair enough. You gave it the old college try. Now, put your pecker back in your pants and let's talk about the law."

When Regina and Lily walked into the jail reception area, Regina noticed a man sitting off to the side. He was well dressed and well groomed, unlike the other people waiting for an inmate to be released. Regina thought that she might have seen him in the courtroom during the hearing, but she couldn't be sure. She was trying to remember when Robert Chesterfield stepped out of the jail elevator, looking dapper in his suit and showing no sign that his incarceration or the charges against him had made any psychological impact. When Lily and Regina stood up to walk to Chesterfield, so did the well-dressed man.

"Robert!" he shouted.

Chesterfield turned and stared. "Horace! What are you doing here?"

"I flew over from London yesterday. We need to talk."

"Ladies," Chesterfield said, "this is Horace Dobson, my theatrical agent. He represented me when I performed my magic act in London."

"And I'm here with great news. Your case has gotten a lot of publicity, and you can use it to your advantage. I've been on the phone to casinos in Las Vegas. They're interested in having you perform. Your career could get a big boost."

"I don't have a career, my dear boy. I left it behind when I married Lily," he said, casting a radiant smile in his wife's direction.

Regina stifled an urge to throw up.

"You're hot now, Robert, and you need to take advantage of the moment," Dobson insisted.

"I appreciate your coming all this way, so the least I can do is hear you out. But Lily and I have been separated while I've been in jail, and I want to spend time with her. Give me your hotel room number and I'll call you there tomorrow." Chesterfield put his arm around Lily's shoulders. "Tonight, I want to be alone with my wife."

Regina remembered the pass Chesterfield had made only a few hours earlier. She had an urge to tell Lily Dowd about it, but she kept her mouth shut.

"I've got to get back to my office, Robert," Regina said. "Call me tomorrow, so we can plan a time to discuss the next steps in your case."

"Will do. And thanks again. You're a marvel."

Regina headed back to her office. She was thoroughly disgusted with Chesterfield, but she didn't have to like someone to represent them.

CHAPTER FOURTEEN

Two weeks after the hearing in front of Judge Beathard, Peter Ragland dismissed the indictments in the Randall, Gentry, and Moser cases. He had not called Regina to let her know what he was going to do, but Regina knew Ragland's ego wouldn't let him admit to her that he had screwed up.

Regina told her client the good news and assumed that she was done with Chesterfield, but two months later, Regina returned from court to find a voice mail from Robert Chesterfield asking her to call him as soon as she got in. Chesterfield sounded nervous, and that surprised Regina, because she could not remember one time during her representation of Chesterfield when he had not been perfectly calm.

"Thank you for getting back to me so quickly," Chesterfield said as soon as Regina identified herself.

"What's happened? You sound upset."

"I am upset. Can you come to our house on the coast?"

"When?"

"Now."

"I'm prepping for a trial that's starting next week. What's so urgent?"

"Lily went out for a walk this morning. She does that most days, but the weather was bad and I was concerned. I asked her to stay in, but she insisted on going. She's usually gone for an hour, but I expected her to return earlier because of the storm. When she wasn't home two hours later, I went looking for her. When I couldn't find her, I called the police. A search party just found her body half a mile away, on the rocks at the bottom of the cliff that runs behind our house."

The weather was raw. Regina assumed that she would have to trek along a cliff exposed to the elements in frigid, stormy conditions, so she changed into jeans, hiking boots, and threw on a ski jacket with a hood before heading to the coast. Gusts of wind shook her car, and a heavy rain battered it during the drive, and she had to stay too focused on the road to think about the possibility that she might be representing Robert Chesterfield in another murder case.

Regina had never been to Lily Dowd's home, but she had no trouble locating it. Official vehicles and vans sporting the logos of local television stations lined the shoulder of the highway at the turnoff. A sawhorse blocked the driveway. Regina showed her identification to the officer stationed in front of it. As soon as he received confirmation from someone in the house, the officer waved Regina through.

Regina got her first view of Dowd's home when she rounded a bend in the driveway. She was amazed at its size and impressed by the way it blended into the seaside scenery. Chesterfield walked out to Regina's car as soon as she parked. He was unshaven, he appeared to have run a comb through his hair without using a mirror, his eyes were bloodshot, and he looked nothing like the debonair fashion plate she was used to seeing.

"Thank you for coming so quickly," Chesterfield said as he escorted Regina under the overhang and out of the rain.

"Have the police questioned you?" she asked.

"Once we found Lily, I told them I wouldn't talk to them until you came."

"What about before that?"

"Two officers showed up after I called 911. I told them where Lily liked to walk and showed them the path. We went north and south along the cliff. It was raining pretty hard by then and there were very strong gusts of wind, so there wasn't much conversation.

"The mist and driving rain made it hard to see, so the officers called a halt after half an hour and radioed for more men. I can't remember what I said while we waited, but I'm sure we didn't talk much. More men came and I waited inside. When someone spotted Lily on the rocks a little over half a mile from here to the south, the officers asked me to go to the spot to make an identification. I said I thought the dead woman was Lily. After that I said I wouldn't talk to anyone until you got here."

As soon as they were inside, a tall man in a black hooded windbreaker walked over to them. He had a full head of wavy salt-and-pepper hair and a bushy mustache.

"Miss Barrister?"

"Yes."

"I'm Clint Easley, a detective with the county. I'm in charge of this investigation."

"Pleased to meet you."

"Likewise. I'd like to talk to your client, but he insisted that I wait until you arrived."

"I'm sure you understand why, given his recent experience with the justice system."

"I do, but you're here now, and given your reputation, I'm sure you'll protect him."

"Has Mrs. Dowd's body been moved yet?" Regina asked.

"No. It's at the base of a cliff with no easy access. We're going to have to wait for the storm to abate before I send anyone down there to recover it."

"I'd like to see the scene of the accident before I give Mr. Chesterfield any legal advice. Would that be okay with you?"

"You don't need my permission, Miss Barrister. Mr. Chesterfield isn't under arrest, and the path along the cliff is open to the public."

Regina smiled at Easley. "Will you show me the way?"

"My pleasure," he said as he flipped up his hood and then headed outside.

Gale-force winds drove massive waves against the coal black rocks, sending spray high into the air. Other waves, unimpeded, crashed onto the shore. The storm made the trek slow going. Several deputies suddenly appeared through the curtain of rain. They looked miserable, hunched forward, hoods up, and hands plunged into their pockets, trying to stay warm and dry and failing miserably. When they reached the deputies, Easley handed Regina a pair of binoculars.

"She's down there!" Easley yelled so he could be heard above the howling wind and pounding surf.

Regina brought the binoculars up and looked over the side of the cliff. Raindrops dotted the lenses, and she had to wipe them off to get a decent view. Through the mist, she could see a body splayed across the top of a boulder, arms and legs spread wide. Regina couldn't make out the corpse's features, because long strands of wet hair spread across the dead woman's face.

"How can you be sure that's Lily Dowd?" Regina shouted.

"We can't, but Mr. Chesterfield said those were the clothes she was wearing when she went out for her walk."

Regina straightened up. "Okay, I've seen enough. Let's go back."

No one objected, and the trio walked back as fast as they could. When they reached the front door, Regina noticed a black BMW. Chesterfield swore.

"What's the matter?" Regina asked.

"It's the fucking Bobbsey Twins."

"Who?"

"Tweedledee and Tweedledum, Lily's offspring, come to make my life miserable."

A short, plump woman and a rail-thin man were standing in the entryway. As soon as Chesterfield walked in, the woman rushed toward him.

"What have you done to my mother?" she shouted.

Easley held up his badge. "I'm the detective in charge here, and I'll ask the questions. Now, who are you?"

Neither person seemed intimidated by the badge. "I'm Dr. Iris Hitchens, Lily Dowd's daughter, and this is her son, Andrew Dowd. He's an attorney. I called here two hours ago to talk to my mother. A policeman answered the phone and refused to tell me why he was in my mother's house. I'm here now and I demand an answer."

Easley relaxed. "I'm afraid I have some very bad news for you. You might want to sit down."

"I'm a medical doctor, Detective. Not some frail damsel. Now, tell me what's happened to Mother."

"Your mother went for a walk in very bad weather. When she didn't return, Mr. Chesterfield called the police. We've found a dead person at the base of a cliff near here. It appears to be a woman, but we can't get down to the body, because of the weather—so we haven't been able to make a positive identification."

Iris glared at Chesterfield. "You killed her, you bastard. You already got away with two murders, but you're not going to get away with murdering my mother."

Easley stepped between Iris and Chesterfield. "There is no evidence indicating that your mother was murdered, Dr. Hitchens."

Iris turned on the detective. "This man poisoned two people. He's a killer. He's after Mother's money, and murdering her is the quickest way to get it. I demand that you arrest him."

"I'm not arresting anyone until I have proof that a crime was committed, and I can't do that without evidence. Now, I'm going to ask you to calm down or I'll have to ask you to leave. Do you understand me?"

Andrew put a hand on his sister's shoulder. "He's right, Iris. We shouldn't jump to conclusions."

Iris turned on her brother. "Grow some balls, Andrew. Lord Robert is a gold-digging leech, and I'm not going to let him get away with this."

"Iris," Chesterfield said, his tone conciliatory, "I begged Lily to stay inside because of the storm, but she insisted on going for a walk. You've seen how strong the wind is. It's very possible she lost her balance and fell.

"And there's another possibility. Your mother has been very depressed lately, and she's been taking antidepressants. I don't want to think that she took her life, but . . ."

Iris's eyes went wide and she leaped at Chesterfield. He didn't try to defend himself, and her nails left blood trails on his cheeks before Easley could restrain her.

"You've just committed an assault," Easley said. "If Mr. Chesterfield presses charges, I can arrest you."

"No, no," Chesterfield said, his tone magnanimous. "Iris is overwrought. I forgive her. It is her mother, after all. I would like her to leave, though. This is my house, and I'm upset enough without having to worry about being attacked."

"You bastard," Iris said. "You won't get away with this."

"We should leave, Iris," Andrew said.

Iris glared at Andrew. Then she shook off Easley's hands and stomped outside. Andrew followed her.

When the door opened, Easley could see that the storm had

abated. "It looks like we might be able to start a recovery operation, so I'm going back to supervise. I suggest you stay here, Mr. Chesterfield. I'll want to talk to you as soon as we bring your wife up."

"I'll be here," Chesterfield assured him.

When the detective was out of earshot, Regina turned to her client. "That was nicely done," she said, her voice dripping with sarcasm.

"I don't know what you mean."

"You played Lily's daughter like a fiddle so you could get rid of her."

Chesterfield arched an eyebrow and flashed an innocent smile. "Did I? Really, I meant no harm, but I thought Iris and Andrew should know that suicide was a possibility. Lily has been terribly sad lately."

"I'm going to wait until the body is brought up. You can identify it. Other than that, I don't want you talking to Easley or anyone else. Got it?"

"You're the boss."

"I also want you to understand that your retainer for my representation in the Randall and Gentry cases does not cover my involvement in this case. If you want me to be your attorney, we'll have to make a new financial arrangement."

Chesterfield smiled once again. "That won't be a problem, Regina. If the corpse at the bottom of the cliff is Lily, I am going to be a very rich man. Soon after you won my case, Lily made a new will, leaving everything to me."

CHAPTER FIFTEEN

The rays of a warm spring sun poured through the floor-to-ceiling windows in Robert Chesterfield's bedroom and woke him from his carefree slumber. Chesterfield smiled as he stretched his arms. One reason for his smile was the fact that his hands no longer had to touch Lily Dowd's disgusting flesh. The absence of that dim-witted cow from his life elated Chesterfield. Touching her, mooning over her, and having sex with her had been made bearable only when he was thinking about the pot of gold at the end of the rainbow.

Chesterfield got out of bed and walked to a window that looked out on the Pacific. The sea was calm today, and puffy white clouds drifted across a bright blue sky. If only his boyhood mates from the slums of Manchester could see him now. The only flies in the ointment were the Bobbsey Twins, who were contesting the will he had talked Lily into writing. He loved watching them fume and rage whenever they were in his presence. Chesterfield had hired the best probate lawyers in the state, and they assured him that the will was airtight, so the irritation caused by Lily's obnoxious brood would fade soon like a poison ivy rash.

Chesterfield put on workout gear and started a series of calisthenics that would keep him supple. In a month, he would open his magic act in Las Vegas and he needed to be in top shape. Some of the illusions he performed required a great deal of elasticity because of the narrow spaces into which he had to fit. Chesterfield loved performing magic and the adoration it brought him, so he was willing to put up with the pain his rigorous routine caused him.

An hour after he started working out, Chesterfield slipped on running shoes. He was about to go outside when the phone rang.

"Robert?" Regina Barrister asked.

"Hi, Counselor. Do you have news for me?"

"Yes, and it's all good. I just had a call from Clint Easley. The county is not going to bring any charges against you. The official verdict is going to be that Lily's death was an accident."

"Which it was."

"Her children tried to pressure the district attorney to bring murder charges, but there's no evidence that you or anyone else was with Lily when she died."

"Does this mean I don't have to worry about being charged with Lily's death or any of the Multnomah County cases?"

"There's no statute of limitations on murder, but you're free and clear unless new evidence causes any of the cases to be reopened."

"I certainly made the right choice when I hired you. I've heard that they call you the Sorceress, and the nickname is very apt. Thank you for all you've done. I'm a fan for life."

Chesterfield hung up. For a moment, he stood stock-still. Then he pumped his fist. He'd beaten the system and gotten filthy rich in the process. Life was good, he thought. No, it was *great*!

Regina Barrister ended the call and looked out her office window at the river and beyond to the sun reflecting off the pristine white

snow that covered Mount Hood. The sight should have thrilled her. Instead, she felt as if she had to take a bath. She had a strong suspicion that Robert Chesterfield was guilty of the crimes charged in Peter Ragland's indictments, and the possibility loomed large that Chesterfield murdered his wife.

The only positive she could take away was the fact that Robert Chesterfield was no longer part of her life.

PART THREE

VANISHING ACT

2017

CHAPTER SIXTEEN

By the time Regina finished telling Robin what she remembered about Robert Chesterfield and his case, the sun had almost set. Robin was so absorbed by Regina's tale that she didn't feel the chilly breeze drifting inland off the river.

"Do you think Robert Chesterfield killed his wife?" Robin asked Regina.

"The weather was terrible on the day Lily Dowd died. She could have slipped or the wind could have knocked her off the cliff. I was almost knocked off my feet several times when we walked to the place where her body was found."

"So, you're saying that Robert didn't have anything to do with her death?"

"I'm saying that the police never found any evidence that Lily Dowd was murdered. If she was, there wasn't a shred of evidence implicating Chesterfield. No jury would ever have found him guilty beyond a reasonable doubt. Dowd's children sued Chesterfield for wrongful death in a civil case with a much lower standard of proof, and that case was dismissed for lack of evidence."

"What about the poisoning cases?"

"Chesterfield always denied the charges, and the police never produced any evidence connecting him to the chocolates that killed Randall. It wasn't even clear that Arthur Gentry was poisoned. If I were on a jury, I would have had a reasonable doubt."

"I'm not asking how you would have voted if you were on a jury," Robin said. "I asked you if you thought Robert Chesterfield murdered Sophie Randall or Arthur Gentry."

"What does it matter what I think? I wasn't present when the killer doctored the chocolates. I didn't see who did that. Any opinion I have is a guess. I will tell you that Chesterfield insisted he was innocent. I will also tell you that I did not like the man, and I was glad when my representation ended."

The next morning at work, Robin searched the internet to learn as much as she could about Robert Chesterfield. One piece of information made Robin very sad. After Chesterfield's criminal case was dismissed, Gary Randall also sued Chesterfield for committing the civil tort of wrongful death. Randall's case was as hopeless as the Dowd children's suit, but he was obsessed. His lawsuit was thrown out, but he appealed—and the attorney fees drove him into bankruptcy. He committed suicide soon after.

Chesterfield's legal troubles didn't end with the dismissal of the wrongful death cases. The Dowd children sued to break the will. The litigation was lengthy and costly, and Chesterfield settled out of court. He ended up with the house on the coast, the Portland condo, and several million dollars, but his lifestyle was expensive and his notoriety made it impossible for him to make a living playing cards.

Fortunately for Chesterfield, the murder charges made him famous. Caesars Palace, one of the big casinos on the Strip, featured his magic show, and people flocked to Las Vegas to see it. Was Lord Chesterfield a cold-blooded murderer or a victim? Audiences filled the casino theater and drew their own conclusions.

At the height of his fame, Chesterfield had married Claire Madison, a trust fund baby who became famous on a reality television show. She was several years younger than Chesterfield. The marriage had gone through ups and downs, and according to the tabloids, the tension increased when Chesterfield's career took a sharp downturn. Chesterfield still had an act, but he performed at lesser-known casinos.

Robin had just learned that the Sophie Randall and Arthur Gentry murders had become cold cases when Jeff Hodges knocked on her office door. Robin looked up from her computer and smiled.

"Hey, kid, have you got a moment?" Jeff Hodges asked.

"For you, always."

Jeff returned the smile and sat down on one of Robin's client chairs. "I researched the question you asked me about getting a patent for a magic illusion."

"And?"

"You can, but there's a problem. In order to get a patent, you have to explain how your gizmo works. In this case, the gizmo is the illusion, which means that anyone can find out how the trick works by reading the patent application. I assume your client wants to protect the secret of how his trick works. He'll be defeating that purpose if he files for a patent."

"Thanks, Jeff."

"On a more important note," Jeff said as he stood to leave. "There's a new restaurant on Alberta. It's Cajun. Are you interested?"

"Sounds great."

"I'll make a reservation for six, okay?"

"You bet."

"See you later."

Robin called Chesterfield and told him what Jeff had discovered.

"Thank you for your prompt response," Chesterfield said when

Robin finished explaining the problem, "but I'd decided to forgo my patent already. I apologize for not calling sooner."

"That's okay. Since we can't help you, I'll send you a refund minus our fee for the time we put in."

"No, no. Please keep the retainer in your trust account in case I need you for another matter."

"What would that be?"

"Nothing right now, but I may have a legal problem that's up your alley in the near future."

Robin decided not to press Chesterfield and they ended the call. She was curious about his unnamed problem, and she had a sneaking suspicion that it would involve criminal law.

CHAPTER SEVENTEEN

The trip from Portland to the coast had taken Robin and Jeff through a riot of green. An occasional gap in the foliage revealed white water coursing down rivers that ran alongside the road. Once they turned south on the coast highway, they had glimpses of the Pacific, calm and sun-drenched on this balmy late afternoon in July.

"The turnoff should be on the right in a quarter of a mile," Robin said after consulting the GPS on her phone. Robin had typed the address listed on the beautifully engraved invitation she had received two weeks ago into the navigation app. The invitation was enclosed in a cream-colored envelope. Robin's name and address had been written in graceful calligraphy. The invitation asked her to attend the premiere of the Chamber of Death at Chesterfield's seaside mansion.

Jeff slowed his pickup and started looking for the entrance to Chesterfield's estate.

"There!" Robin said, pointing to a gap in the roadside foliage. Jeff turned in and drove down an unpaved road until an iron gate forced him to stop. Jeff spoke into an intercom. Moments later, the gate swung open.

"These are some digs," Jeff said when the mansion came into view.

Robin agreed, but she noticed that the landscaping had not been kept up, and the sprawling house looked weather-beaten. A building that was at the mercy of brutal winter storms and the constant attack of wind and salt spray would get beaten up, but she assumed that someone with the money to live here would have the damage repaired.

A valet took Jeff's keys, and the couple walked to the front door. Robin and Jeff had been spending their weekends hiking and camping, and Robin wore a black designer dress with spaghetti straps that showed off the muscles on her tanned shoulders, arms, and legs. Jeff was wearing a tie Robin had picked out for him with a dark suit.

The front door was opened by an attractive brunette before Robin could ring the bell. "Welcome to the premiere of the Chamber of Death, Miss Lockwood and Mr. Hodges. I'm Miriam Ross, Mr. Chesterfield's personal assistant."

Ross gestured down a set of stairs toward a sunken living room, where several elegantly dressed men and women were congregating. A bar had been set up near a stone fireplace, and waiters holding trays of finger food and champagne were circulating.

"Please join Lord Chesterfield's other guests. The show should start soon."

When Jeff and Robin reached the bottom of the stairs, a waiter approached with flutes of champagne. They each took a glass. Floor-to-ceiling windows gave the guests a view of the sun high in the sky above the rim of the ocean. Robin wandered over and looked out at the cliff behind the house. Toward the south end of the mansion, stairs led down to the beach, where a speedboat bobbed at anchor at the end of a dock.

Jeff took a sip of champagne while he scanned the room. "Do you know any of these people?" he asked.

Robin turned around and surveyed the crowd. "I don't *know* any of them, but I recognize a few."

Robin pointed her glass toward a woman she knew to be in her late forties but who looked much younger, thanks to the wonders performed by Beverly Hills plastic surgeons.

"That's Claire Madison, Chesterfield's wife. Her folks made a fortune in the diamond trade, and she inherited a tidy sum when they passed. Madison had a brief career on a reality TV show and as an actress in B movies. She's one of those people who are famous for being famous. She met Chesterfield in Las Vegas. The tabloids say that she married him for the publicity and that they have an open marriage. Most of the time, she lives in LA."

Claire was talking to a slim, tanned man dressed in a custom-made gray suit, blue silk shirt, and red and yellow striped Hermès tie and a balding man with a sallow complexion.

Claire saw Robin looking at her. Her brow furrowed for a moment. Then she smiled and headed toward Robin with the two men in tow. "You're Robin Lockwood."

"I am," Robin said, surprised that Claire Madison knew her.

Claire laughed when she saw the puzzled look on Robin's face. "I bet you're wondering how I recognized you. I'm a big UFC fan, and you received a lot of publicity because you were fighting while you were in law school."

"That was always a little embarrassing."

"I bet it made it hard to get dates." Claire gave Jeff the once-over. "But I see you're doing okay in that department now."

"I am," she said proudly. "This is Jeff Hodges. He doubles as my boyfriend and ace investigator."

"Pleased to meet you. This is Lou Holt," Claire said, introducing the younger man. "He owns the casino where Bobby will be performing his magic act. And this is Horace Dobson, Bobby's agent."

Robin and Jeff nodded at the men.

"I was at your fight with Kerrigan," Claire said.

"Ouch," Robin responded at the mention of the fight that had ended her career.

Claire smiled again. "I also saw you KO Holly Reagan."

"I liked that result way better than the one from the Kerrigan fight."

"I saw the Kerrigan fight too," Holt said. "I thought she got you with a lucky punch."

Now Robin smiled. "I'd like to believe that. The truth is, I was not in her class and never would have been. That fight was a wake-up call. Fortunately, I had law school to fall back on. Thanks for the invitation, by the way. I'm a huge fan of magic, and I can't wait to see Mr. Chesterfield's latest illusion."

"I didn't make up the guest list. Bobby did. I'm curious. How do you know Bobby?"

"He hired my firm to research a legal problem. It turned out that we couldn't help him."

Just as Claire started to say something, the front door flew open and a short, chubby man with gray hair and a salt-and-pepper mustache stormed in. Unlike the other guests, he was dressed in jeans, a plaid shirt, and a tan, zip-up jacket. The intruder paused in the doorway and scanned the room. When he spotted Claire Madison, he charged toward her. Miriam Ross tried to stop him, but he brushed her aside.

"Where is he, Claire?" the man demanded.

"He's getting ready for the show."

"Where? I need to see him."

"You can see him after the show."

"When I get through with him, there's not going to be a show."

"Calm down, Joe," Dobson said.

"I'll be calm when I get my money. Now, where is he?"

"I'm not going to let you see him in the state you're in," Claire said.

"Hey, Joe, what's the problem?" Dobson asked.

"The problem is that I've invested a lot of money in Bobby's latest adventure, and some of it seems to have disappeared."

"You don't have to worry about your money," Chesterfield's agent said. "His show is going to be a huge success. You'll be swimming in dough soon."

"That's what Bobby says every time he deigns to take my calls, which isn't very often."

"He's a busy man. You know that."

"What I know is that there are irregularities in his books. I've talked to a lawyer, and there's going to be a complaint filed with the district attorney if I don't get an explanation pretty damn soon."

"Jesus, Joe, there's no reason to get the cops involved," Dobson said.

While they had been talking, a large man with auburn hair and a full beard walked up, followed by a blonde in a tight dress that showed off her cleavage and curves.

"Did I hear that Bobby has money problems?" he said.

Dobson spun around. "There's no problem, Auggie. It's just a misunderstanding. Once you see Bobby's trick, you'll know that everything is gonna be okay. Right, Lou?"

"If it's as good as he says it is, Bobby's going to be headlining a top Vegas act again," Holt assured Augustine Montenegro.

"When are we going to see this amazing trick?" Montenegro asked Claire.

"Soon, Auggie. You're going to love it. Let me ask Bobby how much longer we have until he's ready."

Claire left the living room and walked through the kitchen to the farthest section of the southern wing of the house. A door at the end opened into a theater that Chesterfield had built as a work-shop where he could experiment with new illusions. The theater was dimly lit and the walls were concrete. One end was taken up by a stage that was raised above the floor. Comfortable seats similar to those you would find in a movie theater stretched back five rows. An aisle separated the seats. A ramp led up to the stage. On the stage was a pyramid covered in hieroglyphics that stood seven feet high and was open in the middle.

Chesterfield was at the back of the theater, standing next to an ornately decorated sarcophagus. The sarcophagus sat on a long steel dolly that tilted very slightly in front. The dolly was supported by two wheels in the front and two in the back. Two handles attached to the rear end of the dolly could be used to push it forward. Chesterfield was surrounded by three young women dressed in bright red hooded robes with flowing sleeves, decorated with yellow hieroglyphics. Chesterfield was dressed in a warm-up outfit and track shoes.

"Bring the lights down one more notch, Larry!" Chesterfield shouted to a man seated at a computer a few feet behind him.

The lights dimmed.

Chesterfield looked down the aisle at the stage and gave the thumbs-up sign. "Perfect. Keep it that way. And you can take a break. You, too, ladies."

Claire walked over to her husband as soon as they were alone. Chesterfield had invited Claire to his premiere, but he was surprised that she had shown up. They hadn't been getting along, and she'd never shown much interest in his magic act.

"You look lovely, darling," Chesterfield said.

"Nice of you to say so."

"What brings you here?"

"Two things. First, your guests are growing restless. When will you be ready?"

"I'm good to go, love. Give me twenty minutes. Then ask

Miriam to lead everyone down here. What's the other thing you wanted to tell me?"

"There's an uninvited guest who's causing a scene."

"Who?"

"Joe Samuels."

"Oh Christ. That's all I need. What's got him excited?"

"Something about a problem with your books. He threatened to go to the police."

"Joe gets emotional. There's nothing to worry about."

"I hope not. Auggie Montenegro seemed very interested in what Joe was saying."

"I owe Auggie some money, but I've got it covered."

"I hope you do. You know that I'm not going to bail you out."

"You won't have to. Now, go upstairs and tell everyone that they're about to see one of the greatest illusions in the history of magic."

Robin was very excited when she entered the dimly lit theater. She took a seat near the front and watched the stage, eager for the action to begin. There was a low rumble of conversation after everyone was seated. Then the lights went down and a curtain parted, revealing a pyramid. On either side of the pyramid was a square box concealed by a black cloth.

There was a puff of smoke, and Robert Chesterfield appeared on the stage wearing a black hooded robe with flowing sleeves. "Ladies and gentlemen—" Chesterfield began.

"You're a fraud, Chesterfield. And a traitor!" shouted a man dressed in a tuxedo who was walking down the wide aisle that separated the rows of theater seats. He was five seven, lean, muscular, and ruggedly handsome. Jet-black hair, a Roman nose, and clear blue eyes gave the man the appearance of a leading man in a 1940s movie.

"I'm going to expose the secret behind this trick you're hoping will save your pathetic career—the same way you exposed the illusion I use to close my show, *Mysterioso*."

Several members of the audience gasped. A masked magician who called himself Mysterioso revealed the secrets behind magic tricks on a popular television show. His identity was a heavily protected secret. Several death threats had been received by the show's producers.

"That's David Turner," Robin whispered to Jeff. "He's one of the top magicians in Las Vegas. He replaced Chesterfield at Caesars Palace when the casino didn't renew Chesterfield's contract. He's also rumored to be Claire Madison's lover. A few weeks ago, Mysterioso revealed how Turner makes a car disappear while it circles around a racetrack on the stage. It's the trick he's known for, and he closes every show with it."

"I thought you didn't watch that show," Jeff said.

"I don't. It was big enough news to make the papers. Caesars Palace pays Turner millions, and people come from all over to see that trick. Attendance has fallen dramatically since the TV show."

"Who let this two-bit charlatan into my house?" Chesterfield asked.

Two security guards materialized from the end of the aisle and started walking toward the intruder.

"I asked David here." Claire flashed a glacial smile. "If your trick is any good, you should be able to fool a professional magician."

"Yeah, Bobby!" Augustine Montenegro shouted. "We're a bunch of rubes, so it shouldn't be hard for you to fool us. I'm interested to see just how good this so-called amazing illusion is."

Chesterfield hesitated for a moment. Then he smiled at his rival. "Very well, David, I accept your challenge. And now, if you will take a seat, I will proceed to amaze and astonish you."

Chesterfield's three assistants appeared at the back of the theater and started pushing the dolly with the sarcophagus down the aisle, toward the stage.

"In ancient Egypt, those who offended the gods were entombed alive in a sarcophagus and died a horrible death," Chesterfield said. "I am known as an escape artist. Tonight, I will perform the ultimate escape: I will cheat death."

Chesterfield's assistants pushed the sarcophagus up the ramp.

Chesterfield pointed at the pyramid. "This, my friends, is the Chamber of Death. Those who enter have never returned to join the living."

One of the assistants pressed a button, and the top of the dolly tilted down. Then the three women pushed the sarcophagus onto the stage and maneuvered it so it was between the sides of the pyramid with one of the long sides facing the audience.

Chesterfield pointed to the sarcophagus. "I will be placed in this coffin alive." Chesterfield surveyed the audience. "Are there any among you who may be affected by sheer horror? If so, I suggest that you leave the theater, because what you will see next is not for the faint of heart."

Chesterfield waited. When no one left, he walked to the first box and whipped off the black cloth, revealing a glass cube filled with writhing snakes. There were gasps from the crowd.

"This cube is filled with some of the world's most dangerous snakes: cobras, vipers, and Cleopatra's favorite, the asp." The magician pulled off the cloth that covered the second cube. "What you see in here are some of the most poisonous scorpions known to man." Chesterfield pointed to an object on the side of the coffin. "Please note the chute on this side of the sarcophagus. When I am locked in this coffin, my assistants will send this horde of death dealers down the chute and onto my body. According to the literature, I should be dead within minutes."

Chesterfield paused dramatically.

"In our audience is my attorney, Robin Lockwood. Miss Lockwood, would you please come onstage and inspect the sarcophagus to make sure there are no hidden doors through which I can escape?"

Robin was embarrassed, but she was too fascinated to reject the offer. She walked up a flight of stairs at the side of the stage and went up to the coffin. She leaned down. It looked solid. She ran her hand around the coffin and knocked on every surface. After a while, she stood up. "I didn't find any escape hatches."

"Thank you, Miss Lockwood. You may return to your seat, and I will enter the Chamber of Death."

Chesterfield stepped into the coffin. A cover lay on the stage. One of the assistants picked up one end, and another picked up the other end. Then each assistant stood on a side of the sarcophagus and raised the lid so it was suspended over the sarcophagus with her back to the audience.

Chesterfield sat up in the gap between the assistants holding the lid so Robin could see him in the coffin. The third assistant stepped in front of the coffin between the assistants who were holding the lid and pushed Chesterfield down. When she stepped back, the other two assistants lowered the coffin lid.

Padlocks were attached to chains that were threaded through loops on either side of the coffin. When the coffin lid was secured, an assistant pushed the roller offstage so the audience had an unobstructed view of the sarcophagus.

Another assistant turned to the audience. "The gods have decreed Lord Chesterfield's death. His fate is sealed."

Two of the assistants put on gloves. One opened a lid on top of the cube containing the snakes. The other gloved assistant opened the chute facing the audience. Someone gasped when a handful of wriggling reptiles was shoved down the chute.

Suddenly, Robin heard the sound of fists beating against the inside of the sarcophagus.

"Stop. There's something wrong. Let me out!" Chesterfield shouted.

"Your pleas fall on deaf ears," the assistant said.

One of the gloved assistants took a handful of scorpions and poured them down the chute. Chesterfield screamed again.

"Let him out!" someone shouted.

The assistants ignored that plea as well.

Chesterfield's voice grew weaker. Then an unearthly scream issued from the coffin, followed by silence.

"Please, let him out!" a woman shouted.

A man stood up and started for the stage, but a security guard stopped him.

"Let me go. This has gone too far!" the man shouted.

"Lord Chesterfield has traveled to the land of the dead," one of the assistants said as she unlocked the padlocks. When the chains were unwrapped, another of the assistants opened the lid of the coffin. She stared inside.

Then she turned to the audience. "Miss Lockwood, will you look inside the sarcophagus and attest to the fact that the snakes and scorpions are in it, but Lord Chesterfield is not?"

Robin walked up onstage and looked in the coffin. Snakes and scorpions wriggled and slithered in it, but there was no sign of the magician. "He's not in there," Robin declared.

The assistants gathered at the front of the stage and stared toward the back of the theater. Robin and the members of the audience followed their gaze. No one spoke. After a few moments, the assistants turned to one another. They seemed confused.

"Is something wrong?" Robin asked.

"This isn't how the finale works," an assistant whispered. "Mr. Chesterfield is supposed to appear at the back of the theater, but he's not there."

CHAPTER EIGHTEEN

Claire walked up to the stage. "What's going on?"

The assistants looked nervous. "We don't know where Mr. Chesterfield is. He's supposed to have materialized in the back of the theater."

Claire turned around. "Larry, turn up the lights."

When the lights came up, no one was there.

"If he's not where he's supposed to be, where would he be?" Claire asked.

"I don't know," the assistant answered.

David Turner started to walk toward the stage, but Miriam Ross blocked his way. The security guards flanked her.

"No one is allowed to go on the stage without Mr. Chesterfield's permission," Ross said.

The magician turned toward Claire. "Tell her to move."

"I can't. This is Bobby's house." Then Claire addressed Miriam Ross. "Do you know what's going on?"

Ross looked upset. "Honestly, I don't. Every time I've seen Mr. Chesterfield do the trick, there's this flash and he appears behind the audience."

"Is this part of the trick, Miriam? Is he trying to build the suspense?" Claire asked. "If it is, tell us now, because I'm getting worried."

"No, no. I don't know why he's not here. He . . . he'll probably turn up," Ross said, but she didn't sound as if she believed what she was saying.

"Did you tell him I was here, Claire?" Joe Samuels asked.

"Yes."

"Then this is just some of your husband's bullshit. He's hiding from me because he knows I'm gonna nail his ass."

"That doesn't make sense," Horace Dobson said. "The trick was terrific. Right, Lou?"

"I have to agree."

"See, Joe. You've got to admit it lived up to the hype, which means Lou is going to feature Bobby in his show and we'll all be making money. Why would he hide after everything went so well?"

"You're forgetting one thing," David Turner said.

"What's that?" Dobson asked.

"Once the public learns that Chesterfield is Mysterioso, his career will be over. His show will be picketed, he'll be sued by me and every other magician he's tried to ruin. Someone might even try to kill him."

"Like you?" Dobson asked. "Where were you during the performance?"

"What are you suggesting?" Turner asked.

"Magicians can move around undetected. How do we know that you didn't figure out the trick, kill Bobby, and hide his body?"

Turner smiled. "I'm glad you think so highly of me. I'm pretty sure I know how the trick works, but I couldn't possibly do what you're suggesting in such a short period of time. Besides, Claire was sitting next to me, and Mr. Montenegro was sitting on my other side during the performance. If I left my seat, they would have noticed."

"Like everyone noticed Bobby get out of that coffin?" Dobson countered. "And how did you find out that Bobby was Mysterioso?"

"I told him," Claire said. "David and I have been seeing each other. When Bobby found out, he was furious. I knew Bobby was Mysterioso, but I kept his secret until he tried to ruin David by exposing the secret behind his most famous trick."

"You bitch!" Dobson shouted.

"Let's everyone calm down," Robin said. "You're forgetting that we don't know what happened to Mr. Chesterfield. If this is part of the trick, he'll show up. If it's not, we should start a search to see if we can find him."

Robin turned to Miriam Ross. "Can you think of someplace Mr. Chesterfield might be hiding?"

Ross laughed. "A million places. This house is huge."

"Without revealing how the trick works, can you tell us where Mr. Chesterfield would have ended up after escaping from the sar-cophagus?"

"I don't know how the trick works." Ross turned to the cos-tumed assistants. "They do."

"Ladies?" Claire asked.

The women looked conflicted.

"We can't say anything," one of the assistants said. "We signed a nondisclosure agreement about the trick. If we say anything, we can be sued."

"I can think of three possibilities here," Robin said.

"Tell us," Claire said.

"First, this is part of the trick, in which case, Mr. Chesterfield is fine and he'll show up soon. Second, Mr. Chesterfield escaped from the coffin, but something happened to him that's making it impossible for him to appear."

"Such as?" Horace Dobson asked.

"He was injured accidentally or he was injured intentionally by someone and is either dead, a prisoner, or badly hurt."

"You said that there is a third alternative," Ross said.

"From what I heard today, Mr. Chesterfield had a number of reasons to run away. Mr. Samuels is threatening legal action, Mr. Turner has just exposed him as Mysterioso, which may ruin his career and force Mr. Holt to cancel his act. And those are the problems I know about. Mr. Chesterfield put me on retainer but never told me why. I have to assume that he was anticipating legal problems, and my specialty is criminal law."

"I suggest that we wait a few more minutes," Jeff said. "If Mr. Chesterfield hasn't turned up, we should search the house and grounds in case he's injured."

Jeff turned to the assistants. "Since you know how the illusion works, you should check on places he might be when we leave the theater. That way, no one can accuse you of giving away how the trick works."

While most of the guests and employees searched the house, Jeff and Robin volunteered to search the cliff behind the house. The sun was setting, but they could still see fairly well in the pale light that remained. The air had grown chilly, and Jeff draped his jacket across Robin's shoulders.

"I hope we don't find Chesterfield sprawled on the rocks where they found Lily Dowd's body," Robin said.

"That would be very creepy."

Robin hummed *The X-Files* theme, and Jeff laughed.

"I can see that you're not taking Chesterfield's disappearing act seriously," he said.

"I just don't trust him. Regina didn't like him. She wouldn't say it, but I'm sure she thought he poisoned the chocolates that killed Sophie Randall. And his phony upper-class Brit act wears on you after a while."

They walked down the cliff to the spot where Lily Dowd's body had been found, but Chesterfield's body wasn't sprawled on the rocks. After walking south for fifteen minutes more, Jeff and Robin walked back toward the house. Robin stopped when they reached the spot where a flight of weatherworn wooden stairs led to the beach. She looked down.

"That's interesting," she said.

"What is?"

"There was a speedboat moored at the dock down there. It's gone now."

"That is interesting. And so is that," Jeff said, pointing to a door in the side of the mansion.

Robin walked over and opened it. Jeff flipped a light switch. They were in a mudroom stocked with items you would use at the beach or on a boat. There was also an ascending flight of stairs.

"Let's see where this goes," Robin said.

Jeff followed Robin up. There was a door at the top. Robin opened it and found herself in a short concrete corridor that led to the side of the stage in the theater. She walked around the dolly that had been used to bring the sarcophagus to the stage and looked out. Chesterfield's assistants were sitting in the front-row seats.

Jeff looked at them. Then he smiled. "What do you say, ladies? Mystery solved?"

"We can't answer that question," one of the women said.

"Right. The nondisclosure agreement," Robin said. "I don't know how he got out of the coffin, but I'm willing to bet that your boss left by that door, went down to the dock, and hightailed it in the speedboat. I have no idea where he went next. Do you?"

The women looked at one another.

"Come on. This has nothing to do with the illusion."

The women huddled. Then one of them said, "Honestly, we don't have any idea. We really expected Mr. Chesterfield to be at the back of the theater."

"Okay, I believe you. Jeff and I are going to tell the others what we found. Why don't you join us?"

Jeff and Robin found Claire and several of the other guests in the living room. Robin told them their theory about the speedboat.

"Between everyone, we've searched the house and grounds," Claire said. "There are still many places Bobby could hide, but I'm fairly confident that he's not here, which makes your theory very plausible."

"What do you want us to do, Claire?" Horace Dobson asked.

"I think Bobby is playing one of his games, and I, for one, am not in the mood to humor him. So I'm going home, and I suggest you do too."

"Sounds like a plan," Robin said, taking Jeff's arm. "Shall we?"

"We shall."

Claire turned to Miriam Ross. "If my husband shows up, don't tell me."

Then she and David Turner followed Robin and Jeff outside.

Auggie Montenegro smiled at Dobson. "Looks like your client took it on the lam."

Then he turned to Miriam. "Unlike Claire, if Lord Bobby reappears, I am definitely interested in hearing about it. There might even be a finder's fee for any information." Auggie winked at Ross. Then he led his date toward the door.

"You get in touch, right away, if Bobby shows up," Dobson told Ross before he left.

When the door closed, Miriam dropped onto a couch and held her head in her hands. She couldn't believe Bobby would run out on her. Not after all the promises he'd made. He would show up. She was sure of it. Ross took a deep breath and got to her feet. The waitstaff was standing around, watching her.

"Let's get this place cleaned up. I want it looking spotless when Mr. Chesterfield returns."

Ross hoped that her tone carried more certainty than she felt.

CHAPTER NINETEEN

"No further questions," Robin said.

"I don't have any either," Deputy District Attorney Amy Arnold said. "Can Officer Mayfield be excused?"

"Miss Lockwood?" Judge Irving Knolls asked.

"That's fine with me."

"Any more witnesses?" the judge asked.

"No, Your Honor," Robin said as the officer headed for the door to the courtroom.

"Your motion to suppress presents a fascinating legal issue, Miss Lockwood," Judge Knolls said, "and this is definitely a close question. You may get a different result in the Court of Appeals, but you haven't convinced me that the officers acted in violation of state or federal law when they searched your client's car. So I'm going to deny the motion. Are you ready to proceed to trial?"

"Miss Arnold and I have been discussing a plea offer. If you give us a few minutes, we may be able to resolve this matter without a trial."

"Okay. It's getting close to twelve anyway. Let's recess, and I'll see you back here at one thirty," the judge said.

"Why don't you wait in the hall while I talk to the DA," Robin told her client.

"So, Amy, what do you want to do?" Robin asked when the two lawyers were alone in the courtroom. "Lamar doesn't have any priors, he's got a good job, and he was taking the painkillers for a bad back."

"And selling them illegally."

"Have a heart," Robin said. "Those drugs are expensive, and he's just making it financially."

The DA looked troubled. She went quiet, and Robin let her think.

"Will he go to rehab?" Arnold asked.

"Definitely. He's addicted and he doesn't like it. It's causing problems at work and with his marriage."

"Okay. If he waives his right to a speedy trial, agrees to go into rehab, and successfully completes it, I'll dismiss the case."

"Thanks. Let me ask Lamar if he'll accept the deal."

Robin's client agreed to the deal, and Robin told him to be back in court at one thirty. Then she told Amy Arnold that her client was going to take the offer. When she left the courtroom to go to lunch, she found Jeff waiting for her in the hall.

"What a pleasant surprise," Robin said. "Want to grab a bite?"

"Did you win the motion?"

"No, but I knew Arnold was worried that I'd win on appeal, so she gave Lamar a sweetheart deal. No jail, and she'll dismiss if he successfully completes rehab."

"Good work. I'll treat for lunch."

Robin smiled. "It's great having a sugar daddy as a boyfriend."

Jeff handed Robin a newspaper. "You left early for the gym, so I don't think you've seen this."

MAGICIAN'S MYSTERIOUS DISAPPEARANCE

One month ago, Robert Chesterfield, a celebrity magician whose stage name is Lord Chesterfield, disappeared from his seaside mansion on the Oregon coast during a private showing of the Chamber of Death, an illusion he was preparing for his debut at the Babylon Casino in Las Vegas. Mr. Chesterfield had been chained inside a sarcophagus filled with poisonous snakes and scorpions. When the sarcophagus was opened, the magician had disappeared. According to his personal assistant, Miriam Ross, Mr. Chesterfield was supposed to reappear behind the audience, but he has not been seen since he escaped from the coffin.

A week ago, the United States Coast Guard discovered a speedboat belonging to Mr. Chesterfield floating off the coast of California in the vicinity of San Diego. Blood on a shoe that has been identified as belonging to Mr. Chesterfield and more blood recovered from the speedboat has been matched to Mr. Chesterfield by DNA testing. The San Diego Police Department has issued a statement saying that they have no further information concerning the whereabouts of the missing magician.

Robert Chesterfield gained notoriety in 1998, when he was arrested for the murder of Sophie Randall and Arthur Gentry and the attempted murder of Samuel Moser. Oregon attorney Regina Barrister represented Mr. Chesterfield and was instrumental in getting the case dismissed. No one else has been arrested since the Multnomah County District Attorney's Office dismissed the charges against Mr. Chesterfield. Peter Ragland, who prosecuted the case against Mr. Chesterfield, had no comment when asked about the current developments or the 1998 cases.

"What do you think?" Jeff asked when Robin finished reading the article.

"He could have staged the scene so people would think he was dead."

"Or he could be the victim of foul play," Jeff said.

Robin sighed. "It's not our problem, Jeff."

"Too true. But aren't you dying to know what happened?"

"Honestly, no. Now, where do you want to eat?"

When Rafael Otero walked into Auggie Montenegro's spacious corner office on the top floor of the Happy Mountain Casino, his boss was reading one newspaper, and two others were spread out in front of him.

"You wanted to see me, boss?"

Auggie kept reading, but he motioned toward a chair on the other side of his aircraft-carrier-size desk. "You seen these news stories about the speedboat?" Auggie asked.

"What speedboat?"

"Don't you read or watch the news?"

"I've been busy. I don't have time for TV or newspapers."

"You should make time. The more educated you are, the better decisions you make."

Rafael knew Auggie would get to the point eventually, so he didn't say anything.

"Remember I told you about Chesterfield's disappearing act? Well, Lockwood, his lawyer, thought he took off in a speedboat. The coast guard just found it floating offshore near San Diego. There was a lot of blood and a bloodstained shoe, like the one Chesterfield was wearing when he did his act."

"They think he's dead?" Rafael asked.

"I don't care what anyone thinks. I know Bobby. He's a magician, and magicians make a living by fooling people. That greasy motherfucker is playing everyone. San Diego is spitting distance from Mexico. A person who owes money can find a lot of places to hide in Mexico. Bobby is alive and well, Rafael, and I want you to find him."

"That seems like a lot of trouble to go to over a couple of grand."

"It's not the money. It's the principle. If I let Bobby walk away, every piece of shit who owes me will start getting bright ideas. So, you head south and find him, and when you do, you fuck him up good. It's got to look horrible. I want this to be a warning to anyone who thinks about stiffing me. So, lots of blood, lots of gore, and leave the body where every jerk with an IOU can see it."

"Where's your client?" Joe Samuels screamed into the phone. "And don't you dare tell me he's in Davy Jones's locker! I know better."

"Then you know more than me," Horace Dobson said. "I want to wring that bastard's neck as badly as you do. Canceling his show at the Babylon has cost me a fortune."

"The lawsuit I'm going to file against your crooked ass is going to cost you a hell of a lot more."

"Calm down, Joe. I had no idea Bobby was embezzling the money you put up to finance his illusion."

"So you say. I think you knew what that bastard was doing, and you took your cut."

"Say that to anyone else, and I'll be the one suing for slander."

"Fuck you, Dobson," Samuels said as he slammed down the phone.

Horace Dobson leaned back, closed his eyes, and muttered, "Fucking Bobby," over and over.

"The coast guard found Bobby's boat covered in blood, but no one's found his body, so he could still be alive," Claire Madison told her lawyer as soon as he took her call. "How does this affect a divorce?"

"If you want to get a divorce, you have to notify your spouse. Usually, you serve him with divorce papers. You can't do that if he's missing."

"I knew it. The son of a bitch is doing this deliberately because I exposed him as Mysterioso."

"There's a procedure called 'divorce by publication' you can use if you can't find your spouse, but it will cost you, and it takes a while."

"What do I have to do?"

"You have to convince a judge, based on a sworn affidavit, that you've done everything in your power to find the missing spouse and you still can't locate him."

"How long is that going to take?"

"Several months. I can send you a copy of the affidavit of diligent search. It will tell you what you have to do. But let me ask you a few questions. Who has more money, you or Mr. Chesterfield?"

"Me."

"Do you have a prenup?"

"No."

"Do you have a serious boyfriend?"

Claire hesitated. "I am with someone."

"Do you want to marry him once you're divorced?"

"God no. I'm done with marriage."

"Okay. Then a divorce is the last thing you want. If you divorce Mr. Chesterfield, there's a possibility that you might have to share your estate with him. If he stays missing for five years, you can have him declared legally dead. Then you don't need a divorce."

"So missing is good?"

"Very good."

PART FOUR

RESURRECTION

2020

CHAPTER TWENTY

This is the true story of how Jimmy O'Leary *really* found God.

Shortly after Jimmy was sentenced to ten years in the Oregon State Penitentiary, he decided that he didn't like being in prison. Jimmy wasn't afraid of being beaten up or raped in the shower, since he was bigger, stronger, and meaner than almost every other con at OSP. Jimmy's problem was that he loved women, hunting, and fishing, and there were no females, trout, or deer where he was living.

As soon as Jimmy decided that he had to get out of prison he decided that he needed a plan, but that created another problem. Jimmy was big and strong, but he wasn't very bright, so he had no luck devising a plan. Then he met Omar Sykes while he was pumping iron in the yard. Omar was serving life without the possibility of parole and was feared by the other inmates because he was crazy and crafty and had nothing to lose. Omar liked to recruit dumb, strong, mean inmates like Jimmy to his team so he could control the prison drug trade.

"If you want to get out of OSP, you got to find God," Omar advised.

"How come?" Jimmy asked.

"You know the old saying, there aren't any atheists in fox-holes?"

"No."

Omar decided that he would have to slow things down for Jimmy. "You know what an atheist is?"

"No."

"It's someone who doesn't believe in God."

"Okay."

"And you know what a foxhole is?"

Jimmy nodded. "It's where you hide in a war movie."

"Exactly!" Omar said. "Now, when you say that there are no atheists in foxholes, what you mean is that even if you don't be-lieve in God, if you are facing death, you'll hedge your bets by praying for God's help, just in case he exists. Got it?"

"Yeah."

"Now, there aren't any atheists in parole board hearings, either. Every con who goes in front of the board says he's found God. Of course, no one on the board believes him. They know cons make that shit up so they can get paroled. But when the board is con-vinced that an inmate really and truly has found God, the chances that con will get himself a parole go way up. You got that?"

"Yeah. So, to get out, I got to be religious."

"Correct. Only you can't find God too fast. You got to do it slow and thoughtful or the board will know you're running a scam."

"How do I find God slowly?" Jimmy asked, and Omar told him.

The next Sunday, Jimmy went to the prison chapel, as Omar had advised. Then he went every Sunday until the prison chaplain noticed him. The first time the chaplain tried to engage Jimmy in conversation, Jimmy followed Omar's advice and said he was just in chapel for something to do. Gradually, he began talking to the chaplain, and he soon "confessed" that the chaplain's sermons had gotten him thinking.

Jimmy didn't profess to having been converted until his third parole board hearing, which was attended by the chaplain, who testified that Jimmy was truly saved. Parole was granted after Jimmy had served five years.

Things looked rosy until ten days before Jimmy was going to walk out of prison. That's when Peter Knox, a new inmate from Jimmy's old neighborhood, told him that Timothy Rankin, Jimmy's former cellmate, was screwing Loretta. Loretta had been Jimmy's girlfriend when he went in, and he still had the hots for her.

Jimmy had gone on and on about Loretta while he was bunking with Rankin, and he felt betrayed. After his conversation with Peter Knox, it occurred to Jimmy that Loretta had stopped visiting him. Her excuses always made sense, but her absence left Jimmy anxious and wanting. And now that he started thinking about it, he realized that he hadn't heard from Loretta for quite some time.

When Jimmy walked through the prison gates, his brother, Miles, was waiting. Jimmy's parents had passed while Jimmy was incarcerated, and they had left Miles the house. Miles, who was steadily employed and totally honest, had kept Jimmy's room for him.

Jimmy had spent a lot of time thinking about what he would do to Timothy Rankin when he got out. The morning after he was released, Jimmy waited for his brother to leave for work. As soon as the front door closed, Jimmy went to the shed in the backyard. The shed was used for storage. Jimmy had to move a sofa, several cartons, and an old vacuum cleaner before he found a gun and the cardboard box full of bullets. He'd hidden them six years before, after the failed armed robbery that had landed him in jail. The box was damp and the top melted off in Jimmy's hand. He tossed it aside, loaded the handgun, and went looking for Timothy.

Jimmy found his old cellmate sitting on his front porch.

When Timothy saw Jimmy, he stood up and greeted him with a big grin. "Hey, man, I heard you got out."

"And I heard you been fucking my woman," Jimmy said as he drew his gun and aimed it at Timothy's chest.

Timothy's eyes went wide, and he threw his hands in the air. "What woman?"

"Loretta."

"Who said that?"

"Pete Knox."

"Knox is lying. He thinks I ratted him out to the cops, which I didn't. And Loretta doesn't even live around here anymore. She moved years ago."

"Now I know you're lying. If she moved, she woulda told me."

Jimmy squeezed the trigger. The bullet hit Timothy in the chest. Timothy screamed. The bullet bounced off his chest. Jimmy's eyes went wide. He pulled the trigger again, and the bullet bounced off Timothy's chest again.

This time, Jimmy screamed. Then he threw the gun in the air, yelled, "Jesus save me, Jesus save me," and ran away as fast as his legs would carry him.

Jimmy passed a church during his flight from Timothy's house. When he saw a statue of Jesus on the lawn, he stopped dead. Moments later, he was in confession. Less than an hour later, the priest had walked Jimmy to the nearest police station, where he told a detective what he had done.

It is true that Jimmy started going to chapel because it was an essential part of his plan to get out of prison, but somewhere during those years of churchgoing and talks with the chaplain, Jimmy had taken the Lord into his heart. When he told the parole board that he had found God, he wasn't really lying, and it was his sincerity that convinced the board members to grant his parole. Still, there was a part of Jimmy that wondered if God really existed.

That all changed the second he shot Timothy Rankin in the chest twice at point-blank range and saw the bullets bounce into the air.

The priest who accompanied Jimmy to the police station believed that Jimmy O'Leary had truly accepted Christ. He also believed that Jimmy needed a good lawyer, and he remembered Barry McGill, one of his parishioners, telling him about a very good lawyer named Robin Lockwood who worked out at his gym.

CHAPTER TWENTY-ONE

Barry McGill waited to talk to Robin until she came out of the locker room. "You got a minute?"

Robin stopped and put down her gym bag.

"You know I go to church."

"I do."

"So, this Sunday, after the service, Father Gregory, my priest, asked me if I knew a good criminal lawyer."

"The priest isn't in trouble, is he?"

"No, no, nothing like that. It's this guy who ran into his church and confessed to shooting this other guy. Only the guy that got shot didn't die, and something really strange happened."

"'Strange' like how?"

Robin dropped her workout gear in her office. Then she went to see Jeff, who was eating a doughnut and sipping coffee while reading the sports page. Robin knocked on the doorjamb.

Jeff looked up and smiled. "You look very sexy this morning," he said.

"And you look like you're engaged in frivolous activities on company time."

"Hey, I have to keep up on the sports news in case a Trail Blazer wants to hire us."

"I apologize," Robin said as she dropped onto a chair across from her boyfriend. "But it's time for you to earn your keep. We have a case right out of *The Twilight Zone.*"

"Oh?"

"Our newest client shot a guy twice at point-blank range, and the bullets bounced off his chest."

"'On any other day, that might seem strange,'" the investigator said, quoting his favorite line from *Con Air*, one of his all-time favorite movies. Then he held up the Arts and Entertainment section of the newspaper and pointed to a full-page ad.

"You're kidding?!"

The ad contained a color photograph of Robert Chesterfield in a flowing black robe surrounded by three beautiful women—a blonde, a redhead, and a brunette—who were dressed in bright red robes adorned with yellow hieroglyphics. It proclaimed that Lord Robert Chesterfield—"one of the world's great magicians"— was going to rise from the dead during the premiere of the Chamber of Death at the Imperial Theater.

"Has Chesterfield or any of his people called?" Robin asked.

"Not that I know," Jeff said.

"What do you think?"

"I don't think we have to think about Robert Chesterfield unless he does call us. Now, tell me about this bullet thing."

CHAPTER TWENTY-TWO

Homicide Detective Carrie Anders spotted Roger Dillon's car when she pulled into the rain-soaked supermarket parking lot at 11:15 in the evening. There was only a sliver of moon, but light from the poles the store had spread around the lot cast a soft glow over the puddled asphalt.

Detectives Dillon and Anders were a study in contrasts. Roger was in his fifties, and he dressed in fashionable suits and wore expensive, conservative ties. He was average height and slender, and his salt-and-pepper hair and wire-rimmed glasses made him look like an academic.

Anders was thirty-four, over six feet tall, and weighed a hulking 220 pounds. She dressed for comfort in pant suits that were often wrinkled and man-tailored shirts. People frequently underestimated her intelligence because of her bulk, her placid expression, and the slow way she spoke, but she had been a math major in college and was whip smart.

Anders walked to Dillon's car as soon as he opened his door. Heavy drops pounded down from roiling black clouds, and Dillon pulled up the hood attached to his windbreaker when he got out.

"Congratulations," Anders said to her partner. "I hear Tara was accepted at Berkeley."

Dillon beamed. "She's also been accepted at a few other schools. Serena and Tara are going to visit her top choices next week."

The two detectives talked about the colleges Dillon's daughter had gotten into as they walked toward an area of the parking lot that had been cordoned off by yellow crime-scene tape.

Sally Grace, the medical examiner, walked over to greet the detectives.

"What have we got?" Dillon asked.

"A white male, late sixties, early seventies," Dr. Grace said. "There was a bag of groceries next to the body. The keys in his pocket opened the car he was lying behind. It looks like he was going to put the groceries in the trunk when the killer came up behind and shot him."

"Any ID?"

Grace shook her head. "No wallet, so I'm guessing he's the victim of a robbery. But you're the detectives."

Dillon and Anders followed Grace to the body, which was surrounded by techs from the crime lab. A tent had been erected over the corpse to shield the area around the body from the rain, but Dillon figured that any evidence that might help find the perpetrator had been washed away by the heavy downpour.

He started to say something, then stopped in midsentence and squatted next to the corpse. "This is Henry Beathard. He was a Multnomah County Circuit Court judge until he retired a few years ago."

Anders stared at the dead man's face. Then she shook her head sadly. "You're right. I testified in his court a few times. He was a good guy and a fair judge. What a shame."

Dillon stood up. "Are there any witnesses?"

"A shopper walked past the body on the way to her car and

called 911. The first responder took her statement. She didn't hear the shots. There weren't many cars here this late, so she probably would have seen a car leaving, but she says she didn't see anyone walking or driving away."

Dillon used his phone to take a picture of Beathard's face. "I'm going inside to talk to the people in the store," Dillon said. "Maybe someone noticed a person watching the judge or acting oddly."

"See if they have security cameras trained on this spot."

"Will do."

"Let us know what the autopsy turns up," Anders said to Dr. Grace.

The detectives headed for the store. Dillon had heard the judge was married and had grandkids. He sighed. You work hard, keep your nose clean, look forward to retirement, and life happens. It wasn't fair, but Dillon knew that life's not being fair was the rule and not the exception.

Regina Barrister and Stanley Cloud were cuddling on the sofa, holding hands when the evening news came on. Regina had made a habit of watching the evening news years ago when she started practicing law, because people featured at eleven o'clock at night often phoned her first thing in the morning. She'd kept the routine even when events that should have been familiar became less so.

"A fatal shooting in the parking lot of a Portland supermarket has brought a tragic end to the life of Henry Beathard, a retired and respected Multnomah County judge," the newscaster said as the screen showed yellow crime-scene tape brightening a dark, waterlogged parking lot.

"Ah no," Stanley moaned.

Regina's brow furrowed. "Did you know him?"

"Yes, and you did, too, Reggie. You had several cases in Henry's court." Stanley sighed. "He was a really good guy. We had dinner with him and Marie a few times too. You liked Henry. You thought he was a very good judge."

Regina paused as a thought tickled the edge of her memory. "Did I have any big cases in his court?"

"You might be thinking about a man you defended a long time ago, Robert Chesterfield. He's a magician."

"Why does he sound so familiar?"

"Robin, your partner, represented him a couple of years ago. She came here to talk to you about him. Then he disappeared. His name was in the paper today. He's back in town, and he's going to perform a show at the Imperial. That's what you're probably thinking about."

"Robert Chesterfield," Regina repeated. "What did he do?"

"They said that he murdered two people, but you were brilliant, and you forced the DA to dismiss the case."

"Was he guilty?"

"You were evasive the only time we talked about the case. You said that you would have had a reasonable doubt if you served on his jury, but you never told me what you really thought about his culpability."

CHAPTER TWENTY-THREE

When Robin entered the contact visiting room at the jail, she found James O'Leary sitting with his hands folded in front of him, smiling serenely like a Buddhist who has achieved Nirvana.

"Hi, Mr. O'Leary. My name is Robin Lockwood. I'm a lawyer, and Father Gregory asked me to help you with your case."

"I don't need a lawyer," Jimmy said.

"You're charged with attempted murder, so you probably do need a lawyer."

"God is my attorney."

"God won't be able to represent you in an Oregon court unless he's a member of the Oregon State Bar."

The smile never left Jimmy's face, but he did shake his head. "It ain't nice to joke about the Lord, Miss Lockwood."

"You're right. I apologize. But Father Gregory is very worried about you, and he wants me to help out. Do you have any objection to my working with God to help him get a just result?"

Jimmy thought for a moment. "I guess that would be okay."

"Why don't you tell me what happened?"

Jimmy told Robin about Peter Knox, Loretta, and Timothy Rankin. Then he told her about digging the gun and the bullets out from under the junk in the shed and what had happened at Rankin's house. When Jimmy had finished, Robin had a few ideas about what had turned Timothy Rankin into a superhero.

Several days of rain had given way to a few dry days. A heavyset man with a beer belly and thick beard was sitting on his front porch, drinking a Widmer IPA and taking advantage of the weather.

"Timothy Rankin?" Robin asked when she and Jeff Hodges walked up.

"Who wants to know?"

Robin held out her business card. "I'm Jimmy O'Leary's attorney, and this is Jeff Hodges. I was hoping I could ask you a few questions."

"Is this about Jimmy saying he tried to shoot me?"

"Yes."

Rankin broke out laughing. "Those cops said Jimmy told them he shot me in the chest and the bullets bounced off." Rankin laughed again. "Does Jimmy think I'm Superman?"

"So, you're saying that Jimmy didn't shoot you."

"Would I be talking to you if Jimmy shot me?" Rankin shook his head. "Did they test Jimmy for drugs, because it sounds to me like he was smoking something powerful."

"If Jimmy didn't shoot you, why did you call the police?"

"I didn't." Rankin cocked his head toward the house next door. "It was the neighbor. She's always sticking her nose in where it don't belong."

"Jimmy said he threw the gun away. Did the police find the gun or the bullets?"

"I saw them looking around, but I don't know how they'd find something that was never there."

"Am I correct in concluding that you will not testify that Jimmy O'Leary tried to kill you?" Robin asked.

"Of course not. I like Jimmy. We were cellmates. I don't know why he made up this crazy story, but it is crazy." Rankin chuckled. "Jimmy is fucked up in the head, if you ask me. Bullets bouncing off me. Who ever heard of such a thing?"

Robin decided to go while the getting was good. "Thank you for your time, Mr. Rankin."

"I ain't got nothing but time. Say hi to Jimmy for me when you see him, will you?"

Jeff led Robin to their car.

"What do you think really happened?" Jeff asked when they drove away.

"I think Jimmy shot Mr. Rankin, but Rankin doesn't want to press charges."

"Why?"

"Maybe because he's helping a friend who was lied to by Peter Knox, or maybe he's afraid Jimmy's friends will come after him if he testifies." Robin shrugged. "It really doesn't matter, if we can get the DA to dismiss."

"And the gun and the bullets?"

"My guess is that Rankin got rid of them."

"What about O'Leary's crazy story about the bullets bouncing off Rankin?"

"It's not so crazy. I talked to Paul Baylor at Oregon Forensics. Those bullets had been sitting around for a long time in an old shed. Jimmy told me that the cardboard box that held the bullets was waterlogged. When you fire a gun, the hammer hits the back of the bullet cartridge and ignites the primer, which ignites the powder charge. If the charge was wet, it could deteriorate and you could get a dud that would travel only a few feet with very little power."

"So maybe Jimmy isn't crazy."

"Crazy or not, it looks like he's going to walk."

Robin went back to her office and called the deputy DA who had the O'Leary case. He wasn't in, so she left a message asking him to call her. As soon as she completed the call, she started checking her emails. Halfway through, the receptionist told her that she had a call.

"Miss Lockwood?" a voice from the past asked.

"Chesterfield?!"

"It is I."

"Why are you calling?"

"Do you still have my retainer?"

"It's in my trust account."

"How much is left?"

"Most of it. I didn't do much work on your case."

"Excellent. I was wondering if you might bring the balance to me in cash."

"I'll have my secretary go to the bank tomorrow. Come by after noon, and it will be at the front desk."

"Actually, I was hoping that you could meet me this afternoon."

"I have a lot of work to do. It would be easier if you came here."

"I agree, but I'm being followed, and I'm concerned that these individuals might stake out your office."

"What kind of trouble are you in, Robert?"

"It's nothing you need worry about."

"You just told me that people are watching my office. If these people warrant concern, then I am going to worry. What is going on?"

"I'll explain when you bring the money."

Robin debated refusing to bring Chesterfield the cash, but her curiosity overrode her common sense. "Where do you want to meet?"

CHAPTER TWENTY-FOUR

Robin left the bank and walked across the Burnside Bridge to the east side of the Willamette River. The sky was threatening another deluge, and the streets were deserted. Chesterfield had spooked Robin with his talk of stakeouts and stalkers, so she was hypervigilant as she headed to the Stumptown Tavern.

Robin thought she saw the same person following her on two occasions, but she couldn't be sure it wasn't a trick played by her imagination. She doubled back twice, cut through an alley, and didn't see anyone who looked suspicious by the time she reached her destination.

Robin searched the tavern's dark interior. A couple in their forties occupied a booth near the front, and three men who looked like laborers occupied another booth. The rest of the booths were vacant. An overweight woman in jeans and a sweatshirt and a man who was too tall to be Chesterfield were seated at the bar. Robin took a seat in an empty booth in the back, and that gave her a view of the front door. She had been sitting in the booth for ten minutes when a man in a baseball cap and a soiled raincoat materialized across from her.

"Sorry if I startled you, but I had to make sure you weren't followed," Chesterfield said as he slid onto the bench across from Robin and took off the cap.

Robin was shocked by his appearance. The man sitting opposite her bore only a passing resemblance to the debonair gentleman who had hired her to look into patenting his great illusion. That Robert Chesterfield had radiated health and self-confidence and had dressed in the latest fashions. This Chesterfield seemed like a shrunken version of his former self. He wore old jeans and a threadbare, cable-knit sweater underneath the raincoat. His hair had thinned, there were circles under his eyes, and he'd lost weight. The only thing sophisticated about this new version was his upper-class British accent, which Robin knew was a fake.

"I saw your ad," Robin said. "The Great Chesterfield will rise from the dead?"

"It is a tad melodramatic, but I leave the marketing and PR to Horace."

"Why are you resurrecting yourself?"

"Money problems. Speaking of which, did you bring the cash?"

"Yes, but I want to know who's watching my office before I give it to you, and whether I'm in any danger."

"You don't have to worry. I'm the one they want."

"Who is 'they'? Is it Auggie Montenegro's guys?"

"Do you have my money?" Chesterfield asked again, sidestepping the question.

Robin stared at the magician for a moment. Then she handed a thick envelope across the table. "Where have you been hiding?" Robin asked while Chesterfield counted the bills.

"Here and there," Chesterfield answered. "You're better off not knowing." Chesterfield finished counting the cash, but he didn't put it back in the envelope. "I need help with a legal matter. Are you still willing to represent me?"

"I'm not sure after the stunt you pulled."

"I don't blame you. Let me tell you what I'd like you to do for me. If you don't want to do it, there will be no hard feelings."

"Go ahead."

"I was down on my luck when I came up with the idea for the Chamber of Death. I was certain that I could get a show if it was as spectacular as I thought it would be, but illusions are expensive to produce, so I needed backers. You remember Joe Samuels?"

"He showed up at your mansion and caused a scene."

"He had every right to. Joe and some other people put up money for the illusion. As I said, I was down on my luck, so I borrowed some of the money my backers had put up and used it for, uhm, living expenses."

"Is that another term for gambling debts?"

Chesterfield flashed a sheepish grin.

Robin wasn't amused. "I believe that the legal term for what you did is 'embezzling,'" she said.

"You're right. I won't deny that what I did could be seen as embezzling, but I was certain I could pay back Joe and the others when the show began. I didn't think anyone would notice until I started getting paid by the Babylon Casino."

"Only Mr. Samuels did notice."

"And he was going to go to the police. Horace told me that Joe did file a complaint after I disappeared. I'd like you to negotiate with him. Get him to agree to drop his criminal complaint so I can put on my act without worrying about getting arrested. Then I can pay him back from the proceeds of my new show."

Robin thought for a moment. "Fifteen hundred should cover my time. Where can I reach you?"

Chesterfield handed Robin the money and Horace Dobson's business card. "I'm not at a fixed address right now, but you can contact me through Horace. And thank you. I can understand why you wouldn't want to have me as a client."

"I'm a lawyer, Robert. My job is helping people in trouble, not judging them."

Chesterfield stood up.

"What about these people who are following you?" Robin asked. "Are you in danger?"

"I appreciate the concern, but I can take care of myself."

There was a back door to the tavern, and Chesterfield disappeared through it. Robin was going to leave by the front door when she hesitated. She was fairly certain that someone had followed her, and she wasn't certain that she'd lost them.

Robin turned around. When she opened the back door, she saw Chesterfield standing against the alley wall using a knife to hold two men at bay. One of his attackers looked like a nightclub bouncer. The other man was slender.

"Don't be stupid, Bobby," the slender man said. "That knife won't protect you."

"We'll soon see, Rafael. I hope you brought a first aid kit with plenty of bandages."

Robin pulled out her cell phone. "What's going on here?" she shouted as she dialed 911.

Rafael turned toward Robin, and Chesterfield struck. Rafael looked at his stomach. Blood was streaming from a cut. "What the fuck!" he screamed as he slapped his hand against the wound.

The other man stepped forward, and Chesterfield danced away.

"I've just dialed 911!" Robin shouted.

"You should get Rafael to a hospital," Chesterfield said to Rafael's partner. "What will Auggie say if he bleeds out?"

Rafael doubled over and groaned, "Marco, let's get out of here."

Robin stepped back as Marco helped Rafael out of the alley. She watched them until they rounded a corner. When she turned back to talk to Chesterfield, he'd disappeared again.

"What's your emergency?" the 911 operator asked.

Robin hesitated. Chesterfield and his assailants were gone. What would be accomplished by telling the police what had happened?

"Sorry. I misdialed," she said as she ended the call.

Robin knew Rafael was wounded and was probably not following her, but she was spooked and she stayed on high alert during the walk back to Barrister, Berman & Lockwood. The first thing she did was go to Jeff's office.

"I just saw Robert Chesterfield stab a man in an alley behind the Stumptown Tavern," Robin told Jeff, who was sitting behind his desk, looking over a file.

"You what!?"

Robin dropped into a seat across from her investigator. "Chesterfield called and asked me to return his retainer. I told him I'd have it here tomorrow, but he said he didn't want to come to the office, because some people were after him and might be staking it out. He asked me to bring the money to the tavern. Two men were waiting for him when he left."

"How bad off was the guy Chesterfield stabbed?" Jeff asked when Robin finished telling him what had happened in the alley.

"Chesterfield seemed to know what he was doing, so I'm guessing it looked worse than it was. I think he just wanted to scare off his attackers."

"Any idea who they were?"

"Chesterfield called one of the men Rafael, and the other man's name is Marco. He also mentioned Auggie Montenegro, so I'm guessing they work for him collecting debts. Do you remember Montenegro? He was at the premiere at Chesterfield's mansion. He owns a casino in Vegas. And he's rumored to have mob connections."

"They were probably leg breakers if Chesterfield felt he had to use a knife instead of his silver tongue."

"Chesterfield sounds like he's in hiding," Robin said. "He wouldn't tell me where he's staying. I have to go through his agent to get in touch with him."

"Do you think you're in danger?" Jeff asked.

"It's possible. Like I said, Chesterfield was worried that my office was being watched. If it was, those guys may have recognized me in the alley."

"If you thought you might be followed, why didn't you ask me to go with you?"

"I wasn't that worried when I left to meet him. And I can take care of myself."

"I know you can," Jeff said, "but it never hurts to have backup. I think you should go armed until we're sure you're safe."

Robin had a permit to carry a handgun she purchased after her life had been put in danger a few years ago.

"The men who went after Chesterfield will assume you know where they can find him," Jeff continued. "They may try to force the information out of you. I'll try to watch your back, but don't take any chances."

Robin reached across the desk and touched Jeff's hand. "Thanks for caring, but I think I'll be okay."

CHAPTER TWENTY-FIVE

"There's a Joe Samuels on one," Robin's receptionist said.

Finally, Robin thought. She had been leaving messages for him for a week, and she had almost given up hope that he would return her calls.

"Thanks for getting back to me, Mr. Samuels. I want to talk to you about your disagreement with Robert Chesterfield."

"It's not a disagreement. The son of a bitch stole from me."

"Mr. Chesterfield has a contract to perform a magic show at a theater in Portland. He knows that he owes you money and he wanted me to—"

"No deals," Samuels cut in. "I want that con artist in jail, where he belongs. You tell Lord Chesterfield that I'm not dropping the criminal complaint. I'll get my money back when the court orders him to pay me restitution."

"Which he won't be able to do if he's locked up."

"You don't get it. I don't care about the money anymore. I've got more money than I know what to do with. What I want is revenge. The old-fashioned, biblical eye for an eye. I want the world's greatest escape artist trying to escape from a prison cell. Have I made myself clear?"

"Definitely, and I understand why you're upset. I wasn't too happy with my client when he pulled that disappearing act, either. All I ask is that you count to ten, take a few deep breaths, and try to put what Robert did to you in perspective. I can see that this is a matter of principle, but—if I've got this right—the amount he took from you was around ten thousand dollars. That's not chicken feed, but I don't see an Oregon court sending Mr. Chesterfield to jail for this type of nonviolent first offense."

"*Que será, será*, Miss Lockwood. Seeing that son of a bitch sweat will bring me great pleasure."

Samuels hung up and Robin sighed. She wished that she'd been able to solve Chesterfield's problem with Samuels, but she could appreciate the investor's position.

Deputy District Attorney Lorna Waxman learned about her promotion to the Homicide team when she went to work. Waxman's desk was next to Peter Ragland's, so he knew about some of the felony cases she was handling. Peter had a stack of open files and was reluctant to add more cases to his load, but Lorna had told him about a case involving Robert Chesterfield. The anger that surfaced when Ragland thought about the magician had never diminished, and he saw Samuels's criminal complaint against his nemesis as a chance to exact a small measure of revenge.

After the Sophie Randall–Arthur Gentry fiasco, not even his father's reputation could save Peter Ragland from being demoted from the team that handled death penalty cases. Then Jasper Ragland died and many of the politicians who owed him favors retired or followed Jasper to the great law firm in the sky, leaving Peter to fend for himself.

Over the twenty-some years since Regina Barrister had made

a fool of him, Ragland's hairline had receded, he'd put on sloppy weight, he'd lost his self-confidence and become a ghost in the district attorney's office, drifting through it followed by the foul odor of failure. Some people wondered why Peter didn't leave, but he knew that no decent firm would hire him after his father died, and he had no faith in his ability to make a living if he hung out a shingle.

Vanessa Cole, the Multnomah County district attorney, was a slender, fifty-three-year-old black woman with sharp features and fierce brown eyes. She'd grown up in a wealthy area of Portland's West Hills and had gone to Stanford for college and law school. Cole was known for her smarts and high ethical standards, and she'd been a shooting star from the moment she joined the Multnomah County District Attorney's Office, moving quickly from trying misdemeanors to trying felonies to handling murder cases, then death penalty murder cases. When her predecessor retired for health reasons, Cole had been appointed to the post, and she won the position in the next election when she ran unopposed.

Vanessa was reviewing the office budget when her secretary buzzed to tell her that Peter Ragland wanted to talk to her. Over the years, Vanessa had had very little contact with Ragland. He had a reputation as someone competent to handle run-of-the-mill cases, and there were rumors about some problem with an old case that had kept him from being promoted during her predecessor's reign. Vanessa had gone from law school to a judicial clerkship to a stint in a law firm before joining the Multnomah District Attorney's office, so she had not been a DA when Ragland had tried the case that kept him from promotion.

"What's up, Peter?" Vanessa asked when Ragland was seated across from her.

"I just had a chat with a man named Joseph Samuels. He filed a criminal complaint alleging theft, and I'd like the case."

Cole frowned. "Does someone else have the case now?"

"It was originally assigned to Lorna Waxman, but she was just promoted to Homicide."

"What's so special about this case?"

"The defendant is Robert Chesterfield. He was charged with murder in 1998. The case was solid, but Regina Barrister was his lawyer and she got the key evidence thrown out on a technicality."

Cole's brow furrowed. "Is he the magician?"

"Yeah. He pulled a disappearing act a few years ago, when we were ready to go after him on this theft thing."

"I read a story about him in the paper."

"Right. Anyway, he's got a show at the Imperial, and we can arrest him there."

Vanessa didn't want to waste any more time on a theft case. "Okay. You've got the case," she said, impatient to get back to the budget.

Peter left before his boss could ask any more questions about Chesterfield. From her reaction, he figured that Cole probably didn't know much about what had happened in the Randall, Gentry, and Moser cases. But he remembered everything about the cases that had led to his disgrace, and he was eager for a second chance to put Robert Chesterfield behind bars.

CHAPTER TWENTY-SIX

"I have good news, Jimmy," Robin told her client when they were sitting across from each other in a contact visiting room at the jail. "The DA is dropping the charges. You'll be free by the end of the day."

"How can they do that when I confessed?"

"Under Oregon law, a person can't be convicted based only on a confession unless there is evidence to support the story the person tells the police. That's the law because some people confess to crimes they didn't commit."

"But I did try to kill Tim."

"That's not what he says. Tim told the police that you made up the story about shooting him. And the police don't have a gun or those bullets you say bounced off his chest."

Jimmy thought for a moment. Then he smiled. "This is all God's doing. God saved Tim by making those bullets bounce off his chest, and now God has saved me by making the gun and the bullets disappear."

Robin didn't want to disillusion her client, so she didn't tell him what she'd learned about the gunpowder. "I've done some digging, Jimmy. Peter Knox thought Timothy Rankin ratted him out to the police, but he didn't. I know some people in Narcotics. They wouldn't tell me who informed on Knox, but they assured me it wasn't Timothy. I also found out that Loretta moved out of state two years ago, so Timothy couldn't have been having an affair with her. Knox made that up, hoping you would go after Timothy. So, I have to ask you, are you going to try to hurt Rankin when you're released?"

"I'm never gonna hurt nobody again. God gave me a chance to be redeemed, and I'm gonna prove he wasn't wrong to do it."

"That's good to hear. You're going to be released in the next half hour. Do you have someone who can drive you home?"

"My brother, but he's working a late shift."

"When does he get off?"

"Around midnight."

Robin hesitated. She usually kept her relations with clients to legal assistance, but she liked Jimmy. "Where do you live?"

Jimmy told her. The address was a twenty-minute ride away, and she'd brought her car to work because she'd had an appearance in Salem that morning.

"I can give you a ride home. I'll wait across the street in the park for you."

Robin rode down in the jail elevator and walked to the park that was across from the Justice Center. She found an empty bench, opened her attaché case, and took out a respondent's brief that the attorney general had filed in one of her appeals. She'd been reading it for twenty-five minutes when a shadow obscured the page.

Robin looked up. Looming over her were the men who had attacked Robert Chesterfield behind the tavern. Robin's primitive brain sent her body into fight-or-flight mode. When she started to stand, Marco pressed his meaty fingers into her shoulder and forced her back onto the bench. Rafael sat beside her and winced. Robin guessed that he was still hurting from his stab wound.

"Can I help you?" Robin asked, trying to stay calm.

"You can help yourself by telling me where I can find Bobby Chesterfield," Rafael said.

Robin was certain that the two men wouldn't expect a woman to know how to fight, and that was her advantage. She visualized smashing her fist into Rafael's groin before springing up and spearing Marco in the throat. An elbow strike to Rafael's temple and a punch or kick to Marco's crotch would disable the pair long enough for her to run back to the Justice Center and its police presence.

While that course of action would help her in the park, she realized that more problems would come later when the men came after her to avenge their beating. Robin decided that violence would be plan B, and she opted to use her brain to defuse the situation.

"I don't know where he is," she said.

"We both know that's not true. You're Bobby's lawyer, so you have to know how to get in touch with him."

"I *was* Mr. Chesterfield's lawyer. He hired me to resolve a legal matter for him, but I wasn't able to, so I'm no longer doing any work for him. And I really don't have any idea where he is."

Rafael smiled. "Nice try, but a lawyer is always going to know how to get in touch with someone who owes her money. So where is he?"

"Chesterfield may be a lot of things, but dumb isn't one of them. He warned me that you were watching my office. That's why he insisted that we meet at that tavern. It's also why he hasn't told me where he's living. He figured you'd try to pressure me into telling you where you can find him. He calls me when he wants to talk," Robin lied, not wanting Rafael to know that her contact was Horace Dobson. "He hasn't given me an address or a phone number."

Again, Rafael smiled. "That logic shit may work with juries, but it's not working on me. Last chance. Tell me where Bobby is hiding, or Marco is going to hurt you."

Robin was preparing to put plan B into action when Jeff walked up.

"Is there a problem, Miss Lockwood?"

Rafael got up and Marco turned toward Jeff, who was pointing a .38 Special at them.

"Who the fuck are you?" Rafael barked.

"I'm someone who won't hesitate to shoot you if you don't walk away right now."

Robin stood to give herself more space in case things got out of hand. "These men wanted to know where Robert Chesterfield is, and I explained that I have no idea where he's staying. They were just about to leave."

"Is that right?" Jeff asked.

Marco glared at Jeff.

Rafael put a hand on his forearm. "It's okay, Marco." Then he turned to Robin. "If I find out you've been lying to me, there will be consequences."

When Rafael and Marco walked away, Robin turned on Jeff. "That wasn't necessary," she said. She sounded upset.

"From where I was standing, it was."

"I had everything under control, Jeff. You didn't have to ride in and save me like a knight in shining armor."

"Do you have your gun?"

"I left it in the office because I was visiting Jimmy O'Leary in the jail. And I don't need you to act like a mother hen."

"I acted sensibly, and I worry about you." Jeff smiled. "You're a big pain in the ass sometimes, but I don't want to lose you."

The tension in Robin's shoulders eased and she let out a breath. Then she touched Jeff's cheek. "You won't lose me. I know you followed me because you care. I appreciate that. But I don't need a man to babysit me. And I'll make sure I have my gun with me at all times. Okay?"

Jeff holstered his gun and wrapped his arms around Robin. "I love you. You know that, right?"

"I do, and I'm sorry that I've worried you. But I think we've seen the last of Montenegro's enforcers."

Jeff looked over Robin's shoulder in the direction Rafael and Marco had walked. "I hope you're right," he murmured.

"Jimmy O'Leary is getting released, and I promised I'd give him a ride home. I'll come back to the office after I drop him off. You go back and investigate a place to eat tonight. It's on me."

"I'll make sure it's pricey as payback for scaring me."

Now Robin smiled. "You do that, cowboy. See you soon."

During the drive to O'Leary's house, Robin kept a tight grip on the steering wheel to keep her hands from shaking. For all her bravado, the encounter with Rafael and Marco had scared her, and she decided that it was time to cut her ties with Robert Chesterfield.

When she returned to her office, Robin found Horace Dobson's number in Chesterfield's file. She had done an internet search for the agent and discovered that Dobson didn't have many clients. He'd been living in London when he read about Chesterfield's murder charges, and he'd moved to Las Vegas when he made Chesterfield's deal with Caesars Palace. Hobson had made a lot of money representing Chesterfield, and he'd picked up several clients because he was representing a celebrity, but his client list had slimmed down as Chesterfield's star descended.

"Dobson Talent Associates," Dobson sang out enthusiastically as soon as he picked up.

"Mr. Dobson, this is Robin Lockwood, Mr. Chesterfield's attorney."

"Oh," Dobson said, his enthusiasm evaporating when he realized that Robin was not a potential client.

"Mr. Chesterfield told me to call you if I needed to get in touch with him."

"Yes?"

"I talked to Joe Samuels. He refuses to settle. He's still very angry and I don't think he'll change his mind, so I'm going to send back the rest of Mr. Chesterfield's retainer. Should I send it to your office?"

"That will work."

"There's something else. Tell Robert that the two men who confronted him behind the tavern tried to get me to tell them where he was living. I told them I have no idea where he is."

"You didn't tell them about me, did you?" Dobson asked, alarmed.

"That's the other reason I called. I wanted to warn you. You're Robert's agent, and they may come after you."

As soon as Robin hung up, she got her handgun out of her desk drawer.

CHAPTER TWENTY-SEVEN

The Imperial Theater was a reclamation project funded by a Portland developer who was building expensive condominiums in a section of the city that was known for drug deals, strip clubs, and the homeless. The developer was trying to make the location attractive by bringing in high-end retail stores, upscale restaurants, and a performing arts center. During its various recent incarnations, the Imperial had been a porn theater and a venue for local bands. The developer had remodeled it and brought in legitimate theater, upscale musical acts, and currently, a semi-famous, still-notorious magician.

On the evening that the Chamber of Death was going to debut, and during the two weeks of rehearsals beforehand, a small group of protesting magicians picketed the theater because Robert Chesterfield had been exposed as Mysterioso. Chesterfield approached the Imperial in disguise, as he had every day of rehearsal, because of the protesters. When he was certain that he hadn't been spotted, he slipped into the alley that ran alongside the theater.

Henry Schloss, an elderly security guard, looked up when the stage door opened.

"Evening, Henry," Chesterfield said. "It looks like we're going to be busy tonight."

"It sure does."

"Did you get the tickets I left for your daughter and her husband?"

"I did. Thanks. They were thrilled."

"My pleasure," the magician said as he headed down a narrow hall past the dressing room used by his assistants and on to his dressing room, which was adjacent to the loading dock. He had just taken off his cap and jacket and seated himself in front of his makeup mirror when Rafael, gun in hand, stepped out from behind the rack of hangers holding Chesterfield's costumes.

"Do they still say 'break a leg'?"

Chesterfield jumped out of his chair. "How did you get in here?"

"Through the loading dock."

"You scared the shit out of me."

"And you pissed me off by playing hide-and-seek, which was pretty stupid since you had to show up at this theater eventually."

"I wasn't trying to hide from *you*, Rafael. I'm trying to avoid those idiot protesters. How's your side, by the way? You know I just nicked you to scare you off, right? No hard feelings?"

Rafael smiled. Then he drove his fist into Chesterfield's solar plexus.

The magician had anticipated the blow. He tensed his stomach muscles to absorb it, but he doubled over anyway to make Rafael think he was in pain. Chesterfield pretended to catch his breath. Then he straightened slowly. "That was completely unnecessary," he said when he was upright.

"It made me feel good," Rafael answered.

"What do you want?"

"That's a rhetorical question, right?"

"There's no need for all this drama. I intend to pay my debt to

Auggie, now that I have steady employment. My agent has shows lined up for me in several major cities."

"Auggie doesn't care about the money anymore. He wants to make an example of you."

Before Rafael could say anything else, the dressing room door opened and one of Chesterfield's assistants walked in. "Bobby, I . . . ," she started. Then she saw Rafael and his gun, and her mouth gaped open.

"It's okay, Sheila. Rafael and I are old friends. He was just showing me a gun he purchased." Chesterfield smiled at Rafael. "I'm afraid I can't talk any longer. I have my show to perform, and I need to speak to my assistant."

"Yeah. The show is important," Rafael said. "Maybe we can meet afterward."

"That would be wonderful. And give my regards to Auggie. Tell him I'm thinking of him and I'll have something for him soon."

Rafael left the dressing room, and Chesterfield talked to his assistant as if nothing had happened, but he collapsed on a chair as soon as the door closed behind her. There was no way he could keep avoiding Auggie's debt collectors, now that Horace had gotten bookings for him that would announce his presence online, in the press, and on TV. He'd hoped that he could pay off Montenegro, but that might be off the table if Auggie wanted to make an example of him.

Chesterfield shut his eyes and slowed his breathing. He couldn't think about Montenegro or anything else now. He had a show to put on and he had to stay focused.

Robin waved at Regina Barrister and Stanley Cloud as soon as she spotted them in the theater lobby. She'd asked Stanley if he thought Regina would enjoy an evening of magic. After some thought, he decided that it would be good to get Regina out of the house.

"I bought great seats," Robin said as she handed Stanley two tickets. "We're fourth row center. We should have a great view."

"Thanks," Stanley said as he followed Robin and Jeff down the aisle.

"My pleasure. I'm really eager to see the Chamber of Death."

"We saw a dress rehearsal at Chesterfield's home on the coast, the night he disappeared," Jeff added.

"Do you have any idea how the Chamber of Death works?" Stanley asked.

Robin laughed. "Not a clue. Chesterfield let me examine the sarcophagus before he performed it at the dress rehearsal, and I still have no idea how he got out."

The press had played up Chesterfield's murder cases and disappearance all week, and the free publicity had guaranteed a packed house. As she walked to her seat, Robin scanned the audience. David Turner was in an aisle seat on the end of the second row. Claire Madison was seated beside him. Robin knew from reading the entertainment news that she and Turner were living together. The news reported that Chesterfield had filed for a divorce and was fighting to get a lot of money from her.

Turner's career had been in jeopardy ever since Chesterfield had exposed his show-closing illusion on television. He had developed a new closing act, but it wasn't as amazing as the illusion Chesterfield had exposed, and there were rumors that Caesars Palace might not renew his contract.

Seated near the aisle on the other side of the theater were Marco and Rafael. Robin also spotted Horace Dobson sitting in the last seat in the front row. She assumed he had reserved that seat so he could go backstage if he was needed. Sitting a few rows behind Dobson was Joe Samuels. Peter Ragland and two police officers were standing in the aisle against the wall next to his seat. Robin wondered if they were there at Samuel's request to arrest

Chesterfield. Robin also noticed Miriam Ross, Chesterfield's former assistant, seated near the front of the theater. Iris Hitchens, Lily Dowd's daughter, was seated midway in the theater in an aisle seat.

The gang's all here, Robin thought as she worked her way down the row to her seat. Moments later, the houselights dimmed and Robert Chesterfield appeared onstage in a puff of smoke.

The first half of Chesterfield's show was entertaining, but everyone was waiting to see the Chamber of Death. Chesterfield milked the suspense until the show was almost over. Then the houselights went out. When they came back on, the open pyramid was center stage, and a ramp connected the stage to one of the aisles. The pyramid was jet-black, and the curtains behind it were also black.

Fog rose around the pyramid, shrouding it in mist, and eerie music crept through the theater. The tension built. Then a bright flash blinded the audience, and Chesterfield appeared in front of the pyramid wearing a hooded black robe with flowing sleeves that Robin remembered from the rehearsal at the cliff house.

Chesterfield stared at the audience and let the suspense build. Then he began to speak. "In ancient Egypt, those who offended the gods were entombed alive in a sarcophagus and died a horrible death. I am known as an escape artist. Tonight, I will attempt to perform the ultimate escape: I will try to cheat death."

Two of Chesterfield's assistants appeared at the back of the theater dressed in bright red robes with flowing sleeves and hoods that hid their faces. The costume was decorated with yellow hieroglyphics. A sarcophagus rested on a slanting platform that sat on a dolly. The assistants began pushing the sarcophagus down the aisle, and a third assistant followed them. The sarcophagus was pushed up the ramp and onto the stage, and the assistants left it at the left side of the pyramid.

Chesterfield pointed at the pyramid. "This, my friends, is the

Chamber of Death. Those who enter have never returned to join the living."

One of the assistants pressed a button and the top of the platform that held the coffin tilted down. The three assistants pushed the sarcophagus onto the stage and maneuvered it so it was between the sides of the pyramid with one of the long sides facing the audience.

Chesterfield pointed to the sarcophagus. "I will be placed in this coffin."

Two rectangular boxes sat on either side of the pyramid. Black cloths hid their contents.

"Are there any among you who may be affected by sheer horror? If so, I suggest that you leave the theater, because what you will see next is not for the faint of heart."

Chesterfield waited. When no one left, he walked to the first box and whipped off the black cloth, revealing a glass case filled with writhing snakes.

There were gasps from the audience.

"These are some of the world's most dangerous snakes: cobras, vipers, and Cleopatra's favorite, the asp." The magician pulled off the cloth that covered the second cube. "What you see in here are some of the most poisonous scorpions known to man."

Chesterfield pointed to an object on the side of the coffin. "Please note the chute on this side of the sarcophagus. When I am locked in this coffin, my assistants will send this horde of death dealers down the chute and onto my body. According to the literature, I should be dead within minutes."

Chesterfield looked out at the audience.

He spotted an attractive woman in her early twenties who was sitting with her boyfriend in the front row. "Madam, would you be willing to assist me?"

The woman giggled and nodded.

"Please come onto the stage."

Chesterfield waited while the young woman walked up the steps and over to him. "What is your name?"

"Charlotte."

Chesterfield smiled. "That's a charming name. Now, Charlotte, please tell the audience, have we ever met before?"

"No."

"We are complete strangers?"

"Yes."

While Chesterfield talked to Charlotte, one of his assistants took hold of one end of the lid that covered the sarcophagus, and a second assistant took hold of the other end. They stood behind the coffin with their backs to the audience and raised the lid.

"Charlotte, would you please inspect the sarcophagus to make sure there are no hidden doors through which I can escape?"

Charlotte went up to the coffin and leaned down. She ran her hand around the inside and knocked on every surface. After a while, she stood up. "It looks solid."

"Thank you. You may return to your seat, and I will enter the Chamber of Death."

Chesterfield climbed into the coffin, and sank down. The two assistants suspended the lid over the sarcophagus.

Chesterfield sat up in the gap between the assistants who were holding the lid so the audience could see him in the coffin. The third assistant stepped in front of the coffin between the assistants who were holding up the lid and pushed Chesterfield down. When she stepped back, the other two assistants lowered the coffin lid and attached padlocks to chains that were threaded through loops on either side of the coffin.

While the coffin lid was being secured, the assistant who had pushed Chesterfield into the coffin pushed the dolly that had held the sarcophagus offstage so the audience had an unobstructed view of the sarcophagus.

One of the assistants who had lowered the lid turned to the

audience. "The gods have decreed Lord Chesterfield's death. His fate is sealed."

The two assistants who had lowered the lid of the coffin put on gloves. One opened a lid on top of the cube containing the snakes. The other gloved assistant opened the chute facing the audience. Someone gasped when a handful of wriggling reptiles was shoved down the chute.

Suddenly, Robin heard the sound of fists beating against the inside of the sarcophagus.

"Wait. There's something wrong. Let me out!" Chesterfield shouted.

"Your pleas fall on deaf ears," the assistant said.

Chesterfield continued to try to convince the assistants that there was a problem with the trick while another gloved assistant took a handful of scorpions and poured them down the chute.

Chesterfield screamed. Then he pleaded for the assistants to let him out. They ignored him and his voice grew weaker, until an unearthly scream issued from the coffin followed by silence. Several members of the audience gasped.

One of the two assistants who remained onstage addressed the audience. "Has Lord Chesterfield survived the Chamber of Death?"

As eerie music floated through the theater, the other assistant unlocked the padlocks. When the chains were unwrapped, the two assistants who had remained onstage raised the lid of the coffin. They looked down. Then one of them jumped back, and the other one screamed.

"Is this part of the act?" Stanley Cloud asked Robin.

"I don't know. They didn't do this when I saw the illusion on the coast."

Several members of the audience stood up, and Robin saw Horace Dobson race onto the stage. He looked into the coffin and lost all of his color.

"Call the police!" he shouted. "Bobby's been murdered."

CHAPTER TWENTY-EIGHT

Tamara Robinson, a policewoman with the physique of a serious bodybuilder, met Carrie Anders and Roger Dillon in the theater lobby and told them what had occurred during the performance.

"A guy named Joe Samuels filed a criminal complaint against Robert Chesterfield. Lou Fletcher and I came with the DA who has the case. We were going to arrest Chesterfield on theft charges when the show finished. The big finale is this Chamber of Death trick, where the magician is sealed in a coffin and they put snakes and scorpions in with him. When his assistants opened up the coffin, Chesterfield wasn't supposed to be inside. Only he was, and he'd been stabbed to death.

"One of the assistants screamed, and Horace Dobson, Chesterfield's agent, ran onstage. When he yelled that Chesterfield had been murdered, we told everyone to stay in their seats and secured the doors, but some people took off as soon as they realized that the theater had turned into a crime scene. We did keep most of the audience inside. We called for backup right away, and I have officers guarding the exits."

"You did a great job, considering the circumstances," Dillon said.

Robinson shook her head. "I got to tell you, the natives are restless. I've had more than one person ask me for my name and badge number and tell me how well they know the mayor."

"Don't sweat that," Anders said. "We'll back you up if anyone complains."

"What do you want us to do now?" Robinson asked.

"I want everyone who was seated near the stage interviewed," Dillon said. "You can let the people at the back of the theater out after getting names, addresses, and phone numbers, but keep anyone here who noticed anything strange."

"Who's taken charge?" Anders asked.

"Peter Ragland."

"What's he doing here?" Dillon asked with obvious surprise.

"He's the DA who came with us."

"Where is he?"

"On the stage with the ME, talking to Dobson and Norman Chow, the theater manager. Oh, and there's a lawyer named Robin Lockwood who wanted to talk to a homicide detective. She says she has information that might be helpful."

"Where is she?" Anders asked.

"Down by the front, near the stage."

"Thanks, Tamara. Why don't you get started on the interviews." As soon as Robinson walked away, Anders turned to her partner. "Why the reaction when Robinson mentioned Peter Ragland?"

"I was promoted to Homicide twenty-odd years ago. In my first murder case, Peter Ragland prosecuted Robert Chesterfield for a double homicide. Chesterfield hired Regina Barrister. All the charges had to be dismissed after Barrister got Ragland's evidence thrown out before trial. Those cases solidified Barrister's reputation as a legal whiz and destroyed Ragland's career."

"Do you think Ragland asked for the theft case so he could get a little revenge?" Anders asked.

"I wouldn't put it past him," Dillon replied.

"Why don't you make sure Ragland doesn't mess up this case while I talk to Lockwood."

When Dillon left the lobby, Anders followed him into the theater.

Anders spotted Robin and waved her onto the stage so they could have privacy.

"Hi, Robin," Anders said as soon as they were standing behind one of the curtains. "I didn't know you were a fan of magic."

"I am, but that's only one reason why I'm here. Robert Chesterfield was a client. A few years ago, he asked me to patent the Chamber of Death. That never happened, but he did invite Jeff and me to see a dress rehearsal at his mansion on the coast. You know about his disappearing act, right?"

Anders nodded.

"I was there when it happened."

"Is that what you wanted to tell me?" Anders asked.

"No. I have no idea how Chesterfield was murdered or who killed him, but I wanted you to know that there are several people in the audience who had it in for him."

"Such as?"

Robin pointed at Rafael and Marco. "Those men work for Augustine Montenegro, a Las Vegas casino owner. Chesterfield had gambling debts. A short time ago, Montenegro sent those men to collect. They attacked Chesterfield in an alley behind a tavern. Chesterfield fought them off and stabbed Rafael."

"How do you know this?"

"I saw it happen. Chesterfield asked me to meet him at the tavern to discuss a legal matter. After we were through, Chesterfield left by the back door. I left the same way a few minutes later and saw Rafael and Marco threatening Chesterfield. I told them I was calling 911. When Rafael turned toward me, Chesterfield stabbed him. A week later, they threatened me in the park across from the jail."

"Did you report any of this?"

"No."

Anders knew Robin well, so she didn't ask why. Instead she said, "You mentioned that there are several people in the audience who didn't like Chesterfield. Who are the others?"

Robin pointed out David Turner and Claire Madison. "Claire is married to Chesterfield and she's very wealthy. Turner has been her lover for years. I read that Chesterfield has filed for a divorce. The main issue is Claire's money and how much of it he can get.

"Turner is a famous magician. He has a show at a Las Vegas casino that he used to close with a mystifying illusion. A few years ago, there was a TV show with a masked magician who called himself Mysterioso and revealed the secrets behind magic tricks. It turns out that Chesterfield was Mysterioso, and he told the world how Turner did his biggest trick because Turner was sleeping with his wife. That crippled Turner's act and hampered his career.

"Then there are those protesters outside the theater. They're professional magicians, and they're here because Turner let everyone know that Chesterfield was Mysterioso. They hate Chesterfield."

"Anyone else with a grudge?"

Robin gestured toward Joe Samuels. "Chesterfield embezzled money from Joe Samuels, and he's filed a criminal complaint. When we met at the tavern, Chesterfield hired me to try to settle with Samuels so he wouldn't be arrested. Samuels rejected the offer and told me he wants Chesterfield to suffer in jail.

"Then there's Iris Hitchens," Robin said, pointing toward Lily Dowd's daughter. "Chesterfield was married to her mother, who died under mysterious circumstances. Hitchens blamed Chesterfield, although there was no evidence that he killed her. There was a protracted court battle over Dowd's will and really bad feelings between Dowd's children and Chesterfield.

"Miriam Ross is also in the audience. She was Chesterfield's assistant. I don't know if she has a motive to kill her old boss, but she's here."

"Jesus, Robin. Is there anyone in the audience who didn't have a motive to kill Chesterfield?" Anders shook her head. "You're not making my job any easier."

"Sorry," Robin said.

Robin had seen Peter Ragland on the stage. She knew his failure in Chesterfield's case had torpedoed his career, but she decided not to mention that to Carrie, who already had too many suspects.

"Okay," Anders said. "I appreciate the help. I'll talk to the people you named, but Chesterfield was onstage doing his act, and the people you've mentioned were in the audience. Doesn't that rule them out?"

"It was pitch-black in the theater, and everyone was watching the stage. The people I mentioned could have slipped out during the performance. I don't know how they could have gotten to Chesterfield without being seen, but David Turner is a master magician, and the protesters are magicians. Turner and the other magicians might have been able to figure out a way to kill Chesterfield in the middle of the Chamber of Death trick."

Anders furrowed her brow. "It just occurred to me that the killer had to know how the trick was performed before he could figure out how to kill Chesterfield onstage, but this is the premiere."

"Most of the people I mentioned saw the trick performed a few years ago during the rehearsal at the coast. That's where I met most of them. And Horace Dobson and everyone who works in the show would know how the illusion works. Rafael and Marco weren't at the rehearsal, but Montenegro was, so he could have told them about the trick."

"Okay. Thanks for the heads-up, Robin. You and the people you're with can leave. I'll clear it with one of the uniforms."

When Horace Dobson announced Chesterfield's murder, Peter Ragland had ordered Tamara Robinson and Lou Fletcher to secure the doors to the theater and call for more officers. Then he had raced onto the stage to take charge of the investigation. As soon as he'd gotten Dobson and the magician's assistant calmed down, he called Vanessa Cole. Ragland could tell that Vanessa wasn't pleased that he hadn't waited for a DA in Homicide, but she had let him take charge since he was on the scene and had experience in handling murder cases.

When Peter had charged Chesterfield with murder all those years ago, the case had ruined Peter's career. Now Chesterfield's murder onstage during the Chamber of Death illusion would be national news. Wouldn't it be ironic, he thought, if the magician's murder resurrected his career?

Peter was talking to Sally Grace, the medical examiner, when Roger Dillon walked onto the stage.

"Hi, Peter," Dillon said. "I didn't know you handled homicides."

Ragland reddened. "Normally I don't, but I was here to arrest Chesterfield in a theft case. Since I was here, Vanessa told me to take charge."

A man in his midthirties was standing next to the deputy DA and was visibly upset. "Can't you speed this up?" he asked. "We're trying to upgrade the image of this neighborhood, and the theater is one of our main attractions. The publicity will kill us."

"I appreciate your problem, Mr. Chow," Ragland said, "but we're investigating a murder, and everyone in this theater is either a suspect or a potential witness. I regret any harm to the theater's reputation, but we have to follow procedure."

"What did I miss?" Anders asked as she joined the group.

"Mr. Chow, Mr. Dobson, this is Carrie Anders," Ragland said. "She and Roger Dillon are with Homicide."

"This is horrible," Dobson said.

"Did you know Mr. Chesterfield well?" Anders asked.

"I've been his agent since the 1990s."

"Can you tell us what happened?" Ragland asked.

"Bobby created the Chamber of Death as the finale for his show." Dobson pointed at the sarcophagus. "He's locked inside this coffin, and the assistants pour snakes and scorpions into it. The audience hears him screaming inside the coffin and banging on the sides. If the trick is done correctly, Bobby disappears from the coffin and reappears at the back of the theater. Only this time, someone stabbed him and he was still inside the coffin when it was opened."

"How does the illusion work?" Ragland asked.

"Is this confidential? A magician's secrets are very valuable."

"We'll try to keep the solution to the illusion secret, but we can't promise anything. It might have to come out in a trial."

"Do the best you can," Dobson conceded with a sigh. "The trick is really simple. The sarcophagus is on a dolly in the back of the theater when the illusion starts. After it's pushed up a ramp onto the stage, the platform sits right next to one edge of the coffin with a little space in between. At one point in the act, the three assistants briefly block the view of the audience, and the bright lights blind the audience so it can't see what's happening on the floor of the stage.

"The audience thinks that the assistant who is in the middle is pushing Bobby down into the coffin, but what really happens is that Bobby rolls over the side of the sarcophagus and crawls into a narrow opening in the platform that supported the sarcophagus. The backdrop of the set is black, and so is the robe Bobby was wearing. The combination of the black background, the black robe and hood, and the blinding lights makes him invisible to the audience. When the middle assistant pushes the dolly offstage, he gets out and runs down a tunnel to the back of the theater."

"What about the screams and banging from inside the coffin?" Roger asked.

"They're prerecorded and piped into the coffin to distract the audience. There's a tiny microphone in the sarcophagus that's impossible to spot."

Dillon shook his head. "Every once in a while, I find out how a magic trick is done, and I always feel stupid."

"Do you have any idea who killed Mr. Chesterfield?" Anders asked.

Dobson hesitated. "I hate to accuse anyone."

"You're not. You're helping us figure out who murdered your friend."

"There are three assistants, Sheila Monroe, Maria Rodriguez, and Nancy Porter. Sheila and Maria raise the lid of the coffin, and Nancy is the one who pretends to push Bobby down. Nancy was the only person who could have stabbed him."

"Where is she?" Ragland asked.

"I don't know. Nancy was supposed to be onstage for the finale, but she didn't come back after pushing the dolly offstage."

"Has anyone searched the theater for her?" Anders asked.

"Not that I know."

"What does she look like?"

"She's a redhead, green eyes, about five feet tall, and very slender, but strong. The assistants all have to be short and skinny so they can fit into tight spaces."

Roger Dillon walked to the edge of the stage and told one of the uniforms to organize a search for the missing woman.

"We're going to need to open the sarcophagus," Anders said. "Are the snakes and scorpions dangerous?"

"No. They look scary, but they're harmless," Dobson assured her.

Anders signaled two officers to raise the lid that covered the coffin. She looked inside and saw snakes and scorpions wriggling and slithering over Robert Chesterfield's body and around the knife that was buried in his heart.

Dr. Grace looked into the coffin. "That looks like a surgical strike right into the victim's heart. He would have died very quickly."

"If the audience heard Chesterfield scream when he was stabbed, they'd think that the screams were just part of the act," Dillon said.

Anders saw the two rectangular glass boxes. "Is there someone who can put these reptiles and scorpions back in their cages so Dr. Grace can examine the body?" she asked Dobson.

"That's the assistants' job. I'll ask them if they're up to it. They're both very upset."

Sheila, who was blond, and Maria, who had glossy black hair, were sitting on bridge chairs just off the stage, still dressed in their voluminous robes. They were talking quietly to each other, but they looked up when the agent and the detectives approached. Anders could see that Sheila had been crying. Maria looked pale.

"I'm Carrie Anders, and I'm one of the detectives who is going to try and find out what happened to Mr. Chesterfield. I'll want to talk to you about what you saw, but right now I need your help. I understand you two can put the snakes and scorpions that are in the sarcophagus back into their cages."

"It's a vivarium," Maria said. "That's what you call it."

"Thanks. I didn't know that. Are you up to putting the snakes and scorpions in the vivariums so the medical examiner can start to work?"

"Yes," Maria answered.

"Before you do that, I understand Nancy Porter is missing. Do you know where she is?"

Maria said no and Sheila shook her head.

"Can you remember what she did before and during the Chamber of Death illusion?" Dillon asked.

"We were onstage for one of Bobby's other illusions," Maria said. "When he finished that trick, we went to our dressing room and put on these robes for the Chamber of Death while he did some card tricks onstage by himself. When it was time for the finale, we went to the back of the theater so we could push the sarcophagus onstage."

"Actually, you and I did," Sheila said, "but Nancy couldn't find her inhaler. She has asthma. So we left and she joined us a few minutes later."

"That's right," Maria agreed. "Anyway, she joined us just as we started pushing the sarcophagus down the aisle and onto the stage. Then Bobby got in the coffin, and we covered it while Nancy pushed the roller offstage."

"She's supposed to come back onstage, but that's the last I saw of her," Sheila said.

"Me too," Maria chimed in.

"Thanks," Anders said. "Let's get rid of the scorpions and reptiles so the ME can do her job."

The women followed Anders and Dobson to the coffin just as a policeman ran out from backstage to say, "I found Nancy Porter."

CHAPTER TWENTY-NINE

While Ragland, Anders, and Dillon followed the policeman, he told them that he had found Porter lying unconscious on the floor of the dressing room that the assistants used. A cloth that smelled of ether was on the floor next to her. When Anders and Dillon opened the dressing room door, they saw a slender redhead clad in a bra and panties sprawled on the floor. Someone had put a pillow under her head, and an EMT was bending over her. Porter tried to sit up.

"Take it easy," the EMT said.

"What happened?" Porter groaned.

Anders squatted next to her. "I'm Carrie Anders. I'm a detective with the Portland Police Bureau. It looks like someone used ether to knock you out. How are you feeling?"

"Woozy."

"Can you stand?" Anders asked.

"I think so."

Anders saw a dress hanging on a rack that looked to be Porter's size and helped her get it on.

There was a couch in the dressing room, and Anders and the EMT helped Porter walk over to it.

"What do you remember?" Dillon asked when Porter was sitting down.

Before she could answer, the door opened and an officer walked in holding a red hooded robe decorated with hieroglyphics and some other clothes. "I found this near the exit to the loading dock in the back of the theater."

Dillon took charge of the robe and the clothes. They were similar to clothes he'd seen the stagehands wearing. Then he held out the robe. "Is this yours?" he asked.

Porter studied it. "It looks like it."

"Do you remember what happened before you passed out?" Dillon asked.

"I have asthma, and I always have to have my inhaler with me if I do something strenuous like pushing the dolly off the stage by myself. Only the inhaler wasn't where I'd put it. I started looking for it and . . ." She shook her head. "That's all I remember."

"When was the last time you saw your inhaler?" Dillon asked.

Porter was lost in thought for a few moments. "Bobby does a trick where he levitates one of us. Then he does card tricks by himself so we have time to change into our costumes for the Chamber of Death. I'm pretty sure I put my inhaler on my dressing table before the levitation trick, but it wasn't there when I came back to change into my robe for the Chamber of Death."

Ragland turned to the officer who'd brought in the robe. "Search this room for Ms. Porter's inhaler."

"Did you see who attacked you?" Dillon asked.

"No." Porter looked around. "Why are all these police officers here?"

"This might be a shock. Are you feeling up to hearing some very disturbing news?" Dillon asked.

"Please. I need to know what happened."

"Robert Chesterfield is dead."

Porter's hand flew to her mouth. "How?"

"It looks like the person who knocked you out used your robe as a disguise and followed Maria and Sheila onto the stage. As I understand it, you pretend to push Mr. Chesterfield down while he is crawling over the edge of the sarcophagus and hiding in the dolly."

"Yes."

"The killer stabbed him in the coffin when he was pretending to push him down, then he may have left by the backstage exit near the loading dock after discarding your robe."

"Oh my God!"

Anders held up the robe. It was oversized and bulky. "With the hood up and the long sleeves, no one in the audience would be able to see who was wearing the robe, but what about the other assistants? Wouldn't they see the killer?"

"There's a good chance they wouldn't," Porter said. "It's dark at the back of the theater. I usually help Maria push the sarcophagus up the aisle and onto the stage, but Sheila would have helped her if the killer showed up after the finale started. They would be looking forward, so they wouldn't see someone dressed in my robe if the hood was up and he was standing behind them. The killer would still be behind them when they lifted the coffin lid, and they stare toward the back of the stage. If the killer kept his head down, the sides of the hood would block a view of his face.

"Bobby sits up in the coffin and I pretend to push him down. He would be vulnerable when he sits up. The killer could stab him then, and Maria and Sheila wouldn't notice, because they're still staring toward the back of the stage. After that, they lower the lid on the sarcophagus, so they wouldn't see Bobby inside. Meanwhile, the killer would go behind Maria and Sheila and push the dolly off the stage, so they would never notice that someone else was dressed in my robe."

"I found the inhaler," an officer said.

"Where was it?" Ragland asked.

The policeman pointed to a drawer in one of the tables the assistant used for applying makeup.

"That's Maria Rodriguez's table," Porter said.

"Could you have put it in her drawer by mistake?" Anders asked.

"Absolutely not. I specifically remember putting it on my table. And why would I put my inhaler in Maria's drawer?"

"Do you have another inhaler you can use, because this one is evidence," Anders said.

"I have extras where I'm staying."

"Okay. I think that's enough for now, unless you have some other questions, Peter, Roger?"

Dillon shook his head.

"I'm good," Ragland said. Then he turned to the officer who had found the robe. "Put this robe, the clothes, the inhaler, and the cloth with the ether in evidence bags and give them to the lab techs. If we get lucky, there may be trace evidence on them."

"We're going to have a doctor check you out," Anders told Nancy, "but we'll need an official statement later."

"Of course." She shook her head again. "I can't believe Bobby is dead."

When they were headed back to the stage, Anders said, "One thing we can be sure of, whoever killed Chesterfield knew how the Chamber of Death worked."

Dillon nodded. "He had to have seen it performed in order to know Porter's role in the trick and her routine before each performance."

"He also had to have been in the theater before today," Ragland said. "The killer got Porter to stay in her dressing room when

Sheila and Maria left by hiding her inhaler while she was onstage. Only someone who knew a lot about the assistants would know that Porter had asthma and had to have the inhaler when she worked on the Chamber of Death trick."

Anders told Dillon and Ragland about her conversation with Robin Lockwood.

"We have to talk to everyone who works in the theater to find out if Turner, Madison, Samuels, and the men who attacked Chesterfield were seen in the theater during rehearsals," Ragland said.

"Now that we've narrowed the list of possible suspects, solving this case should be a snap," Dillon told Anders. "Maybe I'll let you crack it, so you can get the credit. You should have it wrapped up in no time."

"Yeah, if I were a magician."

CHAPTER THIRTY

Norman Chow was still pacing the stage when the trio approached and asked him if they could use his office for interviews. As soon as Chow agreed, Roger Dillon told Tamara Robinson to bring in Joe Samuels.

"I will," Robinson said, "but he couldn't have killed Chesterfield. I was standing near him during the performance. He never left his seat during the Chamber of Death illusion."

"Okay. Good to know. I also want you to interview the stagehands and the guard at the stage door. Ask them if they noticed anyone at rehearsals who shouldn't have been there. You might want to talk to them near the door to the office while we interview some of the people in the audience in case someone looks familiar."

The interview with Joe Samuels went quickly. He admitted that he disliked the magician, but he swore he couldn't have killed him since he never left his seat during the trick. He also said that he didn't see anything during the Chamber of Death illusion that might help solve Chesterfield's murder.

As soon as Samuels left, the detectives had Rafael Otero brought in.

"Am I under arrest?" Rafael asked as soon as he walked into the office.

"No," Dillon said. "We're interviewing everyone who was sitting close to the stage and may have seen something during the performance that will help us identify who killed Mr. Chesterfield. Did you see anything odd during the Chamber of Death trick?"

"The whole damn thing was odd." Rafael shook his head. "Too bad Bobby is dead. I'd love to ask him how he was going to escape from that box."

"So you knew him?" Ragland said.

Rafael smiled. "If I'm not under arrest, I'd like to leave. If I am under arrest, I want a lawyer present when you ask me questions."

"We know Chesterfield stabbed you when you tried to rough him up because he owes your boss money," Ragland said, "but that doesn't interest us. We just want to find the person who killed Chesterfield."

"Good luck with that," Rafael said.

"There's no need to play hardball," Ragland said.

"Of course there is. This is a murder investigation. So, are you going to stop me from leaving?"

"No," Ragland said when he realized that he wasn't going to be able to get Otero to cooperate.

When Rafael opened the door, Tamara Robinson was outside, standing next to an elderly African American couple.

"You need to talk to the Atkinsons," she told the detectives.

"Come in," Dillon said.

"This is Deputy District Attorney Peter Ragland and Detectives Roger Dillon and Carrie Anders," Robinson said when everyone was in the office. "They're in charge of the investigation into

Robert Chesterfield's murder. And this is Titus Atkinson and his wife, Emily."

"Pleased to meet you," Dillon said.

"The Atkinsons were sitting a few rows back from the stage," Robinson continued. "Will you please tell the detectives what you just told me?"

Mr. Atkinson looked nervous. "Emily and I are big fans of magic. We always attend a show when a famous magician comes to Portland, and we always try to get seats close to the stage, so I can try and figure out how they do the tricks."

"Any success?" Dillon asked.

Atkinson flashed a sad smile. "Not much." He shook his head. "I'm almost always stumped."

"How about tonight?"

"No luck. I thought I got the one where he made the roses disappear, but I have no idea how he pulled off those other stunts."

"Tell Detective Dillon about the man who was sitting in front of you," Robinson said.

Atkinson looked nervous again. "Okay—now, I didn't see anyone kill anyone."

"Just tell the detectives what you did see."

"Just before the Chamber of Death trick started, when Lord Chesterfield was doing card tricks, the man who was seated directly in front of me got up and walked into the aisle."

"Did you see where he went after he went into the aisle?" Dillon asked.

"No. I was focused on Lord Chesterfield. I just saw the man leave."

"But you're certain he left?"

"Yes, because my view wasn't obstructed and—well, I recognized him because he's also a famous magician, so I watched him because I wondered what he was doing."

"What's the magician's name?" Ragland asked.

"David Turner. I've seen him on TV, and Emily and I caught his show in Las Vegas several years ago, before that TV magician showed how the car trick worked."

"How long was Mr. Turner gone?" Ragland asked.

"Definitely during most of the Chamber of Death, because I could see the whole thing."

"Did you see Mr. Turner return to his seat?" Anders asked.

"He was back sometime after the girl screamed, because I had to look around him to see what was happening on the stage."

Anders turned her attention to Emily Atkinson. "What about you, Mrs. Atkinson? Did you see where the man went after he left his seat?"

"No. I didn't see the man leave, because I was watching what was happening onstage, and he was sitting in front of Titus, not in front of me."

"This has been very useful," Anders assured the couple. "Why don't you step outside. Officer Robinson will be with you in a minute." Anders turned to Robinson as soon as the Atkinsons were out of the room. "Go get David Turner. I have a few questions I'd like to ask him."

"Have a seat, Mr. Turner. I'm Carrie Anders, and this is Roger Dillon. We're detectives with Portland Homicide. And this is Deputy District Attorney Peter Ragland."

"Why am I being detained?" the magician asked.

"We're talking to everyone who was near the front of the theater and may have seen something that can help us find the person who killed Mr. Chesterfield. I'm particularly eager to get your input because you're a professional magician and would see things I never would."

"Then I'm sorry to disappoint you. I have no idea who killed Chesterfield."

"Do you know how the trick worked?"

"I saw Chesterfield perform the Chamber of Death a few years ago. I thought I'd figured out how he pulled it off, but I was never one hundred percent certain."

"During the performance, did you get a good-enough look from your seat to confirm your hypothesis?"

"Not from the angle I had."

"What's your best guess?"

"When Chesterfield performs the illusion, the background is black. In magic circles, this is known as 'black art,' and it lets a magician wearing black blend in with the background. Chesterfield had on a black robe with a hood and long sleeves, and the lights on the front of the stage were very bright, which also helped to render him invisible. There's a moment when the three assistants are in a line in front of the sarcophagus, blocking the audience's view. That would be his moment to roll out of the coffin and get offstage somehow."

"I understand that you had a grudge against Mr. Chesterfield because he exposed the illusion you used to close your Las Vegas act."

"I hated his guts."

"If you hated him, why did you come to the theater tonight?"

"I wanted to figure out how the Chamber of Death worked so I could ruin his show the way he ruined mine."

"Thank you for your honesty," Dillon said. "Say, out of curiosity, can anyone confirm that you were in your seat during the Chamber of Death trick?"

"Claire was sitting next to me the whole time."

"That's confusing, Mr. Turner, because we just spoke to the person who was seated directly behind you, and he told us that he saw you leave your seat right before the illusion began. Can you explain that?"

For the first time during the interview, Turner looked uncertain.

"Well?" Anders prodded.

"I . . . Ask Claire. She'll tell you I never left my seat."

"If she does tell us that and we can prove she's lying, she could be charged as an accessory to murder," Anders said. "Is that what you want?"

"All right, I did leave my seat so I could get a better look at the trick."

"Then why lie to us?" Anders asked.

"I'm living with Chesterfield's wife, who he was suing for a divorce so he could steal her money. With Chesterfield dead, we're rid of him. And everyone knows I hated him because of the TV show. Plus, I'm a magician. I knew I'd be a prime suspect because of the way he was killed."

"Too true," Dillon said. "So, where were you during the trick?"

"I went into the wings behind a curtain. That put me behind the floor lights so they wouldn't blind me. I thought I could see how Chesterfield got out of the coffin. But he never left it, and now I know why."

"What was happening on the stage when you left your seat?"

"Chesterfield was performing card tricks."

"Have you been in the Imperial Theater before this evening?" Ragland asked.

"No," Turner answered after a slight hesitation.

"You seem uncertain," Anders said.

"I did try to get inside to see a rehearsal last week."

"So you would be able to expose the trick?"

"Yes. But I never got past the guard at the stage door."

"You're telling me that a man with your abilities couldn't sneak into this theater?" Dillon pressed.

"I didn't kill him," Turner said, sidestepping the question.

"You must admit, you're coming off as our most promising suspect," Ragland said.

"I don't want to talk about this anymore," Turner said.

"That's your right," Ragland said, "but it would be in your best interest to tell us anything you know that can help take you off our list of suspects."

"I think I should talk to a lawyer."

While David Turner was being interviewed, Tamara Robinson started talking to Henry Schloss.

"What's your position at the theater, Mr. Schloss?"

"I'm security at the stage door."

"That opens into the alley, right?"

"Yes, ma'am."

"How many exits are there besides the stage door?"

"There's the doors at the front of the Imperial, some emergency fire exits, and a loading dock in the back."

"Have you been on duty since Mr. Chesterfield's show started rehearsals?"

"Yes."

"Did you notice anything unusual tonight or during the week?"

"Well, there's those protesters. They've been shouting and causing a ruckus all week."

"Have you seen any of them in the theater?"

"No."

"Were you on duty at the stage door while the show was going on tonight?"

"Yes."

"Did anyone leave or come in while the show was going on?"

"No."

"Okay. Can you remember anything unusual going on inside the theater this week, during rehearsals?"

Schloss thought for a minute. "There were two things that come to mind. On the first day of rehearsal, a woman got into an argument with Mr. Chesterfield. I don't know what it was about, but I could hear raised voices."

"Do you know the woman's name?"

"No, and I just saw her from a distance. I'm not certain I could ID her."

"Okay. Now, you said there was a second incident."

Before Schloss could answer, the door to Mr. Chow's office opened, and David Turner walked out with Carrie Anders and Peter Ragland behind him.

Schloss's eyes widened and he pointed at Turner. "That guy tried to talk his way into the theater early this week when they were rehearsing."

"I told you that," Turner said to Anders.

"Did you tell them I caught you inside the theater a half hour later?" Schloss asked.

"Well?" Ragland asked the magician.

"I'm not talking anymore until I speak with an attorney."

"I'm placing you under arrest," Ragland said.

"Why? You can't do that. I haven't done anything wrong."

"You lied to us about where you were when Mr. Chesterfield was murdered. That's obstruction of justice. And, because of your skills as a magician, you had the ability to pull off the murder. I think that gives us probable cause. Now, please put your hands behind your back so we can cuff you."

"This is outrageous!"

"If you don't comply with my request, you'll be committing the crime of resisting arrest."

Turner hesitated. Then he let Anders handcuff him. While she was doing that, she told Turner his Miranda rights.

"Have someone drive Mr. Turner downtown," Ragland told Robinson.

Ragland beamed as Turner was led away. "That didn't take long."

"Nice work," Anders said, but she didn't sound sure.

Ragland frowned. "You don't have any doubts that Turner's our killer, do you?"

"He definitely had a motive and the opportunity."

"But?" Ragland pressed.

"I guess it was too easy. The murder was so clever, I thought it would take us a while to figure out who committed it."

"Don't look a gift horse in the mouth," Ragland said with another big smile. "This is going to look great for you and Dillon, and make sure Officer Robinson gets credit for her excellent work. Now, let's follow Mr. Turner downtown and see if we can get him to crack."

"What's bugging you?" Dillon asked Anders as they followed Ragland toward the exit.

"Something is off. I can't put my finger on it, but . . ." She shook her head. "Ragland's probably right. Turner is our guy. I'm overthinking this," Anders said, but Dillon could see that something was definitely bothering his partner.

CHAPTER THIRTY-ONE

When they were leaving the theater, Robin noticed a tension in Regina's shoulders and a gleam in her eyes that meant she was on the hunt—a look Robin had not seen in a long time.

"Is there a restaurant or bar nearby?" Regina asked as soon as they were outside the theater.

"The Meridian Hotel is two blocks from here," Stanley Cloud said, something Regina would have known a few years ago. "They have a bar."

"Let's go there and talk."

Robin agreed quickly, thrilled to see Regina so excited.

The Meridian had been an elegant hotel in the 1950s and sixties, but it had deteriorated as the neighborhood decayed, until it was known by the Vice squad as a hangout for drug dealers and prostitutes. The developer who restored the Imperial had remodeled the hotel and brought in a nationally known chef to run the restaurant.

"So," Regina said when the couples were seated in a booth in the bar, across from each other, "what did you see? Who do you think killed Robert Chesterfield?"

"Chesterfield sat up just before one of the assistants pushed him down, so he was alive then," Robin said.

"Exactly," Regina said. "The only time he could have been killed is when the assistant pushed him back into the coffin. Did you notice that there were three assistants on the stage when Chesterfield was pushed into the coffin, but only two on the stage when the coffin was opened and they discovered he'd been murdered?"

"So, you think the missing assistant killed Chesterfield?" asked Jeff.

"It looks that way," Regina said. Then she smiled, pleased that her brain was still working the way it used to, at least for a little while.

"I saw Peter Ragland run onto the stage. It looked like he was taking charge. I wonder if he picked up on that," Robin said.

"Who's Peter Ragland?" Regina asked.

Robin's heart sank. "He's a deputy district attorney. He was in the theater during the performance. Maybe he's a fan of magic."

"That was more excitement than I expected," Jeff said when they were in his pickup, headed back to their apartment.

Robin smiled. "It was great seeing the old Regina in action. The murder sure got her blood racing. She seemed more alive than I've seen her in a while."

"She did seem like her old self until she asked about Ragland," Jeff said.

Robin stopped smiling.

"In the good old days, before the Alzheimer's got her, she'd have figured out whodunit," Jeff said. "Then she'd have worked out a way to get the killer a not guilty verdict."

"I wonder if she'd have been able to figure out how Chesterfield escapes from the sarcophagus," Robin said. "I'd love to know how the trick works."

"No, you wouldn't," Jeff said. "It would spoil the fun."

Jeff parked, and the couple walked up to their apartment. When they got inside, Robin started to turn on the light, but Jeff moved between her and the switch and took her in his arms.

"What do you say we leave the lights off?" he asked before planting a gentle kiss on Robin's lips.

"I think that's a very good idea," Robin said just as her cell phone rang.

"Don't answer that."

"No one would be calling at this hour unless it was an emergency." Robin stepped back and took her phone out of her pocket.

Jeff sighed and turned on the lights.

"That's odd," she said when she saw who was calling. "Ms. Madison?"

"They arrested David. They're saying he murdered Bobby. He's at the jail. Can you help him?"

"You know I used to represent your husband?"

"I know, but you're the only criminal defense attorney I could think of. Can you see David now?"

"I can definitely set up a visit. Are you sure you don't want the name of another lawyer?"

"I know your reputation. David needs the best."

"Okay. I'll get there right away. We can talk about who should represent Mr. Turner later. Meet me in the reception area at the jail."

"Thank you for acting so quickly."

"Quick is important in a situation like this. Mr. Turner will be very upset, and he won't be thinking straight. There's no telling what he might say quite innocently that will come back to haunt him."

CHAPTER THIRTY-TWO

"Good evening, Mr. Turner," Robin said as soon as she walked into the contact visiting room. "My name is Robin Lockwood. I'm an attorney, and Claire Madison asked me to help you."

Turner stared at Robin for a moment. Then he snapped his fingers. "I know where I've seen you before. Didn't Chesterfield call you up onstage during the rehearsal at the coast to check out the sarcophagus?"

"You've got a good memory."

"You're Chesterfield's attorney!"

"I was, but I terminated our relationship, and now he's dead. I reminded Ms. Madison that I used to represent her husband, but she wanted me to see you anyway. If you feel uncomfortable with me, you can hire someone else."

"I've never been in a situation like this, and I need good advice now—so let's talk, and I can make a decision later."

"Do you know why you were arrested?" Robin asked.

"Probably because I got scared and lied."

"About what?"

"If you were at the rehearsal at the coast, you know why I hated Chesterfield."

"He revealed the secret of your finale on his TV show."

"The effect was devastating. Attendance dropped, and the casino was going to fire me. I saved myself by working a new illusion into the act, but Chesterfield almost killed my career. And that's why I was at the theater. I wanted to figure out the Chamber of Death and re-create it on the internet for revenge.

"The week before, I tried to get in the stage door to see a rehearsal. When that didn't work, I snuck in through the loading dock, but the security guard caught me before I saw the trick. So I left my seat during the illusion and hid onstage behind some curtains when Chesterfield started the illusion.

"When I was questioned by the police, I denied leaving my seat. I didn't know that the person sitting behind me had told the police that he saw me leave. To make matters worse, I also told the police that I'd never been in the Imperial Theater during rehearsals, but the security guard told the police he saw me in the theater."

"That's motive and opportunity, but what about means? How could you kill Chesterfield onstage in full view of the audience?"

"I couldn't, but the DA told me it was no use denying I killed Chesterfield, because he knew exactly how I did it."

"Did he explain how he thought you killed Chesterfield?"

Turner reddened with anger. "I asked him, but he just smiled and said, 'A magician never reveals how a trick is done.'"

"I've had a few cases with Peter Ragland, and he's not one of my favorites."

"What happens now?"

"There's no automatic bail in a murder case, so you might have to stay in jail for a while. If I represent you, I'll request a bail hearing, but I won't win it if the State can convince the judge that they have a strong case. I won't know if they do until I find out why Ragland thinks he can nail you. I'll tell you what I find out as fast as

I can, but that may not be until Monday. Can you hold it together until then?"

"Yes. I'm really scared, but I was in combat in the army, so I've been under pressure before."

Robin smiled. "Not to mention appearing every night before huge audiences in Las Vegas."

Turner smiled for the first time. "Yeah, there is that."

"What did you do in the military?" Robin asked.

Suddenly Turner looked sick. "This will definitely not help my cause."

"Yes?"

"The skills I'd developed as a magician made me perfect for my specialty—silent killing. I would go into the middle of an enemy encampment, kill key personnel, and disappear."

CHAPTER THIRTY-THREE

Peter Ragland reserved a conference room for his meeting with Robin.

"Good morning," Ragland said when the receptionist showed Robin into the room.

"Hi, Peter. How are you?"

"I'm good, especially now that I've got a mystery to solve that's right out of a TV show."

"It is that. So tell me, how did David Turner kill Robert Chesterfield in front of three thousand witnesses?"

"His plan was quite ingenious, but I'd expect nothing less from a master magician."

"Don't keep me in suspense."

"Didn't your client tell you how he killed Chesterfield?"

"Mr. Turner says that he didn't kill Chesterfield."

Ragland smiled. "Of course he does, but we've got him dead to rights." There was a large stack of police reports piled in front of Ragland. He pushed them across the table to Robin. "I'm not required to give you discovery until I get my indictment, but you can take a copy of everything we have back to your office."

"Thanks. I appreciate the gesture."

Once again, Ragland smiled. "I'm not doing it out of the goodness of my heart. I want you to see how hopeless your case is. When you've read the reports and see that I can prove how Turner murdered Robert Chesterfield in full view of the audience, I'm certain you'll tell him to plead guilty. If he does the smart thing, I'm prepared to take the death penalty off the table in exchange for a plea to aggravated murder."

"This is bad," Robin said.

"Very bad," Jeff agreed.

They were seated across from each other in the conference room of Barrister, Berman & Lockwood. Piled high on the polished oak table that separated them were the police reports Peter Ragland had turned over.

"Tell me if you think I've got this right," Robin said. "Ragland is going to argue that Turner hated Chesterfield enough to kill him, and murdering him during his greatest illusion would be a big fuck-you to his nemesis. So Ragland will tell the jury that David used his skill as a magician to sneak into the Imperial during rehearsals so he could learn the routines of the magician's assistants and how the trick worked. Then he slipped out of his seat during the show, went to the assistants' dressing room, and hid Porter's inhaler. When she was looking for it, he knocked her out, put on her robe, went on the stage, and used his skill at silent killing to murder Chesterfield. Then he discarded the robe near the loading dock exit to make it look like the killer left the theater, and went back to his seat. How am I doing?"

"Unfortunately, too well."

"Any ideas?"

"Not about how to disprove Ragland's theory, but there are witnesses I want to interview. Oscar Mars organized the magicians who picketed the theater. They were outside, so they may have seen someone leave by the alley. I'd also like to talk to Chesterfield's assistants to see if they can help figure out who used Porter's robe. Then there's Miriam Ross. She was in the theater during the performance, but I didn't see a statement from Ross in the discovery, so I want to talk to her. What are you going to do?"

"You saw how excited Regina was. I'm going to call Stanley and see what he thinks about giving her a copy of the discovery. She might spot something we missed, and at minimum, it would give her something to do that would make her feel like she's back in the game."

Jeff didn't look enthusiastic. "What if she's so far gone that she can't help us, and she gets frustrated? That could crush her."

"That's why I want to find out what Stanley thinks."

"Okay, but hold off if he doesn't think it's a good idea."

"Don't worry. The last thing I want to do is upset Regina."

Jeff left and Robin decided to go through the large pile of interviews the police had conducted with the audience at the Imperial. She had skimmed them already, taking out the interviews with people like David Turner or Rafael Otero who had a connection to Chesterfield, but there were several hundred other interviews they had not read carefully. Robin knew that she was probably wasting her time, but it would be worth the trouble if she could find a hidden gem.

An hour later, Robin was ready to take a break when she saw a name that sounded familiar. She frowned. Where had she heard Samuel Moser's name before. Try as she might, she couldn't remember.

CHAPTER THIRTY-FOUR

Finding Oscar Mars was easy. The leader of the protesting magicians owned a small magic shop two blocks down from the Bagdad Theater on Hawthorne Boulevard. The store was wedged between a boutique that specialized in recycled clothing and a gelato shop. When Jeff walked in, he found the magician standing behind a glass display case filled with packs of cards, magic kits, and other gadgets for neophyte magicians.

Mars, a short, unimposing man, was dressed in a cheap tuxedo. His toupee wouldn't fool anyone, and he had a black beard and mustache that circled thin, dry lips. The only thing about him that was impressive were his fingers, which were long and graceful and, Jeff assumed, would be a great help when he was manipulating cards.

Mars beamed at Jeff, whom he took for a potential customer. Then he looked disappointed when Jeff introduced himself as an investigator and gave him a business card. But he perked up when Jeff told him that he worked for Robin Lockwood, David Turner's lawyer.

"David exposed that bastard, so I'll help you anyway I can."

"You don't seem broken up about Chesterfield's death."

"I'm not. There's a special place in hell for magicians who reveal the secrets of their art, and I hope Lord Robert is roasting there on a slow-turning spit. Ask your questions."

"Okay. First off, did you or any of the other protesters go inside during the show?"

"No. We thought about doing that so we could disrupt the show, but we decided that would only make Chesterfield sympathetic."

"There's some evidence that the killer may have left the Imperial through the exit to the loading dock at the back of the theater. There's a narrow alley that runs along the side of the theater. Did you notice anyone in that alley?"

"I don't remember seeing anyone in the alley, but I was focused on the front of the theater most of the time. Someone else may have seen someone in the alley. I can give you a list of my fellow magicians, and you can ask them."

"Thanks. My email address is on my card. Send me the list and I'll talk to them. Can you think of anything you saw that might help Mr. Turner?"

"Not offhand. Will Miss Lockwood be able to help David?"

"It's early days, but she's pretty good."

"Then I'll keep my fingers crossed."

According to the police reports, Maria Rodriguez was living in a garden apartment in Southeast Portland. The apartments formed a horseshoe around a courtyard with a neatly trimmed lawn. Moments before Rodriguez answered Jeff's knock, a young woman smiled at Jeff as she wheeled her bike past him.

Onstage, in costume, with makeup, the magician's assistant had seemed taller, with the glamorous appearance of a showgirl. In the pale afternoon light, without makeup, dressed in jeans and a faded T-shirt, she looked ordinary.

Jeff handed Rodriguez his business card and introduced himself.

Rodriguez looked at the card, then took a hard look at Jeff. "Have we met before?"

"Yes, at Robert Chesterfield's house on the coast, the night he disappeared. I was with Mr. Chesterfield's attorney, Robin Lockwood."

"Yeah. I remember you two. Why are you here?"

"David Turner was arrested for killing Robert Chesterfield. He swears he's innocent, and he's hired Robin to help him. I wanted to ask you what you saw during the Chamber of Death illusion."

"I already told the cops everything I know."

"I read the report of your interview, but there were some things the police didn't cover."

"Ask away."

"Thanks. Did you work with Mr. Chesterfield in Las Vegas?"

"No. Bobby hired me through my agent when he was developing the Chamber of Death at the coast. Since I live in Portland and knew how the illusion worked, Bobby called me when he got the engagement at the Imperial."

"Did Sheila Monroe and Nancy Porter work the rehearsal at the coast? I don't remember seeing them there."

"No, just me. The other girls from the coast rehearsal don't live in Portland anymore."

"Okay, that's helpful. Now that you've had some time to think about what happened at the theater, have you remembered anything that might help us figure out who killed Mr. Chesterfield?"

"Honestly, no, and I've thought about it a lot. I assumed Nancy was onstage with us, but now I know she wasn't. With that hood up, I never saw the face of the person who stabbed Bobby."

"What about the person's hands? When the killer stabbed Mr. Chesterfield, it's possible that his arm or hand would have been exposed."

"Yeah, but Sheila and I were looking toward the back of the stage, so we wouldn't have seen the killer's arms or hand."

"It was just an idea I had."

"Sorry."

"That's okay. One other thing, do you know where I can find Miriam Ross? She was Chesterfield's personal assistant when he had the rehearsal at the coast."

"Why do you want to talk to Miriam?"

"She was at the Imperial when Mr. Chesterfield was murdered. I couldn't find a police report with a record of her statement. I thought she might have seen something that could help clear Mr. Turner's name."

"She was at the show?"

"You sound surprised."

"I am. She was really upset when Bobby disappeared at the coast. I think they had a thing going and she felt like he dumped her."

"They were having an affair?"

Maria smirked. "We were all bunking at Bobby's house, and he came on to every one of us. Me and the two other girls in the act turned him down, but Miriam . . . I never caught them going at it, but she put out a vibe, if you know what I mean. And she was furious when he pulled that disappearing act." Maria shook her head. "I guess she never got over it."

"Why do you say that?"

"She showed up at the theater during a rehearsal, and they got into an argument. I don't know what it was about, but she walked by me on the way out, and she didn't look happy."

"Do you know where I can find Miss Ross?"

"I might. Let me get my phone." Maria was gone for five minutes. She had a smile on her face when she came back. "When we were working at the coast, she gave her phone number to us in case we needed something. If she kept it, you can get in touch."

"Thanks."

"So you don't think Turner killed Bobby? I remember how mad he was at the rehearsal."

"Oh, he was mad, all right, but a lot of people were mad at Mr. Chesterfield."

"How many of them are master magicians?"

Miriam Ross agreed to meet Jeff at a coffee shop near the downtown building where she worked as an office manager for an engineering firm. Jeff spotted her as soon as she walked in.

"I remember you," Ross said when Jeff handed her the soy latte he'd offered as a bribe if she would meet with him. "You were with the blond lawyer at Bobby's rehearsal."

"I was."

Ross looked sad. "It was terrible what happened to Bobby."

"You sound like you really cared for him."

"I did once."

"Were you close?"

Ross smiled. "You don't have to be diplomatic. If you got my number from Maria, I'm sure she told you that Bobby and I had a fling at the coast. He and Claire were a couple in name only, so I never felt guilty."

"Did you get angry when he took off after the rehearsal?"

"Yeah, but I got over it pretty quickly. Sex with Bobby was good, but I knew it wouldn't last. Bobby had only one true love—himself—and I knew that from the start."

"So the affair was just a way to kill time at the coast?"

Again, Ross smiled. "That's one way to put it."

"If you disliked Mr. Chesterfield, why did you go to his show?"

"Good question, but there's a simple answer: After seeing the rehearsals so many times at the coast, I wanted to see if the Chamber of Death worked in front of a real audience."

"I heard you two got into it at the Imperial during one of the rehearsals."

Ross raised an eyebrow. "So Maria did gossip. She was always jealous that Bobby was visiting my room at night and not hers."

"What happened at the Imperial?" Jeff prodded.

"It wasn't a big deal. When Bobby disappeared, he owed me two thousand dollars in back pay. When I found out he wasn't dead, I went to the theater for my money. He tried to talk me out of it. When I wouldn't budge, he got upset and threatened me. So I gave him a piece of my mind and stormed out. But if you think I was mad enough to kill him, think again. Bobby was an asshole, but I got over him about a week after he took off, and I'm not going to murder someone over a few thousand dollars."

"When you were watching the performance, did you see anything that might help us figure out who killed Mr. Chesterfield?"

"No, and that's why I left the theater so quickly. I knew I couldn't help the police, and I didn't want to stay at the theater all night."

"I can't think of anything else to ask you. Thanks for the help."

Ross raised her latte. "Thanks for the drink."

Jeff smiled as he handed Ross his card. "If you think of anything that might help Mr. Turner, give me a call."

"What if I want to get together and it has nothing to do with David Turner?"

"I'm flattered, but I'm in a serious relationship."

Ross grinned. "Oh well. You can't blame a girl for trying."

CHAPTER THIRTY-FIVE

David Turner's bail hearing was held in the courtroom of the Honorable LaVerne Washington on the fifth floor of the Multnomah County Courthouse. There were trucks with the logos of local television stations at the curb, and Robin had several microphones thrust in her face as soon as the reporters spotted her. With Jeff blocking, Robin managed to fight her way into the elevator without incurring a major injury.

Claire Madison was waiting for Robin in the hallway on the fourth floor, just below Judge Washington's courtroom, so they could avoid the reporters and thrill seekers who were lurking outside the courtroom.

"When we get upstairs, the mob will descend on you. So keep your head down, don't answer any questions, and keeping moving until we are safely inside the courtroom," Robin said.

"Don't worry about me," Claire assured her. "I'm used to the paparazzi. Don't forget, I was television's flavor of the week for a while."

Robin smiled. "I did forget. Shall we?"

"Let's rock and roll."

"So," Claire asked as they headed down the hall, "will David get out today?"

"I'm going to be brutally frank with you. Getting bail in a murder case is a long shot if the State has any kind of case. I'm going to try my best, but I've read the police reports, and the DA has a very good chance of convincing the judge to hold David without bail."

"Thanks for your honesty."

Robin led Claire up a back stairway so they would come toward the courtroom from an unexpected direction. They almost made it to the courtroom door before someone spotted them and the mob descended. Robin repeated, "No comment," until she had hustled Claire into the courtroom.

"This is a circus," Madison said.

"Welcome to my world," Robin answered as she led Claire to a seat in the front row of the spectator section that the judge's bailiff had reserved for her. When Claire was seated, Robin pushed through the low gate that separated the spectators from the area where the judge, jury, and lawyers worked.

Peter Ragland was already at his counsel table. He flashed a confident smile at Robin just as the guards led David Turner out of the holding area.

"Am I going to get out?" Turner asked nervously when Robin took the seat next to him at the counsel table.

"To hold you without bail, the State has to convince Judge Washington that the proof is evident or the presumption is strong that you killed Chesterfield. That's not like proof beyond a reasonable doubt, the standard in a criminal trial. It's a lot lower."

"Can they meet the burden?" Turner asked.

"Probably. I've gone through the discovery, and Ragland has a good circumstantial case."

"Won't you be able to cross-examine the witnesses to cast doubt on the State's case?"

"When the case is tried in front of a jury, Ragland has to call witnesses I can cross-examine, but he doesn't have to call his witnesses at a bail hearing. Instead, he's allowed to have a detective summarize the State's case."

Before Turner could ask another question, the bailiff rapped his gavel and LaVerne Washington took her place on the dais. Judge Washington, a former public defender, was a hefty, fifty-year-old African American. Most of the time, she was even-tempered, but she had a reputation for having a short fuse when attorneys were unprepared.

"Morning, Mr. Ragland, Miss Lockwood. This is the time set for the bail hearing in *State of Oregon versus David Earl Turner*. Are the parties ready to proceed?"

Ragland stood. "The State is ready."

"Mr. Turner is ready," Robin said.

"You want to keep Mr. Turner in jail without bail, Mr. Ragland, so the ball is in your court."

Ragland nodded. "We're going to have Detective Carrie Anders summarize our case, Your Honor."

Anders lumbered up the aisle, took the oath to tell the truth, and settled in the witness chair. Robin stood when Ragland began questioning her about her qualifications.

"It won't be necessary for Mr. Ragland to qualify Detective Anders. For purposes of this hearing, Mr. Turner will stipulate that she is a homicide detective who is competent to tell the court about the facts of this case."

"Mr. Ragland, I see no reason for you to proceed with the preliminary questions. Detective Anders has appeared before me on numerous occasions."

"Very well, Your Honor. The State accepts the stipulation. Detective, please tell the court the evidence that justified arresting the defendant for the murder of Robert Chesterfield."

Anders turned toward Judge Washington. "Our witnesses will testify that the finale of Robert Chesterfield's magic show is an illusion called the Chamber of Death. In that trick, three magician's assistants lock the magician in a sarcophagus and put snakes and scorpions in with him. When the sarcophagus is unlocked, the magician is supposed to have disappeared. Then he's supposed to reappear at the back of the theater.

"When Mr. Chesterfield got in the sarcophagus, two of the assistants were holding up the lid, and it looked like the third assistant pushed Mr. Chesterfield down into it. When the assistant appears to push Chesterfield down, she is blocking the view of the audience. When that happened, Mr. Chesterfield was supposed to roll over the edge of the sarcophagus, get off the stage, and go to the back of the theater. But on this occasion, the person who appears to push Mr. Chesterfield down stabbed him in the heart and killed him.

"Nancy Porter is the assistant who had the job of appearing to push Mr. Chesterfield into the coffin. After that, she was supposed to move the dolly that was used to get the sarcophagus onto the stage into the wings. Then she was supposed to return to the stage for the finale. But the third assistant never came back. When we searched the theater, Miss Porter was found in the assistants' dressing room, unconscious, and her robe was found near one of the theater's exits.

"The robe used by the assistants during the Chamber of Death illusion is very roomy. We have established that a man or woman wearing it would be completely concealed from the audience and the other assistants.

"Miss Porter will testify that she has asthma and always has an inhaler with her. She had used it earlier in the show and placed it on her dressing table. While she and the other assistants changed for the Chamber of Death, Miss Porter looked for the inhaler, but she couldn't find it. She continued to look for the inhaler when the other assistants left the dressing room. While she was alone, her assailant rendered her unconscious so he could conceal himself in her robe and kill Mr. Chesterfield."

"Why did you arrest the defendant for the murder of Mr. Chesterfield?" Ragland asked.

"We decided that the killer had to have learned how the Chamber of Death trick was performed in order to accomplish the murder. We also decided that he must have been in the Imperial Theater during rehearsals so he could learn about the inhaler and Miss Porter's routine.

"Titus Atkinson was in the seat directly behind the defendant during the show. He will testify that Mr. Turner left his seat while Mr. Chesterfield was performing card tricks onstage in the part of the act that precedes the Chamber of Death illusion. He will also testify that the defendant did not return to his seat until after Mr. Chesterfield was murdered. The defendant denied ever leaving his seat during the performance.

"The defendant also denied being in the theater during rehearsals. A security guard will testify that he saw Mr. Turner inside the Imperial during a rehearsal.

"Figuring out how to murder a person in front of an audience during a magic illusion is something that a magician would know how to do. The defendant is a master magician who performs a magic act regularly in a Las Vegas casino, so he would have been able to figure out how the illusion was done."

"Did the defendant have a motive for killing Mr. Chesterfield?"

"He had several. First, he is living with the deceased's wife, who was being sued by Mr. Chesterfield for divorce. If the couple divorced, Ms. Madison would have to have given Mr. Chesterfield a lot of her money and maybe some of her property. With Mr. Chesterfield dead, that's no longer a problem.

"Furthermore, the defendant hated Mr. Chesterfield for revealing the secret to his Las Vegas casino finale on television several years ago. This almost killed the defendant's career.

"In summation, Your Honor, the defendant had several motives to kill Mr. Chesterfield, the means and skills to accomplish the task, and the opportunity to commit the murder. He also lied about being in his seat during the performance of the Chamber of Death and not being in the Imperial during a rehearsal. We concluded that this provided probable cause to arrest."

"I have no further questions, Your Honor," Ragland said.

"Do you have any questions for Detective Anders?" the judge asked Robin.

Jeff was sitting in the spectator section directly behind Robin. While Detective Anders was testifying, Stanley Cloud moved beside him and whispered in Jeff's ear. Jeff reached over the bar of the court and tapped Robin on the shoulder.

"Ask for a recess," he said when she turned around. "Stanley has something important to show you."

"Miss Lockwood?" the judge asked.

"Can we take a brief recess, Your Honor?" Robin asked.

Judge Washington didn't like taking a recess so early in the proceedings, but she had recognized Stanley Cloud. "Will fifteen minutes be sufficient?" the judge asked.

"It should be."

Robin hurried into the hall as soon as the judge left the bench. She found Stanley waiting for her at the end of the corridor that ran in front of the courtroom.

"What's so important?"

Stanley handed Robin the police report that set out Titus Atkinson's statement. A yellow Post-it was glued to it. The message on the Post-it read: NO TIME!!!

"What does this mean?" Robin asked.

"I asked Regina. She wrote it when she was reading the discovery, but she can't remember why. She's very upset because she obviously thought it was very important. She reread the report but drew a blank."

Robin concentrated on Atkinson's statement, but she couldn't see anything important enough to warrant three exclamation points. Had Regina's dementia made her see something that wasn't there?

"Did you read this?" she asked Stanley.

"I didn't see anything."

"Okay. I've got to—" Robin stopped dead and reread the interview. Then she broke into a grin. "The boss is still the Sorceress. You tell her that for me," Robin said before racing back to the courtroom.

"Detective Anders, before the Chamber of Death finale, wasn't Mr. Chesterfield onstage by himself performing card tricks?"

"Yes."

"And before the card tricks, Mr. Chesterfield made Sheila Monroe, one of his assistants, levitate and float above the stage?"

"Yes."

"During that illusion, Nancy Porter and Maria Rodriguez, the other assistants, were also onstage, weren't they?"

"Yes."

"And all three assistants were dressed in costumes that they did not wear during the finale?"

"Yes."

"Did Miss Porter tell you that she put the inhaler on her dressing table before going onstage for the levitation act?"

"Yes."

"But she couldn't find it when she came back during the card trick routine to change for the Chamber of Death?"

"Yes."

"So the killer must have moved the inhaler during the levitation illusion?"

"That sounds right."

"Okay. Now, Titus Atkinson was sitting directly behind Mr. Turner, wasn't he?"

"Yes."

"And he saw Mr. Turner leave his seat?"

"Yes."

"Isn't it true that Mr. Atkinson told you that Mr. Turner was in front of him during the show up until Mr. Chesterfield began to demonstrate the card tricks in the act preceding the finale?"

"Yes."

"If I have this right, the scenario you've put forth to explain how Mr. Turner murdered Mr. Chesterfield requires Mr. Turner to go backstage while no one is in the assistants' dressing room so he can hide Miss Porter's inhaler. Then he had to wait until the other assistants left the dressing room in their robes so he could knock out Miss Porter with the ether and take her place."

"That's correct."

"That means Mr. Turner had to hide the inhaler during the levitation trick, because the assistants returned to the dressing room while Chesterfield was performing the card tricks. But that creates a problem for the State's case, doesn't it? In order for Mr. Turner to fit into your scenario, he could not have stayed in his seat until Mr. Chesterfield started performing the card tricks. If Mr. Turner didn't leave his seat until Mr. Chesterfield began to perform the card tricks, how would he have been able to hide the inhaler? The assistants would be in the dressing room changing."

Anders started to speak. Then she closed her mouth.

"Can you explain to Judge Washington how Mr. Turner would have time to hide the inhaler if he didn't leave his seat until the card tricks started?" Robin pressed.

"I . . . We didn't think of that."

"That's obvious," Robin said. "What's also obvious, Your Honor, is that Mr. Turner did not have time to hide the inhaler. That means that someone else did. And that person murdered Mr. Chesterfield."

Ragland jumped to his feet. "An accomplice!" he shouted. "Turner had an accomplice. That's who hid the inhaler."

"Who is the accomplice?" Judge Washington asked.

"I . . . We . . . That has to be how he did it."

Judge Washington shook her head. "You seem to be grasp-ing at straws, Mr. Ragland. And until you can grab that straw real hard and show it to me, I've got to conclude that you haven't made your case for denying this man bail."

CHAPTER THIRTY-SIX

Judge Washington and the attorneys discussed the terms of David Turner's release. Peter Ragland insisted on a high bail, house arrest, and an electronic monitor. The judge sided with Robin, who argued that the State's case wasn't strong enough to warrant such stringent conditions.

Ragland maintained his composure until he finished answering the questions the reporters fired at him when he left the courtroom, but he was seething when he ran up the steps to the district attorney's office with Anders and Dillon in tow.

As soon as they were in one of the conference rooms, Ragland turned on the detectives. "Why didn't you warn me about the time discrepancy?" he yelled. "Lockwood made me look like a fucking idiot."

"None of us saw that coming," Dillon answered calmly.

"Well, you should have!" Ragland screamed, forgetting that he had the same information the detectives possessed.

Anders and Dillon let Ragland vent.

After a few seconds, he took a deep breath and tried to calm down. "Turner's guilty. He must have an accomplice who hid that inhaler. Find the accomplice. That's the most important thing right now. If we identify the accomplice, we can nail Turner."

"Do you have an idea who the accomplice might be?" Anders asked.

Ragland shook his head. "It has to be someone who knew about the inhaler and the assistants' routine."

"What about Sheila Monroe or Maria Rodriguez?" Anders said.

"Yeah, the other assistants," Ragland said. "Where did they find the inhaler?"

"In Maria Rodriguez's dressing table."

"Did they print the inhaler?" Ragland asked.

"Yeah, but it only had Porter's prints on it," Anders said.

"Damn. If Rodriguez hid it, it makes sense that she would have been careful about leaving prints." Ragland was quiet for a moment. Then he scowled. "Check on Rodriguez. See if she has any ties to Turner. Maybe she was his assistant in one of his shows."

"Great idea, Peter," Dillon said. "We'll look into her."

"Okay, great. Get on it."

"Right away," Dillon said, grateful for an excuse to get away.

"They're going to take you back to the jail until bail is posted, but you should be free in a few hours," Robin told her client. She pointed to an accordion file filled with police reports. "That's a copy of the discovery the DA gave me. I'll give it to Claire. Go home, take a shower, and eat a good meal. Then go through the discovery and help me figure out who killed Robert Chesterfield."

"Nice job," Stanley Cloud said when Robin finished speaking to the reporters who waylaid her when she walked out of the courtroom.

"I couldn't have done it without Regina."

"You can thank her in person tonight. I called her with the news, and she wants you and Jeff to come for dinner. I've got some sweet corn and several exceptional salmon fillets I intend to bar-becue."

"Your bribe has worked for me," Jeff said.

"I'll be there," Robin said. "Now I've got to get over to the jail to make sure that David gets out as soon as possible."

"What do you think of Ragland's accomplice theory?" Jeff asked as he followed Robin to the elevator that led to the court-house jail.

"Not much. Why? Has something occurred to you?"

"Remember I told you that Miriam Ross had an affair with Chesterfield when he was working on the Chamber of Death illu-sion at the coast?"

"Yes."

"When I talked to Ross, she said that Maria Rodriguez was jealous because Chesterfield had not been attracted to her."

"You think that Rodriguez could be the accomplice?"

"Nancy Porter's inhaler was found in a drawer in Rodriguez's dressing table. If she had a grudge against Chesterfield, she could have been the person who hid it."

CHAPTER THIRTY-SEVEN

Robin and Jeff parked in front of Regina's house, and Stanley Cloud walked out to greet them.

"We're eating on the patio. I just put the salmon on the grill, so let's get back there so I can watch it."

Stanley walked them through the house, and Robin saw the police reports in David Turner's case strewn across the dining room table.

"Where's Regina?" she asked.

"Upstairs, getting dressed. She was ecstatic when I told her that she'd saved the day."

"I couldn't be happier," Robin said.

"Can I fix you a drink?"

"I'll take a beer if you have any," Jeff said.

"A gin and tonic would be great," Robin told the former chief justice.

Stanley checked on the salmon before going inside to get the drinks. Robin walked to the edge of the patio and looked at the river. A light breeze wafted inland off the water, and the temperature was in mid-seventies without any humidity.

"How are you two?" Regina asked.

Robin turned and smiled. "Fabulous, thanks to you. I told David Turner that you figured out the problem with the time line, and he wanted me to thank you."

"Here are your drinks," Stanley said. "Hi, Reggie. Can I get you anything?"

"Maybe a little wine with dinner."

Stanley checked the salmon and declared it ready for consumption.

"Shall we eat?" he said as he carried the planked salmon to the table.

"That was fantastic!" Robin said when she had eaten the last piece of salmon and cleaned the corn off her cob.

"Glad you liked it," Stanley said as he picked up his and Regina's plates. Robin took Jeff's, placed it on top of her plate, and followed Stanley into the kitchen.

"I haven't seen Regina this happy in a long time," Stanley said. "Thanks for sending her the discovery. It made her feel useful again."

"It never hurts to have an extra hand working a case. Especially when that person has a sky-high IQ."

"Amen to that," Stanley said as he rinsed the dirty plates and put them in the dishwasher.

"Do you want an after-dinner drink or coffee before we eat the dessert you so kindly sent?" he asked when he finished up.

Robin frowned. "I didn't send you a dessert."

There was a box of chocolates sitting on the kitchen island. Stanley held it out to her. "You didn't send this over this afternoon?"

"No."

"Sorry, I just assumed it was from you. There was no card, but you were coming over and you know Reggie's weakness for chocolates."

"Well, it wasn't me," Robin said.

Stanley opened the box as he headed to the patio.

"Jeff," Robin asked, "did you send Regina and Stanley chocolates?"

"No. Why?"

"Someone sent them, and Stanley thought it was me."

"Well, it wasn't me."

"Chocolates!" Regina said with a big smile.

Stanley held the box out to her and she started to take a piece.

"Wait!" Robin shouted.

Regina froze, startled.

Robin grabbed the box.

"What's wrong?" Stanley asked.

"I may be paranoid, but I think we should have these candies tested for poison."

"Poison?" Jeff asked.

Robin picked up a knife and punctured one of the chocolates. She sniffed the scent of bitter almonds. "I think I just saved Regina's life," Robin said, and dialed Carrie Anders.

"The chocolates were laced with poison," Carrie Anders said after the lab tech was done testing a sample.

Robin, Stanley, and Jeff were sitting on the living room sofa, facing the detective. Regina was seated apart from the group in an armchair. She looked agitated. Stanley had tried to calm her down, but she was still confused and anxious.

"You would be dead if you'd eaten a piece," Anders added.

"Jesus," Stanley swore.

"That was quick thinking," Roger Dillon told Robin. "What made you suspect that the chocolates were poisoned?"

"Doesn't this sound familiar to anyone?" Robin asked.

"The Chesterfield poisoning case!" Roger Dillon answered after a brief pause.

"Exactly. You were one of the detectives who investigated Sophie Randall's death, weren't you?"

"Yeah, and it went down just like this. Someone sent Samuel Moser a box of chocolates with no card or return address. He gave the chocolates to his secretary, and she ate some and died."

"Robert Chesterfield hired me a few years ago and Regina told me all about the case, so I knew what happened to Sophie Randall. If Chesterfield hadn't been on my mind because of David Turner's case, I don't know if I would have remembered the poisoned chocolates."

"Well, it's a good thing you did," Stanley said.

"Can any of you think of someone who would want to do this to any of you?" Anders asked.

"Stanley and Regina have been retired for several years," Robin said. "I guess a disgruntled client or someone Stanley ruled against could still have a grudge, but it seems unlikely that they were the targets."

"I don't know," Dillon said. "The chocolates were sent here. If you or Jeff were the intended victims, the killer would have sent the chocolates to your office."

"Or he would have to know that you were eating dinner here, tonight," Anders said. "Who had that information?"

"Stanley asked us to dinner in a corridor at the courthouse after Turner's bail hearing recessed," Jeff said. "I didn't see anyone around."

"I didn't tell anyone we were coming here tonight," Robin said. "Did you?"

"No," Jeff answered.

"That means Justice Cloud and Miss Barrister were most probably the intended victims," Dillon said.

"Can you make us a list of anyone who might have this powerful a grudge against either you or Miss Barrister?" Anders asked Stanley.

"I'll get on it first thing tomorrow. Right now, I'd like to get Regina to bed. This has really upset her."

"I think we're through, so we'll get out of everyone's hair. You and Jeff can leave too," Anders said.

Robin and Jeff stayed for a few minutes after the detectives and the lab techs had left.

"What do you think is going on?" Robin asked when they were headed home.

"Damned if I know," Jeff answered.

CHAPTER THIRTY-EIGHT

Robin and Jeff walked from their office to the Imperial Theater at four in the afternoon. The theater was closed, but Norman Chow had agreed to let the defense team inside so they could look at the crime scene.

"Ready for your tour?" asked Carrie Anders, who was waiting outside.

Robin nodded. Anders opened the door next to the ticket booth and led them into the lobby where Chow and Horace Dobson were waiting.

"Thanks for meeting us," Robin said to Dobson.

"The cops said it was okay, or I wouldn't be here," said Dobson, who had reluctantly agreed to take Jeff and Robin step-by-step through the Chamber of Death illusion.

"I can tell you that Mr. Turner vehemently denies killing Mr. Chesterfield," Robin answered.

"Yeah, well, what would you expect him to say?"

"Why don't we start the tour?" Anders said, and everyone walked through the doors that led into the area of the theater where the audience sat. Dobson stood behind a low barrier that ringed the back row. Several aisles started at gaps in the barrier. Heavy floor-to-ceiling curtains hung along the wall down the farthest aisle on his left as he faced the stage.

Dobson walked over to that aisle. "You were in the theater when Bobby performed the Chamber of Death, right?" Dobson asked.

Jeff and Robin nodded.

"Okay, then. Right before he performs the illusion, Bobby entertained the audience with card tricks. After Bobby finished his card tricks, the lights would go out. Bobby would slip into his priest's robes while the stagehands set up the pyramid and put a ramp at the end of the aisle the girls used to push the sarcophagus onto the stage.

"There are tunnels under the audience and the stage that I'm going to show you. After the girls changed into their robes, they would go through a tunnel at the back of the stage and end up behind the audience. When the lights went on and Bobby started his spiel, they rolled the sarcophagus down the aisle and up the ramp. As soon as the coffin was on the stage, it was taken off the dolly and placed lengthwise between the walls of the pyramid."

Dobson led everyone down the aisle and up a set of stairs to the stage. "The dolly would be positioned here," he said, pointing to a space on the left side of the stage that was very close to the wings. A curtain hung from the ceiling to the floor, blocking the view from the audience. "When Bobby rolled out of the coffin, he would slither into a narrow gap in the front of the dolly. The stage lights were kept very bright, and the rest of the dolly concealed the move from the audience. When Bobby was hidden in the dolly, one of the assistants would push it offstage."

Dobson led everyone behind the curtain and through a steel door to a set of stairs that led under the stage. Dobson walked down the stairs. A dimly lit tunnel led under the audience toward the front of the theater in one direction and the back of the stage in the other direction.

Dobson nodded toward the tunnel that led to the back of the audience. "When the trick worked correctly, the coffin was opened and the audience learned that Bobby wasn't in it. By that time, Bobby would have run down the tunnel and up a set of stairs at the end of the tunnel. Then he'd reappear behind the audience."

"Is there an identical set of tunnels on the other side of the theater?" Jeff asked.

"Yes," Norman Chow said.

"Where does the other tunnel on this side lead?" Robin asked.

"I'll show you," Dobson answered as he led the group through the dimly lit concrete tunnel to another set of stairs.

When Robin reached the top, she saw that she was standing near the loading dock. She stared past it to a narrow hall. "What's in that hall?" she asked.

"The dressing rooms," Norman Chow answered.

"So," Robin said, "the killer could have stabbed Mr. Chesterfield, pushed the dolly offstage, run down the tunnel that goes to the back of the stage, run up the steps, dumped Nancy Porter's robe near the loading dock, and exited the theater."

"That's possible," Norman Chow said.

"Wouldn't a stagehand see him?" Anders asked.

"It's possible, but didn't you find clothes that a stagehand might wear when you found Nancy Porter's robe?"

"Yes."

"Everyone is pretty busy during a show, so someone dressed like a stagehand might not have been noticed."

"What's on the other side of the loading dock?" Robin asked.

"An alley broad enough for a truck to drive through," Chow said. "One end leads to Fenimore Street, and the other leads to

Marsh. It goes past the alley that runs by the stage door to the street in front of the theater."

"David Turner could have gone into the tunnel on his side of the aisle after ditching the robe and back to his seat," Carrie Anders said.

"When would he put on the stagehand clothes?" Jeff asked.

"Maybe never," Anders answered. "He or his accomplice could have hidden them near the loading dock to make it look like he was wearing them."

"Or the real killer could have disappeared through the loading dock and got away," Robin answered.

Anders just smiled.

"How's that accomplice thing going?" Robin asked.

Anders's smile faded.

Robin walked past the loading dock and looked into the first dressing room. "Who used this?" she asked.

"Bobby," Dobson answered.

"This is where the star changes," Norman Chow said.

Robin stepped inside and looked around. The room was large with a dressing table, a couch, and racks for clothing. Robin went into the next dressing room, which was much larger and had several dressing tables.

"This is where Maria, Sheila, and Nancy changed," Dobson said.

"Where was Miss Porter found?" Jeff asked.

Anders pointed to a section of the floor in the center of the room.

"Where was her inhaler found?" Robin asked.

Anders pulled out a drawer at the end of the row of dressing tables. "This dressing table was used by Maria Rodriguez," the detective said. Anders moved over two tables and pointed. "Miss Porter used this table. She said she put the inhaler on top of it."

Robin looked around for a few minutes. "Can you walk me to the curtains where Mr. Turner says he was hiding when he watched the Chamber of Death?" she asked Norman Chow.

Chow led the way to the front of the stage. Robin walked behind the curtains. Then she walked down the stairs at the side of the stage that led down to the audience and stood next to the seat Turner had occupied.

"I've seen enough," she said after a while. "Jeff?"

"I'm good."

"Thanks again. We won't keep you any longer."

Norman Chow headed for his office, and the rest of the group walked up the aisle to the front of the theater.

"Have you cracked the case?" Anders asked Robin when they had returned to the sunshine.

"It's the butler," Robin answered, "but don't tell Peter. I want to do the big reveal during my closing argument, like Perry Mason."

Anders laughed. "Looking forward to it," she said. Then she walked away.

"Well, boss?" Jeff asked when they were alone.

Robin shook her head. "You?"

"No big insights, but our guy could have run around through the tunnels on his side of the audience once he got behind the curtains."

"I thought of that."

"It doesn't help us."

"Neither does anything else we learned today."

CHAPTER THIRTY-NINE

Jeff had to talk to a witness in one of Mark Berman's cases, so Robin walked home alone. There was leftover Thai food in the refrigerator, and Robin warmed it in the microwave. Then she grabbed the remote and found some UFC bouts to watch while she ate.

The matches ended at ten, and Robin switched to the local news. A reporter was standing in the street in front of a driveway that led to a house in Dunthorpe, which Robin recognized instantly.

"Behind me is the home of Regina Barrister, the legendary criminal defense attorney. An anonymous source has told this reporter that an attempt was made to poison Ms. Barrister with cyanide-laced chocolates. More than twenty years ago, the magician Robert Chesterfield was accused of murdering a woman with cyanide-laced chocolates. Mr. Chesterfield was stabbed to death onstage last week while performing his greatest illusion, the Chamber of Death. Are the two crimes linked in some bizarre way? The police and Ms. Barrister have refused to comment for this story."

The newscast moved on to another story just as Jeff walked in.

"They just had a story on the evening news about the attempt to poison Regina."

"How did they find out?" Jeff asked as he walked over to Robin.

"The reporter said she got the info from an anonymous source," Robin answered as she switched off the set.

Jeff sat down next to Robin.

"It was probably someone in the PPB," Robin said. "I wonder who."

"I don't," he whispered in her ear.

Robin stared at him. "Don't tell me you're horny. We made love this morning."

Jeff smiled. "I can't help it if I find you incredibly sexy."

"God—men!" Robin said as she feigned a lack of interest, but she couldn't believe how lucky she was to have Jeff in her life. He was smart, definitely sexy, and really nice—a terrific trifecta.

Jeff kissed her ear. "We could watch the weather station."

Robin laughed. "I give up," she said as she folded into him. Moments later, they had their clothes off and had tumbled off the sofa and onto the shag rug that covered the living room floor.

Robin was exhausted by the long workday and the round of very athletic lovemaking. She assumed she would fall asleep as soon as her head hit the pillow, but the scene in front of Regina's house intruded on her peace of mind as soon as her eyes closed. Someone had tried to murder Regina the same way Sophie Randall had been murdered. Chesterfield, the chief suspect in Randall's murder, had been murdered. But how were the crimes linked?

Robin tried to block her thoughts so she could sleep. Eventually she succeeded, but weird dreams plagued her. When she woke up, she opened her eyes and the dreams evaporated like morning mist. She tried to remember them because she was certain that the dreams had sent her an important subconscious message, but they were gone.

What had been so important? She was certain that one of the dreams had been about a murder—not Sophie Randall's or Chesterfield's but some other murder. She just couldn't remember the name of the victim.

CHAPTER FORTY

When Morris Quinlan was in high school, he had been a third team all-state linebacker. That had not been good enough to draw attention from a school like Alabama or Ohio State, but he did get scholarship offers from a few Division II schools and ended up in Idaho. In high school, Morris was smart enough to get decent grades without studying too hard, so he had never learned how to study. Morris did know how to party, so he joined a fraternity. Several of the brothers had a perpetual bridge game going in the basement of the fraternity house, and one of them explained the game to Morris, who soon became addicted to it.

The demands of playing football, weekends of partying, and hours spent playing bridge did not leave much time for class-work. Morris had an academic advisor who kept tabs on the football players. Halfway through Morris's first semester, the advisor told him that he was going to be placed on academic probation if he didn't straighten up. That would have cost him his football scholarship. Morris could not afford college without the scholarship and he couldn't give up the parties, so he decided that bridge had to go, and he did not play again until a fellow police retiree told him about the regular bridge game at the community center a few blocks from his house.

A few days after the arrival of the poisoned chocolates at Regina's home, and shortly before Morris was going to leave for the community center, Roger Dillon asked Morris to meet him for dinner, but wouldn't say why. Morris was distracted. Much to his partner's annoyance, he misbid or misplayed hands several times.

As soon as the bridge games ended, Morris walked four blocks to a neighborhood Italian restaurant. Roger was seated in a booth near the front of the restaurant, and a bottle of Chianti was standing in the center of the table.

"Okay, Roger, enough mystery. Why have you purchased my favorite Chianti?"

"It's part of your consulting fee. Dinner is the other half."

"Consulting on what?"

"A very interesting case. I assume you know that Robert Chesterfield was murdered onstage in the middle of the finale to his magic show."

"Everyone knows that. It's been front-page news."

"Do you also know that someone sent Regina Barrister, Chesterfield's old attorney, a box of poisoned chocolates?"

"It was on the news."

"What did you think about when you heard about the chocolates?"

"Sophie Randall's case."

"Exactly."

"Do you think there's a connection?"

"That's why I'm buying you dinner and giving you these," Dillon said as he reached below the table and brought up a stack of police reports. "This is everything we know about the murder in the theater and the attempt on Regina. I've also included the reports from the Arthur Gentry and Sophie Randall cases. I'm curious to see if you can make anything of them."

"Is giving me the reports legal? I'm not a cop anymore."

"No, you're not. But the minute you take a sip of this Chianti, you will be a paid consultant."

Morris laughed. Then he filled his wineglass. "Okay, you've hooked me. I'll give these the once-over and get back to you."

"Sounds good."

Morris was a regular, and the owner's daughter walked over to take their order. "Hi, Mr. Quinlan. Do you want the spaghetti Bolognese?" she asked.

"No, Flo. My friend here is treating, so I'll have the veal Parmesan with *spaghetti aglio olio*. Coffee, too, please. And don't forget to bring the dessert menu when I've finished my entrée."

Roger smiled. He knew that Morris was taking advantage, but it would be worth it if he came up with an idea that would help solve these cases.

Morris got home a little after nine. He was too keyed up by the challenge Roger had presented to think about going to bed, so he cleared his kitchen table, brewed a cup of coffee, and started going through the police reports.

When he was finished, Morris had no brilliant insights. On the surface, there were enough similarities to the Randall poisoning case to suggest a connection to the attempt on Barrister, but Sophie Randall and Arthur Gentry had been poisoned twenty-plus years ago, and the killer was most probably Robert Chesterfield, who was dead.

It was midnight when Morris finished reading the reports for the second time. He'd hoped he would have a brilliant Sherlockian insight that would solve the case, but he did not have an aha moment, so he went to bed, hoping that something would occur to him after a good night's sleep.

CHAPTER FORTY-ONE

Jeff Hodges took the elevator to the third floor of an old cast-iron building two blocks from the Willamette River and entered the offices of Oregon Talent, Inc. Marvin Olmstead, the owner of the agency, was a man of middle age with a year-around tan, slicked-back auburn hair, and pearly white teeth, which he flashed at Jeff when his secretary escorted him into Olmstead's office.

"How can I help you, Mr. Hodges?" Olmstead asked as soon as he had examined Jeff's business card.

"I'm the investigator for Robin Lockwood's law firm."

"She's representing David Turner, isn't she?"

Jeff nodded. "He's accused of murdering Robert Chesterfield onstage, while Chesterfield was performing a magic trick. Maria Rodriguez, Nancy Porter, and Sheila Monroe were the assistants who helped Chesterfield perform the illusion, and your agency represents them. I wanted to get some background on the women."

"What do you want to know?"

"Can you tell me a little about Maria Rodriguez?"

"Maria is local, born and raised in Portland. I've represented her for four years. She's had small parts in three movies that were filmed here, and she's done some theater. Her dad was a magician until he quit to sell real estate. She worked in his act when she was little, and she's my go-to when I get a request for a magician's assistant."

"What does she do when she's not working in show business?"

Olmstead laughed. "What every 'actor' does when they're not in a show. She's a waitress."

"What about Sheila Monroe?"

"She's getting a teaching degree at PSU. She moved here from New Jersey with her boyfriend three years ago when he was accepted at Lewis and Clark Law School. I've been repping her for two years." Olmstead shook his head. "Sheila's a good kid. She was really shaken up by the murder."

"I was in the audience," Jeff said. "I remember that she was hysterical when she discovered the body."

"I saw her the next day, and she was still a mess."

"What about Nancy Porter?"

"I don't know her very well."

"Why is that?"

"Renee Chambers was supposed to work Chesterfield's show, but she called me at the last minute because her mother fell ill and she had to go home to Wyoming."

"That must have been upsetting," Jeff said.

"Renee had worked a magic show with Porter somewhere in the Midwest. Minnesota, I think. Anyway, she said she'd talked to Nancy and she was willing to fill in. We met when she got to town and signed a contract. She seemed like a good kid, but I haven't had much contact with her."

"Have Rodriguez, Porter, or Monroe ever worked with David Turner?"

"Not to my knowledge. Certainly not in Oregon or Washington while they were with my agency. Turner's never done a show in Oregon. He had a show in Seattle, but Sheila and Maria didn't work it."

"What about Miss Porter?"

"If she worked with him, she never told me. You'll have to ask her."

"Do you know where I can reach her?"

"Yeah. She's house-sitting Renee's apartment until Renee comes back. I'll give you the address."

"Thanks."

"She mentioned that she might go back to the Midwest as soon as the police tell her it's okay."

"What about Chesterfield? I know Rodriguez assisted him three years ago when he disappeared during a rehearsal of the Chamber of Death. Have Monroe or Porter ever worked with Chesterfield?"

"Sheila hasn't while she's been with my agency. And Porter never said she'd worked a show with him. If she had, I'd assume she would have mentioned something when she got this gig."

"Did Rodriguez ever tell you that she disliked Chesterfield?"

Olmstead laughed. "Maria doesn't like anyone, but now that you mention it, I do remember that she was upset when Chesterfield disappeared at the coast."

"Was she worried about what might have happened to him?"

"No, she was angry."

"Did she ever give you a reason?"

"No. But she must have gotten over whatever made her angry, because she took the job at the Imperial when I told her that Chesterfield wanted her, and she seemed glad to get the work."

Jeff stood. "Thanks for taking the time to talk to me. This has been very helpful."

"If you have any other questions, give me a call."

Jeff went to a coffee shop to write an account of his conversation with the talent agent. According to Miriam Ross, Maria Rodriguez had been jealous when Chesterfield chose Ross over her as a sex partner, and Rodriguez didn't strike him as the type to forgive and forget. It occurred to Jeff that Rodriguez's apparent change of heart might have been a cover for her real feelings if she was an accomplice of the person who murdered Robert Chesterfield.

CHAPTER FORTY-TWO

Morris Quinlan leaned forward and studied the chessboard. If he moved his rook, he would expose his queen, but his nine-year-old grandson's bishop was attacking the rook and he would lose the game if he lost the exchange.

After a few agonizing minutes, Quinlan shook his head. "I resign, Joey. You're getting too good for me."

Joey Quinlan grinned. "Don't feel bad, Pop. You'll do better next time."

"Which will be at a time to be announced," Joey's mother said, "because it's time to get you home to bed. You have school in the morning."

Joey groused for a few minutes before giving his grandfather a hug. Quinlan smiled. His grandson was terrific, and he loved spending time with him. Quinlan's marriage had been a casualty of his job. The divorce had been amicable, and his son hadn't held it against him. He knew how much Morris loved his grandson, and the family visited Morris regularly.

Morris walked Joey and his daughter-in-law to the door, then watched them drive away. He was still thinking about his grandson when something occurred to him. He turned the thought over, looked at all sides of it, and concluded that his imagination was way too wild. He laughed and chalked up the idea to the onset of dementia. Then he headed to the living room to watch a movie. He stopped halfway to the television. Maybe his idea wasn't so crazy.

Morris went into his den where he'd put the police reports Roger Dillon had given him. He didn't find what he was looking for. Then again, he wasn't expecting to. It was too far-fetched to think that there was a connection between the murder of Robert Chesterfield, the attempt on Regina Barrister's life, and this other case. But what if he was right? Then he might be right about another idea that had raced through his conscious mind before disappearing like a runaway train that had sped around a bend in the tracks.

Morris sat down on a comfortable armchair, the movie forgotten. He wondered if he should call Roger and tell him what he was thinking, but nixed the idea. There was no way he could get what he needed until the state offices opened in the morning, and he would need something concrete if he didn't want to be laughed out of the room.

CHAPTER FORTY-THREE

The two deputy DAs who shared an office with Peter Ragland were both in court when Carrie Anders and Roger Dillon walked in.

"We found something interesting," Anders said.

"Don't keep me in suspense."

"We've been checking the financials of the magician's assistants. Someone deposited ten thousand dollars in Maria Rodriguez's checking account the day before Chesterfield was murdered."

"What does she say about that?"

"We were just going to ask."

When Ragland stood up, he had a big smile on his face.

Maria Rodriguez worked at a sports bar a few blocks from the courthouse. She looked annoyed when the detectives and the deputy DA told her that they needed to talk.

"I'm in the middle of my shift. I've got orders to bring out. Can't this wait?"

"I'm afraid not," Ragland said. "Why don't you ask the manager to have someone take over your tables."

"Who's going to cover my tips?" she asked angrily.

"That's the least of your worries, Miss Rodriguez. We can talk here and you can get back to work when you finish answering our questions, or we can interview you at police headquarters. Your choice."

Rodriguez glared at Ragland. "Let me tell my manager," she said before stomping off.

"What's this about?" Rodriguez demanded when they were sitting in a booth by the kitchen.

"How are you doing financially?" Ragland asked.

"What do you mean?"

"Have you hit the lottery or gotten an inheritance recently? Had a good run at one of the casinos?"

"Okay, what's going on?"

"We're curious about the ten thousand dollars that was deposited in your checking account the day before Robert Chesterfield was murdered."

Rodriguez's jaw dropped and she stared at the DA. "What the fuck are you talking about?"

Anders pushed a bank statement across the table.

Rodriguez stared at it.

"Where did the ten thousand come from, Maria?" Ragland asked.

"This isn't mine. There's some mistake."

"There's no mistake. Look at the account number and your name."

"There must be another Maria Rodriguez. The bank must have made an error and put this money in the wrong account."

"Or David Turner might have deposited it in your account to thank you for hiding Nancy Porter's inhaler and helping him murder Robert Chesterfield."

"You're crazy. I had nothing to do with Bobby's murder. I don't know Turner and I didn't hide that inhaler."

"He was at the Chamber of Death rehearsal at the coast. And so were you," Ragland said.

"Yeah, but I never talked to him."

"How do you explain the money?" Ragland asked.

Rodriguez looked panicky. "I can't. I don't know a thing about it."

"If that's your position, we're going to have to take you to the police station to continue our talk."

"You can't do that! I'll lose my job."

Ragland leaned across the table and stared into Rodriguez's eyes. "Where did the money come from, Maria? You're going to tell us eventually. Tell us now, and we can cut a deal. Stonewall us, and you'll be waitressing in the cafeteria of the women's penitentiary."

CHAPTER FORTY-FOUR

Nancy Porter was living in Renee Chambers's two-story duplex on the outskirts of Multnomah Village, a quaint area of Portland with a bookstore, restaurants, art galleries, and local shops. She looked wary when she answered the door. Her glossy red hair was tied back in a ponytail, and she was dressed in jeans and a powder blue man-tailored shirt. Unlike Maria Rodriguez, Porter was very attractive even though she wore very little makeup and was not dressed in her showgirl costume.

"I'm Robin Lockwood, the lawyer who's representing David Turner, and this is Jeff Hodges, my investigator. We were wondering if you have some time to talk to us."

"Can I talk to you without getting the permission of the district attorney?"

"Sure," Robin answered with a smile. "Both sides are supposed to talk to the witnesses before the trial to make sure we know all the facts. A lot of times the DA dismisses a case if we can convince him he's got the wrong man, and we try to convince our clients to plead guilty if we think they'll be convicted if we go to trial."

Porter hesitated. Then she asked Robin and Jeff into the living room, which was neat and clean and furnished with inexpensive furniture. Porter sat down on a comfortable easy chair, but Robin could see that she wasn't comfortable. The magician's assistant's hands were clasped in her lap, and her shoulders were hunched from tension.

"How are you doing?" Robin said.

"I haven't slept well since . . . what happened. I have night-mares."

"That's understandable." Jeff pointed at his scars. "I used to be a cop. We raided a house where they were cooking meth, and there was an explosion. I still have the nightmares on occasion, and that was years ago. But it does get better."

"Thanks for telling me that."

"Fortunately, most people don't have the type of harrowing experience you went through," Jeff continued. "When I do meet someone who has, I like to tell them that there is light at the end of the tunnel."

Porter smiled and the tension in her shoulders eased.

"So, I understand that you're house-sitting for Renee Cham-bers," Robin said to change the subject to something lighter.

Porter nodded. "Renee asked if I'd fill in for her when her mom got sick. She said I could use this place so I wouldn't have to pay rent. But you aren't here to discuss my living arrangements. What do you want to know?"

"Anything that can help us figure out if David is guilty or in-nocent," Robin said. "For instance, how would someone know that you use an inhaler for your asthma?"

"I guess everyone knew. I mean, it wasn't a secret. I don't use it a lot, but I used it once or twice when we were rehearsing, so the stagehands, Mr. Chesterfield, anyone who was backstage, would have seen it."

"Did you ever see David in the theater during rehearsals? Was he ever near your dressing room?"

"I heard he snuck into a rehearsal, but I never saw him in the theater."

"How did you get along with everyone?"

"Okay, I guess. I mean, I never had an argument, and no one was mean to me."

"What about Maria Rodriguez and Sheila Monroe? Did they get along with everyone?" Jeff asked.

"Sheila wasn't around much. She's in school and has a boyfriend. She came on time for rehearsals and she studied during breaks. Then she left as soon as the rehearsal finished."

"And Maria?"

Porter looked uncomfortable again. "I don't like to say anything mean."

"This will stay between us, unless it affects our client's case."

"Maria could be difficult, and . . . Well, there was nothing I could testify to. It's just a feeling. But I don't think she liked Mr. Chesterfield."

"Why do you say that?" Jeff asked.

"It was nothing she said, but I saw her looking at Mr. Chesterfield on more than one occasion, and I thought she looked angry." Porter shrugged. "That's all. I may have misinterpreted what she was doing."

"When you were drugged with the ether, did you see who did it or did you see the hand holding the cloth?" Robin asked.

"If I did, I don't remember."

"Do you have any idea who knocked you out or killed Mr. Chesterfield?"

"I've thought about it a lot, but I arrived in Portland just before rehearsals started, and I didn't know anyone. The newspapers had stories about Mr. Chesterfield's past, the murder trials and his disappearance. I read them, because I was working with him. But except for Mr. Chesterfield, I never met anyone, except Maria, who was involved in those situations."

"Can you think of anything else you want to ask Nancy?" Robin asked her investigator.

"No. And thanks for taking the time to talk to us." Jeff gave her his business card. "If you think of something that might help figure out what happened, give me a call."

"Do you know when I can leave?" Porter asked.

"That's up to the police," Robin said, "but I don't imagine they'll keep you too much longer. Do you have Carrie Anders's or Roger Dillon's number?"

"They gave me their cards."

"Call them. They'll give you an idea of when you can leave."

"Okay."

"I understand you live in Minnesota?"

"Yeah. I'll be glad to get home after what happened."

"I don't blame you. This has been a heck of an introduction to Oregon."

CHAPTER FORTY-FIVE

"Roger Dillon?" the voice on the phone asked.

"Yeah."

"I'm sorry to call so late. This is Elmer Davis. I'm a homicide detective in Washington County. I met you and Morris Quinlan about five years ago at the crime lab when they were hosting a seminar on DNA analysis."

"Right. I remember."

"Was Morris Quinlan your partner?"

"Yeah, but he's retired."

"I have some bad news for you. Mr. Quinlan was murdered tonight in the parking lot of the Ramble Inn. I was wondering if you could help us with our investigation."

"Me? How can I help?"

"His wallet and cell phone are gone, so I didn't know who to contact. Then I remembered the seminar. We can spare his relatives the discomfort of making a positive ID if you do it."

"I'll be right there."

• • •

The Ramble Inn was a run-down motel in the Washington County countryside, a half hour's drive from Portland. A heavy rain began falling when Roger was halfway there, and it had not let up when he saw the flickering neon sign advertising the motel and tavern. When Roger pulled into the lot, a heavyset man with salt-and-pepper stubble and a graying crew cut walked up. He was wearing a windbreaker with a hood, and he peered through the front driver's side window.

"Elmer?" Roger asked.

"Sorry to have to call you out here in this weather," Davis answered. He pointed to an empty parking space in front of the motel. "Park there and we'll get the hard part over."

Yellow crime-scene tape had been used to cordon off a section of the lot that was illuminated by lights the forensic team had set up.

"Watch out for the glass," Davis warned.

Roger looked down and saw shards scattered around a car he recognized as Morris's. Then he looked next to the car. Roger had never thrown up at a crime scene or autopsy, but he came close when he saw his old friend sprawled on the asphalt in a pool of blood.

Davis pointed up at a light that should have illuminated the area where they were standing.

"Someone broke the bulb so Morris would have to bend down to put his key in the lock. The key is still there. Morris was hit hard on the back of his head. The ME thinks twice. The blows would have stunned him. When he fell, he was stabbed in the heart. The ME thinks the killer knew how to use a blade because he was only stabbed once and it was a perfect strike. So, can you give me a positive ID?"

"That's Morris."

"Are you okay?"

"No. We were pretty close. Have they found the weapon?" he asked.

"No, but we haven't searched for it yet. It wasn't in the wound, so the killer may have taken it with him."

"Do you think this was a robbery?" Roger asked, hoping it had been, because the alternative would be very hard for him to take.

"He used a cell phone in the bar, and like I told you, we didn't find it or his wallet, so that's probably what happened."

"Do you have any idea why he was out here? This isn't one of his usual haunts."

"I think he was supposed to meet someone who didn't show," the detective said. "Let's get out of this rain. I want you to hear what Riley Dawkins, the bartender, told us."

The bar was dimly lit and smelled of beer and fried food. Two men were sitting in a booth across from the bar, working on burgers and beer, and a man in a suit was seated on a stool at the end of the bar, nursing a glass of hard liquor while he whispered into his cell phone. A mountain of a man in jeans and a red and black flannel shirt was standing behind the bar, polishing glasses. Above the bartender, at one end of the bar, a muted television was showing a basketball game.

"Riley, this is Roger Dillon. He's a detective from Portland and he used to be the dead man's partner."

"He was a cop?"

"Detective, Homicide," Roger said. "A really good detective."

"Condolences. I didn't mean any disrespect. My old man was a cop."

"Riley discovered the body when he went to throw out the garbage," Davis told Roger.

"Can you tell Detective Dillon what you told me?" Davis asked the bartender.

"Yeah, sure. Your friend came in around eight thirty. He sat in the booth in front of where those two guys are sitting. He was facing the door. Alice waited on him—"

"We interviewed her and sent her home because she was upset," Davis interrupted. "She told us he ordered a beer and nursed it while he watched the game. Go on, Riley."

"I'm pretty sure he was waiting for someone, because he kept checking his watch, and each time the door opened, he'd lean out so he could see who came in. Then he'd look disappointed and sit back.

"Around nine forty-five, he pulled out his phone and made a call, but I didn't see him talking to anyone, so I'm guessing that no one answered. He called again around ten. A half hour later, he paid his bar tab and left. The next time I saw him was when I took out the trash. I went over to see if he was okay, but as soon as I saw the blood, I came inside and called 911."

"Do you get a lot of crime out here?" Roger asked. "Muggings, robberies?"

"We had one mugging about five years ago. I have to break up fights every once in a while, but something like this, no."

"Anything else you want to ask Riley?"

"I'm good," Roger said.

"What about the motel?" Roger asked Davis when they were headed outside. "Did Morris have a room?"

"No. He never went into the office and he didn't make a reservation."

"So he might have been lured to this isolated spot?"

"If the person who set up the meeting killed him. Any idea who it might have been?"

"No," Roger answered, but he felt sick. Morris's killer had stabbed him with a surgical strike that mimicked the blow that had felled Robert Chesterfield. Roger wondered if Morris had died investigating Chesterfield's murder—something he would not have been doing if Roger hadn't asked for his help.

CHAPTER FORTY-SIX

Robin got up at five and ran to McGill's gym. She worked out for an hour, showered, and walked to her office, picking up a latte and scone on the way. Robin ate the scone and sipped the latte while she read the story about Morris Quinlan's murder on her phone. The name sounded familiar, but she couldn't remember why.

Robin closed her phone and started work on a brief that was due in the Oregon Supreme Court. She was reading a case that she hoped would win the day for her client when she remembered where she'd heard Quinlan's name. Regina had mentioned it when she told Robin about Robert Chesterfield's old murder cases. If she had the right person, he'd been Roger Dillon's partner when Chesterfield was arrested for the murders of Sophie Randall and Arthur Gentry.

Robin went back to the brief. Then she stopped. There was another victim who had been involved in Chesterfield's old cases. Robin ran a web search and found the newspaper account of Henry Beathard's murder in the supermarket parking lot. Beathard was the judge who had excluded the evidence of Arthur Gentry's murder when Peter Ragland tried to introduce it in the case charging

Chesterfield with the murder of Sophie Randall. The ruling had forced Ragland to dismiss the indictments charging Chesterfield with the murders of Gentry and Randall.

Were Beathard's murder and the attempt on Regina's life linked? The MOs in Regina's and Beathard's cases—shooting and poisoning—were different. Quinlan and Lord Robert had both been stabbed.

Robin stared out her window at the snow-covered slopes of Mount Hood. After a few minutes, she swiveled her chair and dialed the office of the state medical examiner.

"What can I do for you, Counselor?" Sally Grace said.

"I've got a weird question for you."

"Many of your questions are weird. What do you want to know?"

"Did you do the autopsy on Morris Quinlan, the retired detective who was stabbed to death yesterday?"

"I did."

"And you autopsied Robert Chesterfield?"

"Yes."

"Were the two methods of murder similar?"

"Why do you want to know that?"

"I can't tell you now, but I'll tell the DA if my guess is right."

Grace hesitated. Then she said, "Both men were killed by a single thrust to the heart in a way that makes me think that the same person may have killed both people. But that's not something I would swear to in court."

"Thanks, Sally."

Robin hung up the phone and stared into space. Was there really a connection between the three murders and the attempt on Regina, or did she have an overwrought imagination? Regina, Beathard, Chesterfield, and Quinlan had all been involved in the Randall and Gentry cases. Chesterfield had been charged with the murders, and Regina's and Judge Beathard's actions had led to the dismissal of the charges. But Quinlan had arrested Chester-field and had nothing to do with the magician's escaping justice. And the Gentry and Randall cases happened a long time ago. Why would someone try to kill the participants now? It didn't make any sense.

Robin buzzed Mary Stendahl. "Do you know where the files from Robert Chesterfield's old cases are?"

"Probably in our storage locker in the basement."

"Can you get them for me?"

"I'll go down and look."

"Thanks."

Twenty minutes later, Mary stuck her head in the door. "Where do you want these?" she asked, pointing at a dolly loaded down with Bankers Boxes.

"Put them in the conference room."

Robin decided to take a break from the brief. Mary had taken the files out of the boxes and stacked them on the conference table. They covered it, and Robin realized that it would take the rest of the day to go through them. She sighed. The issue in the brief was very complicated, and the deadline for filing it was roaring toward her. She couldn't spend the day going through hundreds of pages of transcripts, police reports, and evidence when she had no idea what she was looking for, so she went back to her office.

It was almost dark when Robin finished the draft of the brief. She closed her eyes and stretched. She was tempted to grab some sushi and head home, but duty called. The hearing on pretrial motions in David Turner's case was coming up. She was too tired to work on the legal issues, but the police reports of the witness statements in Turner's case were strewn around the floor of her office, and she wanted them in a trial notebook, where she could get to them easily if Ragland called someone as a witness at the hearing.

Robin was putting the statements in alphabetical order when she found Samuel Moser's statement. Robin remembered that she had not been able to place the name when she encountered it the first time she and Jeff had gone through the reports. Now she remembered why it had sounded familiar, and she wondered why Samuel Moser would pay money to see the person who had been accused of trying to murder him.

CHAPTER FORTY-SEVEN

The next morning, Robin started on the pretrial motions in David Turner's case. There weren't many issues she could raise. She had a theory for suppressing the statements Turner had made at the Imperial, but she didn't think she would win. She also wanted to get the judge to rule that Ragland couldn't tell the jury about his accomplice theory unless he had evidence pointing to a specific person.

Robin finished her work on the motions at ten thirty. It was too early for lunch, so she went into the conference room and began going through the old files in the Gentry–Randall cases. An hour later, Robin got to the file containing the report of Sophie Randall's autopsy. A photograph from Randall's autopsy was in the file. It made Robin sad to see someone so pretty and, from what Regina had told her, so happy on a coroner's slab.

Robin started to read the autopsy report when she frowned. Randall looked familiar, but Robin had never met her. She stared at the photograph. An odd thought struck her. She shook her head, as if to dislodge it, but the idea hung on with enough tenacity to force her to return to her office and run a web search for articles about Randall's murder. *The Oregonian* had covered the poisoning on its front page, complete with a color photograph of Sophie Randall in happier times, standing with her husband, Gary, and their daughter, Jane.

Robin swore. Now she knew why Samuel Moser had paid money to see a show put on by a man who had tried to kill him.

Samuel Moser was still the manager of the Westmont Country Club, and that's where Robin headed. Robin had never been to a country club before attending Yale for law school. There had been one in her hometown, but no one in her family's income bracket entered the grounds unless they were a gardener, a cook, or a member of the waitstaff. Robin had finished high enough in her law school class to be invited to an award dinner at a country club near the school. As self-confident as she was, she had felt a bit intimidated by the luxurious surroundings, which most of her fellow students took for granted.

The trees that lined the road to the Westmont had lost most of their leaves, and the fairways of the golf course were rain soaked, but Robin still thought that the grounds were impressive. The country club's brick façade appeared out of the mist when she rounded a curve. Robin found a parking spot in the visitors' lot and ran for the shelter of the portico.

The light from a grand chandelier turned the lobby into a warm and welcoming place. A young woman sat behind the desk where members checked in and visitors were screened. Robin told her that she'd like to see Samuel Moser. After a brief moment on the in-house phone, the receptionist pointed Robin toward the wood-paneled hallway that led to Moser's office.

Samuel Moser had not changed much in twenty-some years. He was completely bald now and thinner because of the diet that had saved his life, but he still wore dull gray suits and uninspiring ties and looked as bland as he had on the day that Sophie Randall was murdered.

"Thanks for seeing me," Robin said.

"Have a seat and tell me how I can help you," Moser answered.

When Robin sat down and said, "I'm an attorney and I represent David Turner," Moser tensed. "Mr. Turner is accused of murdering Robert Chesterfield, and you were in the audience when Mr. Chesterfield was murdered."

"I was, but I told the police that I didn't see anything that would help figure out who killed him or how he was killed."

"I know. I read the police report of your interview. What puzzles me is why you were at Chesterfield's performance. Weren't you convinced that Robert Chesterfield tried to murder you over twenty years ago?"

"I'm still convinced that he sent me the poisoned chocolates."

"Then why did you go to Chesterfield's show?"

Moser blinked. "I can see why that might surprise you."

Several years as a criminal defense attorney had made Robin an expert at reading body language. The question had surprised Moser, and it was obvious that he was stalling for time so he could figure out how to answer it.

"Why did you go?" Robin pressed.

Moser flashed a nervous smile. "Curiosity, I guess."

Moser was hiding something. Robin was certain she knew what it was, but she didn't know how to pry it out of him, so she changed the subject. "Have you read about the attempt on Regina Barrister's life?"

"I heard about it, but I don't know the details."

"Someone sent Regina a box of cyanide-laced chocolates."

Moser paled. "Oh my," he said. "And you think there's a connection between the attempt on her life and what happened at the club in the nineties?"

"I think it's a possibility. Regina represented Chesterfield, and her legal work led to the dismissal of his murder charges. Henry Beathard was the judge in the case. His ruling made it impossible for the district attorney to continue the prosecution. Judge Beathard was murdered recently."

"Beathard too?"

Robin could see that the news had upset Moser. "Over the past few months, Judge Beathard was murdered, Chesterfield was murdered, someone tried to kill Regina, and I just found out that Morris Quinlan, the lead detective on Chesterfield's case, was murdered."

Moser looked sick. "Couldn't it just be a coincidence?"

"Yes, but it could also be the acts of a person who wants revenge for what happened here a long time ago. Can you think of anyone connected to Sophie Randall's or Arthur Gentry's murder or the attempt on your life who might want revenge?"

"Me? No, I haven't any idea."

"No one comes to mind?"

"No," Moser said, but Robin was certain that he was lying.

"Mr. Moser, if someone is responsible for three murders and the attempt on Miss Barrister, this person is very, very dangerous. If you know anything, you have to tell the police."

"Yes, certainly. If I think of someone, I'll tell the police," Moser said, "but I don't know anything that can help your client."

"I think you do, Mr. Moser, and I think you know why the killer waited so long to exact her revenge. I've also come up with the reason you went to Chesterfield's show."

"What are you talking about?"

"Sophie Randall had a daughter named Jane. What happened to her daughter after Gary killed himself?"

Beads of sweat appeared on Moser's brow. "What does that have to do with anything?"

"Was Jane put into foster care, did someone adopt her, did she go to live with a relative?"

"I don't know what happened to Jane."

"You and Sophie were close. You must have felt overwhelming guilt for giving her the chocolates, and you must have felt horrible when Gary killed himself."

Moser looked away.

"I saw a picture of Sophie Randall, and I saw a woman at Chesterfield's performance who bears a strong resemblance to her. Did you see a picture of Chesterfield's assistants in the ads advertising the Chamber of Death? Did you go to Robert Chesterfield's magic show to find out if one of those assistants was Jane Randall?"

Moser stiffened. He shook his head. "This is nonsense. I don't know what happened to Jane Randall."

"She's a killer, Mr. Moser. I know you feel responsible for giving the chocolates to Sophie, but that doesn't justify shielding a murderer."

Moser's head dropped into his hands. "Chesterfield deserved to die."

"Did Judge Beathard and Morris Quinlan also deserve to die? And what about Regina Barrister? Who is Jane Randall, Mr. Moser?"

Robin called Carrie Anders as soon as she left the Westmont. "I know who killed Robert Chesterfield," she said. "She may also have murdered Morris Quinlan, Henry Beathard—the judge who heard Chesterfield's case back in the nineties—and I'm sure she sent the poisoned chocolates to Regina. I'm headed to you. I'll explain everything when I get there."

CHAPTER FORTY-EIGHT

"Magic illusions rely on misdirection, and Robert Chesterfield's murder was part of a magnificent illusion," Robin told Dillon and Anders when they were seated in a small conference room in the Homicide Bureau. "Who was the first person everyone believed was the murderer?" Robin asked.

"Nancy Porter, the assistant who appeared to push Chesterfield into the sarcophagus," Dillon said.

"Why didn't you arrest her, Roger?"

"We found out that the killer hid her inhaler so he could get her alone. Then he rendered her unconscious and stole her robe so he could conceal himself and kill Chesterfield."

"When you are in the audience, the magician's escape from the sarcophagus in the Chamber of Death seems impossible," Robin said. "If you see the trick from a different angle, the magic can lose its luster. You learn that the magician doesn't dematerialize. He simply rolls out of the sarcophagus when his assistant blocks the audience's view. Then he crawls into the dolly and gets pushed offstage.

"What if we look at Chesterfield's murder from a different

angle," Robin said. "Sophie Randall was murdered with a box of poisoned chocolates twenty-plus years ago. She had a daughter, Jane. Jane was five when her mother died. Shortly after Sophie Randall was murdered, her father committed suicide. Jane would be in her twenties now.

"When Robert Chesterfield disappeared three years ago, the newspapers dredged up all the details of Sophie Randall's murder. That may have been when Jane Randall learned that Chesterfield escaped punishment for killing her mother and also learned the identity of the people who helped him beat the case.

"Right before rehearsals for the Chamber of Death were going to start, Renee Chambers called her agent. She told Olmstead that her mother was very ill and she had to leave Oregon to be with her. She also recommended Nancy Porter as her replacement.

"Jeff checked. Renee Chambers's mother is in perfect health. I think Jane Randall changed her name to Nancy Porter. I think she got Renee Chambers to lie to Marvin Olmstead about her mother so Nancy could replace her in Chesterfield's show. At that late date, Chesterfield would have had to hire Porter because the show was scheduled to begin in a week."

"If I'm right, Jane stabbed Chesterfield. Then she pushed the dolly offstage, dumped her robe near the loading dock exit to make it look like the killer escaped through it, and returned to her dressing room, where she used a cloth with ether to knock herself out, knowing that everyone would assume she was also a victim."

Roger Dillon frowned. "If she's asthmatic, wouldn't she be taking a risk by using ether to knock herself out?"

"That was my first thought. So I checked with an anesthesiologist. Ether is a strong bronchodilator that opens up airways and has actually been used, on rare occasions, to treat severe asthma. And there is another possibility she may have been faking; she may not have asthma, at all."

"We were idiots," Dillon said.

"No, all of us were part of an audience that was fooled by a very clever illusion."

"We need to speak to Nancy Porter or Jane Randall or whatever her name is, right away," Anders said.

"I've got her address," Robin said. "And I think you should bring backup. If I'm right, she has a gun and no compunction about killing."

Robin and the detectives parked on a side street a block from Renee Chambers's duplex. An unmarked car with four plainclothes officers parked behind them.

"Stay in the car," Anders told Robin.

"If you identify yourself as a police officer, she may start shooting. She knows me. I've been in her house. She won't suspect anything if I knock on her door."

"I can't let you do this. You're a civilian."

"Who has been in more violent confrontations than you and Roger put together." When Anders hesitated, Robin pushed her point. "Look, Carrie. You know I can take care of myself, and I'm not stupid. I'll bail at the first sign of danger."

Anders shook her head. "Fucking lawyers. I should never have let this degenerate into a debate."

Dillon laughed. "Go ahead. We'll be right behind you."

Robin checked her handgun to make sure it was loaded. Then she walked around the corner and stopped. A patrol car was parked at the curb in front of the duplex. Robin walked up to the driver's window and saw an officer speaking into his radio. The officer turned to Robin. "This is a crime scene, ma'am. You can't hang out here."

Anders and Dillon had been following Robin at a distance. When they saw the police car, they joined her.

Anders flashed her badge. "We're here to make an arrest. What are you doing here?"

"We got a 911 about a woman being held at this address."

"Is she okay?" Robin asked.

"Yeah. She was tied up in a bedroom, but she isn't hurt. Just scared."

When they entered the house, they found a policewoman sitting at the kitchen table with Renee Chambers, who was wearing a sweatshirt, T-shirt, socks, and sweatpants and drinking a cup of tea. There was a fading bruise on her cheek, but she looked otherwise unharmed.

"Can you tell us what happened?" Anders asked after the introductions were made.

"She knocked on my door the Thursday before rehearsals were going to start—"

"You mean Nancy Porter?"

Renee nodded. "That's what she called herself."

"Okay, go on."

"As soon as I opened the door, she hit me. Then she held a gun on me and forced me into the bedroom. I tried to say something and she hit me again and told me to shut up and do as I was told. Then she handcuffed me to the bed and put a gag in my mouth. I was terrified, but she said she wouldn't hurt me anymore if I did exactly what she said.

"She left me for a while. Then she came back with my phone and had me call Marvin—"

"Marvin Olmstead, your agent?"

"Yes. She told me to tell him that I had a family emergency and had to go home, but that I had called Nancy Porter, who did a magic act with me in Minneapolis, and she would be here in time for rehearsals. She . . . she said that she would kill me if I tried to call for help or say anything that wasn't in her script, so I did what she wanted.

"After that, she mostly left me alone. She would feed me and she took me to the toilet, but I was locked up in the bedroom all day. Then today she said she'd done what she came for and was going to leave. She said I shouldn't worry, that she would call the police and they would free me. Then she left."

"Did she say where she was going?"

"No."

"Did she ever say anything that hinted at where we could find her?"

"She rarely spoke to me."

"Okay, I think that's enough for now. We're going to take you to a hospital to have you checked out. Then we'll want to debrief you after you've gotten a good sleep. Do you want to come back here or go somewhere else?"

"No, I'm okay staying here."

"Do you want an officer to stay with you for a day or so?"

"I don't think she's coming back, but that would be okay, I'm still pretty scared."

"You're doing really well for someone who's gone through what you just did. Is there anything else you need?"

"No, but can you tell me why she did this? Did she hurt some-body else?"

CHAPTER FORTY-NINE

Peter Ragland was in a great mood. Robin Lockwood may have won the battle at the bail hearing, but he'd win the war when they went to trial, now that he knew Maria Rodriguez was David Turner's accomplice. The office had a brilliant techie who could trace money back to the year the first dollar was minted, and Ragland had assigned her to find out where the ten thousand dollars in Rodriguez's account had originated. Once it was traced back to Turner, Rodriguez and the magician would be dead meat.

Ragland was imagining the look on Lockwood's face when he told her that he'd figured out the identity of Turner's accomplice, when Carrie Anders and Roger Dillon walked in.

"It's not Turner," Dillon said.

Ragland looked confused. "What's not Turner?"

"He didn't kill Chesterfield," Anders said. "It was Nancy Porter, the magician's assistant."

"What are you talking about? Of course Turner is our killer, and Maria Rodriguez hid the inhaler. He paid her off."

Dillon shook his head. "You remember the first time you prosecuted Chesterfield?"

"The Randall and Gentry cases."

Dillon nodded. "Sophie Randall had a daughter, Jane, who was five when Randall died. She's in her twenties now, and she's trying to kill everyone who was responsible for her mother's murder and the dismissal of Chesterfield's murder charge."

Ragland looked skeptical. "How did you come to this amazing conclusion?"

"We didn't. Robin Lockwood figured it out."

Ragland laughed. "Of course she did. And I suppose she can prove her wild theory."

"It's more than a theory now. We just came from Renee Chambers's house—"

"Renee Chambers?"

"Chambers was supposed to be Chesterfield's third assistant. Jane Randall kept her captive in her apartment. She forced Chambers to tell her agent that she had to go home because of a family emergency, and to say that she knew another magician's assistant named Nancy Porter who could fill in. Randall has been living in Chambers's place and keeping her captive. Randall's fingerprints are all over the duplex, and Chambers can ID her as the person who kidnapped her."

Ragland stared at the detectives. "You're telling me that Turner and Rodriguez are innocent?"

"It looks that way," Dillon said.

"What about the ten thousand dollars?"

"I think we'll find it came from Randall," Anders said.

"What does Porter or Randall, or whatever her name is, say?"

"We haven't been able to ask her. She's on the run. We have an APB out. You can ask her when she's under arrest."

Robin spent the rest of the afternoon at police headquarters giving a statement. When Anders dismissed her, Robin thought about going to her office, but she was too exhausted. Instead, she called Jeff and gave him a condensed version of her day, promising to tell him everything that had happened when he came home.

Jeff picked up a steak, potatoes, and an excellent pinot and listened to Robin's tale while he cooked dinner.

"She sure had everyone fooled," Jeff said when Robin finished.

"That she did." Robin sighed. "I know Jane's a stone killer, but part of me feels sorry for her."

"Is that the part where she killed Judge Beathard and Morris Quinlan and tried to murder Regina?" Jeff asked as he plated the food.

"You know what I mean," Robin said as she poured the wine. "She didn't kill Renee Chambers, and Chesterfield murdered her mother, made her father so depressed that he killed himself, and turned her into an orphan."

"What's that old saw about two wrongs not making a right?"

"Okay, smart-ass. Sorry I can feel empathy and you can't."

"I admit that I find it impossible to empathize with a serial killer. Do we know where Randall went?"

"No, but Carrie found some information about her history. Randall's been in and out of foster care and her life has been hard. She was abused in two homes and ran away at twelve and fourteen. She may have been homeless for a while, but she did get a GED and a two-year degree at a community college, where she was on the gymnastics team, which explains how she could pick up the skills she needed to be a magician's assistant.

"The trail went cold right around the time Chesterfield disappeared and the newspapers published stories about the old murder cases. That's probably what triggered her."

"You did good work, kid. The cops would never have figured this out if it weren't for you."

"Oh, they'd have known who killed Chesterfield as soon as they found Chambers. I'm just sorry that we didn't figure out what was going on sooner, but she was very clever, and so was her plan."

CHAPTER FIFTY

After dinner, Robin tried to watch a Blazers game. When she nodded off a second time, she struggled to her feet and went into the bedroom, where she had a troubled sleep. A little after midnight, Robin jerked awake. She looked at the other side of the bed. Jeff was dead to the world. She closed her eyes, but the attempt at sleep was useless, so she went into the living room.

What was bothering her? The obvious answer was that Jane Randall was still at large despite a massive manhunt, but there was something else she just could not put her finger on.

Robin went over everything that had happened since Chesterfield announced his performance at the Imperial. Chesterfield should have been Randall's first victim, but no one knew where to find him, because he was hiding from Rafael Otero.

Judge Beathard was an easy target, and his death had been written off as a robbery gone bad, with no one suspecting that it was part of an elaborate plot.

Randall's next target had been Regina, which made sense. But why had she killed Morris Quinlan? Roger had told Robin and Anders that he had asked his old partner to look into the case.

They guessed that Morris had figured out that Randall murdered Chesterfield and had arranged to meet her at the Ramble Inn.

Robin was starting to feel sleepy, when she realized what was bothering her. There was a loose end: Regina was alive. A sane person would run, but Randall wasn't sane; she was a fanatic who was dedicated to killing Chesterfield and everyone who had helped him escape justice.

Robin grabbed her phone.

Stanley Cloud was only half awake when he answered her call. "Who is this?"

"It's Robin."

"Why are you calling at one in the morning?" he groused.

"We know who killed Chesterfield and tried to kill Regina."

"Who?" asked Cloud, who was suddenly wide awake.

"Nancy Porter, the magician's assistant. Porter is really Jane Randall, the daughter of Sophie Randall, whom Chesterfield poisoned with cyanide-laced chocolates. Randall is killing everyone who helped Chesterfield beat the murder charge. She failed the first time she went after Regina. I think she'll try again."

"What do you want me to do?"

"Put 911 on your speed dial and make sure your alarm system is on. Get a weapon, if you have one. Then lock yourself in your bedroom with Regina."

Regina's house was in one of the wealthiest sections of Portland. One side of the lot was on the river. The rest was surrounded by woods. If Jane Randall was coming for Regina, she had many ways to invade the property.

On the way over, Robin thought about calling 911, but a bad dream didn't count as an emergency. She decided she would keep watch tonight. If nothing happened, she would talk to Anders and Dillon in the morning about providing protection for Regina and Stanley.

It was a moonless night and it was raining hard. As soon as Robin parked, she called Stanley. "I'm here. Has anything happened?"

"No."

"That's good. I hope I'm way off base, but I'm going to patrol the grounds in case I'm not."

Robin checked her gun, pulled up the hood of her windbreaker, and got out of the car. The rain had eased up, but the wind off the river chilled Robin to the bone. There was nothing to distract her, and it took all her willpower to stay focused.

A little after two, she started to believe that she was on a fool's errand. Then she saw movement at the edge of the woods on the other side of the house.

Robin speed-dialed Stanley as she ran along the shore. "You've got a visitor," she whispered when he picked up. "Call 911."

Robin pocketed the phone when she neared the patio in the rear of the house. She held her gun in front of her, peeked around the corner, and scanned the lawn. Nothing. Then she heard a faint noise and looked up. A shadow slithered up the side of the house with the fluid grace of a gymnast. Black clothing rendered her close to invisible.

Robin aimed. "Jane, stop!"

The figure paused.

"Come down now. The police are on the way."

Randall slipped into the shadows so quickly that Robin didn't have time to shoot. Robin dashed back to the patio. She shattered the glass in one of the French doors, reached inside, and jerked the door open. The alarm shrieked. She hoped it would unnerve Randall and make her flee.

Randall had gone into the house through the top floor, so Robin raced for the stairs. When she reached the bottom step, she paused and peered into the darkness. The alarm was unsettling and made it impossible to hear movement. Robin focused on the top of the stairs. When no shot rang out, she climbed cautiously, her gun leading the way.

Halfway up, a figure spun around the banister. Robin dropped just before Randall fired. The air moved as a bullet whizzed by her.

Robin returned fire, hitting the top of the banister. Wood chips flew toward Randall's face. Robin heard a scream over the blaring of the alarm and saw Randall's gun fly over the banister. Robin charged up the steps. Randall had a hand pressed to her cheek, and blood was running through her fingers. Robin started to order her to surrender, when Randall swung on the banister and kicked Robin in the chest. Robin's reflexes saved her from absorbing the full impact, but the blow still sent her tumbling backward. She grabbed the banister to stop her fall, and her gun dropped. Randall's hand slashed out. Robin saw the knife and twisted away. The blade ripped into her jacket and gashed her forearm.

Fighting was second nature to Robin. She ignored the pain and squared up to face her opponent, the way she'd squared up against her opponents in the octagon. Randall was smaller, but she had the high ground, speed, and the knife. Randall edged down one step so she would be closer to Robin. Robin moved backward. As soon as they were on a flat surface, she would have an advantage.

A leg snapped toward her head with so much speed that Robin had little time to react. She threw a hand up and partially deflected the blow. Then she cried out, pretending she was hurt, and rolled down the stairs and away from the knife. Randall flew off the stairs and aimed a kick at Robin's chest. Robin grabbed Randall's ankle and twisted. Randall flew sideways, rolled, and landed on her feet.

Robin stood, turning sideways to make herself a skinny target for the blade. Randall struck. Robin blocked, hitting Randall's wrist before driving her foot into Randall's left knee. The knee buckled. Randall sagged and Robin smashed a right into her nose. The pain blinded Randall. When her hands flew toward her face, Robin drove a side kick into the injured knee. Randall dropped, but she still gripped her knife in her right hand. Robin drove a roundhouse kick into the side of Randall's head. The blow stunned her, and the knife dropped to the ground. Robin spun behind her. Moments before she heard the sirens, Robin choked out Randall.

When Robin was certain that Randall was unconscious, she called 911. "This is Robin Lockwood. I'm at Regina Barrister's house. Stanley Cloud, a former chief justice of the Oregon Supreme Court, just called for help because a burglar broke in. The burglar has been captured and is not a threat. I just heard sirens. Please tell the officers that the situation is under control. I don't want them to shoot Justice Cloud when he lets them in.

"And please tell Homicide Detectives Carrie Anders and Roger Dillon that Jane Randall has been captured. She's a fugitive they've been looking for."

As soon as Robin disconnected, she phoned Stanley to tell him that it was safe to come out.

"How is Regina?" Robin asked when the former chief justice appeared at the top of the stairs and the lights came on.

"I calmed her down. The alarm really upset her."

"She's not alone. Can you please turn the damn thing off? And you'd better open the door. The police should be outside by now."

Stanley looked at Randall as he walked by her on the way to the keypad for the security system. Robin took off her jacket and sweatshirt and examined her forearm. It was bleeding, but the cut wasn't deep. She pressed the sweatshirt against the wound.

The alarm stopped moments before an officer pounded on the door. Stanley opened it and brought two policemen to the bottom of the stairs.

"I'm Robin Lockwood, an attorney." She pointed at Randall.

"This woman is responsible for several murders. You should cuff her. And I need a medic."

Shortly after Carrie Anders and Roger Dillon had arrived at Regina's house, Carrie had Robin taken to the hospital with instructions to come to police headquarters the next day to give a detailed statement. Robin was discharged after her wound was treated, and she arrived home a little after four in the morning.

Robin tried to be quiet when she entered her apartment so as not to wake up Jeff, but he walked out of the bedroom before the front door closed.

"Where were you?"

"I was staking out Regina's house, and I captured Jane Randall."

"What?!"

Robin blushed. "I didn't tell you, because I didn't want you to worry."

Jeff saw the bandage on Robin's forearm when she took off her jacket.

"Are you okay? What happened?"

"There was a fight. I was stabbed, but it's not serious."

"Are you crazy?"

"I had to protect Regina and Stanley."

"Did you think about calling the police? They're paid to protect citizens."

"I didn't have a shred of proof that Jane would try to kill Regina tonight. The police wouldn't have taken me seriously. If I hadn't gone out there, Stanley and Regina would probably be dead."

"We've talked about this, Robin. You seem to think you're invincible, and you put yourself in danger when it's not necessary."

"This was necessary."

"Jesus, you don't get it, do you? You keep forgetting that

there's another person in your life who cares about you and worries about you. There were several ways you could have protected
Regina without putting your life in danger. One involves asking
me to come with you. Did you forget that I was a police officer,
trained to handle serious situations? All that martial arts training
doesn't mean a thing if you're facing a gun."

"I faced a gun tonight and came out on top, and it's not the
first time," Robin insisted stubbornly.

"You're not listening to me. I know how tough you are. I'm
talking about our relationship and what it would do to me if you
were killed or seriously injured. You are not a one-woman army.
That stuff is for the movies. You were stabbed tonight and could
have been shot. If you'd called Carrie Anders or Roger Dillon, they
would have protected Regina."

"You can't keep me in Bubble Wrap, Jeff."

Jeff started to answer Robin. Then he shook his head. "You're
hurt, it's late, and we're both tired. We're not going to solve this
now. We should go to bed." Jeff walked back to the bedroom and
got into bed on his side.

Robin went into the bathroom and shut the door. She was exhausted, but she was also upset and she didn't want to get in bed
with Jeff, because she was afraid that he'd argue with her again.

Robin stripped down and got in the shower, letting the hot
water wash over her. She did care about Jeff. He was very important to her. But she couldn't stand the idea of being controlled.
Robin turned off the water and toweled herself dry. She usually
slept in the nude. But she'd brought pajamas in with her. She didn't
want makeup sex tonight. She wasn't even certain that Jeff would
want to make love.

Robin got under the covers and closed her eyes. She tried to
see Jeff's point. She knew he worried about her. This wasn't the first
time they'd had this talk. But she couldn't admit that Jeff might be
right. Having Jeff move in had been a serious decision for her. She

had always been independent, and her biggest fear was that any man she let into her world might try to change her.

Robin had been given a mild painkiller at the hospital when they stitched her up. That and exhaustion made it difficult to think, so she decided not to. Hopefully, when they woke up, the argument would be forgotten. The last thought she had before she drifted off was, What if it isn't?

CHAPTER FIFTY-ONE

When Anders and Dillon entered the interview room at the jail, Jane Randall was sitting with her hands folded on the table, looking perfectly composed. Her slender body was clothed in an orange jumpsuit that was too large for her and made her look like a child.

"Good morning, Miss Randall," Anders said. "We want to talk to you, but you're under arrest, so I have to read you your Miranda rights."

When Anders finished, she asked Randall if she wanted to have an attorney with her.

Randall smiled. "Do you think Robin Lockwood would represent me?"

Anders returned the smile. "I think she has a conflict of interest, don't you?"

Randall stopped smiling. "An attorney isn't going to help me. No one else ever has. I've been on my own since Chesterfield killed my mother, and I'll deal with this myself."

"That's probably not wise," Anders said. "Peter Ragland is prosecuting, and he's probably going to ask for the death penalty."

Randall shrugged. "I don't care. What do I have to live for? I waive my right to an attorney, so ask your questions."

"First, I want to thank you for sparing Renee Chambers and telling us where to find her."

"Renee never did anything to hurt me."

"What did Morris Quinlan do?" Dillon asked.

"I do feel bad about that, but Regina Barrister was still alive, and I couldn't let him interfere before I killed her."

"She's still alive," Anders said. "Do we have to worry about you, Jane?"

Randall looked Anders in the eye. "My only regret is that she didn't eat the chocolates and die, so she would know the agony my mother went through. If I ever get out, my only priority will be ending her life."

"I appreciate the honesty," Anders said. "I guess we'll have to make sure that you stay locked up for the rest of your life."

CHAPTER FIFTY-TWO

Robin usually got up around five so she could go to the gym before she went to the office, but she hadn't gotten to bed until four, and exhaustion and the painkiller she'd been given kept her under the covers until nine o'clock. She was groggy when she did get out of bed, and she stumbled into the bathroom only half awake. When she returned to the bedroom, Robin saw that Jeff's side of the bed was empty. That's when she remembered their argument.

Robin felt terrible during her walk to the office. Her arm was throbbing, but the pain in her heart was worse. She loved Jeff and she was afraid that what he saw as reckless behavior was pushing him away. She saw what she'd done in a different light. Regina and Stanley were very important to her, and she had no doubt that the decision to watch their house had saved their lives.

Should she have asked Jeff to go with her? Approaching problems without emotion and solving them with cold logic were things Robin did very well. When she thought about what Jeff had said, she could see now that he was right. The police wouldn't have gone to Regina's house because Robin had a hunch, but that didn't mean Robin should have confronted Jane Randall alone. She knew that she should have asked Jeff to back her up, just as she knew that Jeff would have gone with her because he loved her.

Robin went to Jeff's office as soon as she arrived at the law firm, but he wasn't in. Robin felt terrible. Had she destroyed their relationship?

She went to her office and distracted herself by calling Peter Ragland. "Did Carrie or Roger tell you what happened last night?" Robin asked.

"Yeah. It looks like Porter or Randall or whatever her name is killed Chesterfield," Ragland said, but he didn't sound happy about being proved wrong.

"I can see why you arrested David," Robin said to make Ragland feel better. "Can I tell him you're dropping the charges, now that we know he's innocent?"

"Yeah, of course."

"Thanks, Peter."

As soon as she hung up, Robin called her client.

"I have great news," Robin said when David Turner answered his phone. "I just got off the line with Peter Ragland, and he's going to drop all the charges against you."

"How did you manage that?"

"Last night, the police arrested Nancy Porter when she tried to murder Regina Barrister. Porter's real name is Jane Randall, and there is overwhelming evidence that she murdered Chesterfield and two other people."

Robin told Turner about the Randall and Gentry cases and how she had discovered Porter's real identity. Then she told her client about finding Renee Chambers alive and her capture of the fugitive.

"I'm so grateful," Turner said when Robin was done. "I can't imagine that there are many lawyers who would risk their lives to help a client."

"Fighting killers isn't part of my usual legal service."

"Caesars Palace has been threatening to cancel my contract, but I'm guessing they'll change their tune, now that I've been cleared—and I'm also guessing that the publicity will bring in the crowds."

"It worked for Chesterfield."

"Do you think I should use the Chamber of Death as my new finale?"

Robin laughed. "Absolutely not!"

"Just kidding. What I can do is comp you and Jeff to a night in the penthouse and front-row seats to my next show."

"That's tempting, but I'm not sure I ever want to see another magic show."

Jeff was standing in Robin's doorway when she hung up.

"Do you hate me?" she asked.

Jeff didn't answer right away. He closed the door and sat down in a chair across the desk from her. "If I hated you, I wouldn't care if you were hurt or killed. My problem is that I love you and I can't bear the thought of anything happening to you."

"I had to go to Regina's house last night, but you were right. I shouldn't have gone alone. I should have asked you to help me. I'm just not used to asking for help."

"I get that. Sometimes I think you see yourself as one of the Knights of the Round Table, galloping off to right wrongs. But those knights had squires, Batman had Robin, even Don Quixote had Sancho Panza."

Robin stared at Jeff for a moment. Then she burst out laughing. "Is that how you see me, as Don Quixote?"

Jeff smiled. "More like Wonder Woman."

"Does she have a sidekick?"

"To tell you the truth, I don't know. I was more of a Dark Knight guy."

"Were you threatened by the idea of a strong female?"

"If I were, I would never have tried to hook up with you."

Robin stopped smiling. "Are we still hooked up?"

"I want to be. But I also want to know that you believe you can count on me when things get rough."

"I gave what you said a lot of thought. I shouldn't have charged off alone. I should have told you why I thought Regina and Stanley were in danger. I should have asked you to come with me."

"And I would have."

"Are we okay?" Robin asked.

Jeff nodded. "We're okay."

Robin got up and walked around her desk. By the time she got to Jeff, he was standing up. Robin touched Jeff's cheek. "I love you."

Jeff held her and they stayed that way for a while.

Then Robin stepped back and smiled. "That's enough sexual harassment. Don't you have witnesses to interview in the Miller case?"

"Yes, ma'am."

"Then hop to it. We can continue the harassment tonight."

ACKNOWLEDGMENTS

I had more fun writing *A Reasonable Doubt* than almost any other book I've written because I love magic and a grand magic illusion is at the heart of this book. I have seen most of the famous magicians like David Copperfield and Penn and Teller in person and I got the idea of murdering a famous magician on stage while he was performing a fantastic illusion. My problem was that I can never guess how these amazing tricks work. Fortunately, Marshall Amiton, a Multnomah County Circuit Court judge, and attorney Robert Kabacy, who are amateur magicians, took time from their busy schedules to show me how the Chamber of Death illusion works.

In many criminal trials, the prosecutor tries to introduce evidence of crimes that are not charged in an indictment to prove a defendant is guilty of the crimes that are charged in the indictment. The 1901 appellate decision in *People v. Molineux* established the rules governing the admission at trial of bad acts not charged in an indictment. It also provided me with the backstory in *A Reasonable Doubt* that takes place between 1997 and 1998. In the late 1890s, Roland Molineux was charged with two murders committed at different times and places. Molineux was the privileged son of one of the original founders of the Knickerbocker Club, where some of the wealthiest and prestigious men in New York City society congregated. One of the murders involved a dispute with the club's manager, so you can see how the facts of this real-life historical mystery got my mental juices flowing.

A finished novel is the product of team work. The most important part of my team is my editor, Keith Kahla, who points out where I have gone astray in a polite and civilized manner and is rarely wrong. I also received great support from Hector DeJean, Martin Quinn, Alice Pfeifer, Sally Richardson, Eliani Torres, Ken Silver, and Jonathan Bush at St. Martin's.

I wouldn't be at St. Martin's if it hadn't been for Jennifer Weltz, my fabulous agent and the crew at the Jean V. Naggar Literary Agency, which has guided my career since 1984. Wow, that's a long time.

Finally, I treasure the support I receive from my wonderful wife, Melanie Nelson; my daughter, Ami; my son, Daniel, and his wife, Amanda; my amazing grandkids, Loots and Marissa; Melanie's children, Noelle, Brianna, and Brent; and Brent's wife, Tess. I haven't gotten any verbal kudos for my writing from one-year-old Micah, Melanie's first grandchild, but I hope he likes my books when he gets a little older.